This book is dedicated to you, mom. Thanks for making me write that paper so long ago that started this story. This book is also dedicated to all of the trafficked men and women of the world as well as those working to free them. I'm praying for you.

Hope you enjoy!
♡ K. A. B.

CONTENTS

Dedication
A Note to my Readers
Organizations List
Title Page
Kate   1
Kate   2
Hannah   7
Kate   10
Francesca   15
Kate   17
Francesca   19
Kate   20
Jason   22
Kate   24
Jason   25
Kate   26
Francesca   30
Kate   32
Francesca   34

Kate	37
Jason	45
Jen	47
Kate	49
Jen	51
Kate	52
Miranda	54
Jason	57
Kate	59
Kate	62
Jen	66
Kate	67
Jen	70
Kate	72
Kate	74
Kate	79
Jen	81
Kate	83
Kate	87
Kate	89
Jen	91
Kate	94
Jason	101
Jen	105
Kate	108
Jen	112

Jason	116
Kate	120
Kate	121
Jen	122
Kate	127
Jason	131
Jen	138
Kate	141
Jen	148
Jason	150
Kate	155
Jen	159
Kate	162
Jen	167
Kate	170
Jen	173
Kate	176
Kate	179
Kate	188
Jen	189
Kate	195
Jason	199
Kate	202
Jason	206
Kate	209
Jen	224

Kate	226
Miranda	228
Kate	235
Jen	238
Kate	242
Jason	245
Kate	248
Jen	253
Kate	257
Jason	268
Kate	272
Kate	278
Jason	284
Acknowledgements	291
Books By This Author	293

A NOTE TO MY READERS

Dear Readers,

On the next few pages is a list of government and non-government run organizations working to free men, women, and children from slavery. If you've wondered how you might get involved in the fight against human trafficking, this list is a place to start. You can find lists of signs for trafficking to watch out for, links to donate, statistics, volunteer opportunities, and much more. Please share this with your friends and family and get involved in any way you can! There are also lists that I would strongly recommend you look up of companies that benefit from slavery today both in the U.S. and abroad. At the bottom of this list, I included links to stores who donate a portion of their profits to the fight against trafficking.

ORGANIZATIONS LIST

This list was provided by A21:

General Human Trafficking Information
National Human Trafficking Hotline
U.S. Department of State Trafficking in Persons Report
Polaris Project
Global Slavery Index
Global Modern Slavery Directory
United Nations Office on Drugs and Crime
International Labour Organization
International Organization for Migration

Digital Safety And Child Exploitation
National Center for Missing and Exploited Children
Thorn

This list is from my own research:

To get connected with services and supports to get help and stay safe, report a tip about a potential case of human trafficking, or find service referrals for victims of trafficking, contact the **U.S. National Human Trafficking Hotline** by calling 1-888-373-7888 (TTY:711), by texting "BeFree" (233733), via live chat or email. Services are available toll-free 24 hours a day, 7 days a week.

The Childhelp® National Child Abuse Hotline – Professional crisis counselors will connect you with a local number to report abuse. Call: 1-800-4-A-CHILD (1-800-422-4453)

The National Center for Missing & Exploited Children® (NCMEC) – Aimed at preventing child abduction and exploitation, locating missing children, and assisting victims of child abduction and sexual exploitation. Call: 1-800-THE-LOST (1-800-843-5678)

National Center on Sexual Exploitation
1201 F St NW, Suite 200
Washington, D.C. 20004
202.393.7245
public@ncose.com
https://endsexualexploitation.org/

National Sexual Violence Resource Center
2101 N Front Street
Governor's Plaza North, Building #2
Harrisburg, PA 17110
717-909-0710 PHONE
717-909-0714 FAX

717-909-0715 TTY
877-739-3895 TOLL-FREE
https://www.nsvrc.org/organizations/134

Coalition to Abolish Slavery & Trafficking
3580 Wilshire Blvd, #900-37
Los Angeles CA 90010
P: 213-365-1906
F: 213-365-5257
Email: info@castla.org
https://www.castla.org/
https://www.endslaverynow.org/coalition-to-abolish-slavery-and-trafficking-cast

Polaris
P.O. Box 65323
Washington, DC 20035
(202) 790-6300
info@polarisproject.org
https://polarisproject.org/

Alliance to End Slavery and Trafficking
202-370-3625
terry.fitzpatrick@freetheslaves.net
https://endslaveryandtrafficking.org/who-we-are/

Child Welfare Information Gateway
1-800-394-3366
info@childwelfare.gov

https://www.childwelfare.gov/

Heal Trafficking
info@healtrafficking.org
https://healtrafficking.org/

A21
info@A21.org
https://www.a21.org/content/contact-us/grgqa0
https://www.a21.org/

Women at Risk
(616)855-0796
info@warinternational.org
https://warinternational.org/

King's Ransom Foundation
420 Water Street, Suite 106 Kerrville, TX 78028
866-590-3499
admin@kingsransom.org
https://kingsransomfoundation.org/

Shared Hope International
P.O. Box 1907
Vancouver, WA 98668-9807
1-866-437-5433
savelives@sharedhope.org
https://sharedhope.org/

Children's Rescue Initiative
10670 Hwy 18
Conneaut Lake, PA 16316
https://thechildrensrescue.org/

She Has a Name
1700 S. Broadway
Camden, NJ 08104
856-963-0312
Email: info@seedsofhopeministries.org
https://www.seedsofhopeministries.org/she-has-a-name/

Treasures
PO Box 5311
Sherman Oaks, CA 91413
info@iamatreasure.com
818.986.LOVE (5683)
https://www.iamatreasure.com/

Valiant Hearts
P.O. Box 92511
Southlake, TX 76092
817-329-6921
Toll Free: 855-524-3747
info@valianthearts.org
https://www.valianthearts.org/

Timothy Ballard
https://www.timothyballard.com/

Save the Children
501 Kings Highway East,
Suite 400,
Fairfield, CT 06825
203.221.4000

Toll Free# 1.800.728.3843
supportercare@savechildren.org
https://www.savethechildren.org/

International Justice Mission
PO Box 2227
Arlington, VA 22202
703.465.5495
https://www.ijm.org/

Operation Underground Railroad
1950 W. Corporate Way
Anaheim, CA 92801
(818) 850-6146
https://ourrescue.org/

Hope for Justice
Report a concern of human trafficking in the USA:
Office hours (9am-5pm Mon-Fri, Central time)
(+1) 615-356-0946 or email info.us@hopeforjustice.org

Report a concern of modern slavery in the UK:
Office hours (9am-5:30pm Mon-Fri).
(+44) 0300 008 8000 (local rate call) or help@hopeforjustice.org

Outside of office hours, we recommend that you contact Crimestoppers on 0800 555 111.

Hope for Justice USA
P.O. Box 280365
Nashville, TN 37228
(+1) 615-356-0946

info.us@hopeforjustice.org
https://hopeforjustice.org/

Hope for Justice UK
P.O. BOX 5527,
Manchester, M61 0QU
(+44) 0300 008 8000 (local rate call)
info.uk@hopeforjustice.org

Hope for Justice Norway
Postboks 246 Sentrum
4002 Stavanger, Norway
(+47) 22 55 02 00
info.norge@hopeforjustice.org

UNICEF
125 Maiden Lane
New York, NY 10038
(800) 367-5437
https://www.unicefusa.org/

Hookers for Jesus
10120 W Flamingo Rd
Suite 4-506
Las Vegas, NV 89147
702-883-5155
702-623-0958
info@hookersforjesus.net
https://hookersforjesus.net/

Stores

https://www.thetoteproject.com/
https://goodpaper.com/
https://www.sudara.org/
https://www.purposejewelry.org/
https://elegantees.com/
https://thistlefarms.org/
https://starfishproject.com/
https://www.hopeoutfitters.com/
https://www.uncvrdjewelry.com/

A CHANCE FOR FREEDOM

K. A. Baumann

Scripture quotations are from the ESV® Bible (The Holy Bible, English Standard Version®), Copyright © 2001 by Crossway, a publishing ministry of Good News Publishers. Used by permission. All rights reserved.

KATE

Present Day

Kate slowly reached out to knock on the door. She hesitated, her hand halfway there, and bit her lip. *Lord, help me.* Instead of knocking, she rested her hand against the wooden doorway for support. *I can't do this.* Taking a deep breath, she tucked a stray curl behind her ear. *I have to do this.* Her heart pounded in her ears, almost blocking out the tranquil sound of the birds in the trees. Butterflies swirled in her stomach. Everything in her screamed at her to turn and run. Her legs threatened to buckle. She drew another deep breath and slowly forced it out. *I can do this.* Her hand trembled as she reached out and knocked.

KATE

Nineteen Years Earlier

"Wake up! Wake up!" Kate shouted as she ran down the hall to her parents' bedroom. "It's today!" She burst through the doorway, flinging the door so hard it slammed into the wall. She paused and cringed. "Oops." She pounced up onto the bottom of the bed by her parents' feet and bounced on her knees. "Come on. Wake up."

Her dad groaned, rolled over, and covered his head with his pillow. Her mom sighed and picked up the alarm clock. "Kit Kat," she cleared her throat and continued on, her voice barely patient. "It's only four. We have five hours before we need to get up and ready."

"Oh." Kate dropped her head.

"You didn't wake Emma up, did you?"

Kate shook her head. "No, she's sleeping."

Her mom nodded and sat up. "Jim."

"Huh?" He pushed himself up on his elbows. His pillow flipped off his head and left his hair askew. He glanced up at her mom.

Kate's mom chuckled and tousled his hair.

He blinked, then turned his head to look at Kate. "Oh. Alrighty." He pushed the covers back and reached out for Kate. "Get over here, Missy," he growled.

When she saw her parents' smiles, she broke out in a grin and crawled up to snuggle in between them. Kate threw an arm around each parent, drew their heads close to her, and fell asleep to the sound of their whispered conversation.

******

"Hey, Kit Kat. Kate, Hon. It's time to wake up." Kate's mom shook her.

Kate rolled over and squinted her eyes open. "Why?" she whined.

"Did you forget already? We go to the carnival today. The babysitter will be here to watch your sister and brother soon. Dad's downstairs making breakfast."

Kate bounced up. "Already?!"

Her mom laughed and messed up her already tangled hair. "Yes, already. Now let's go. You need a shower."

Kate groaned and tumbled out of bed to follow her mom to the bathroom.

A few hours later, Kate and her parents pulled into a parking spot in the carnival's packed lot. Kate jumped up and down as she reached for her parents' hands. She focused on the people walking in and out among the games, rides, and snack booths as her parents talked with the person at the ticket stand. The sounds of the shouts, rides, and games sent a thrill through her. She hopped from one foot to the other and back again. As soon as her parents finished their conversation, she pulled them into the crowd.

"Kit Kat." Her mom knelt down and turned Kate around to face her. "I know you are excited about today, but I need you to make sure you stay with me and

Daddy, okay? There are a lot of people here and it would be easy to get lost."

"Okay, Mommy." Kate tried to keep her focus on her mom, but all the noise and people were too distracting. She twisted around to watch a group of loud teens pass by.

"What did I just tell you?" her mom asked.

"Um..." Kate pulled her eyes from the crowd back to her mom's face.

"Stay with me and Daddy. I don't want you to get lost."

Kate nodded. "Stay with you and Daddy." She smiled and looked up at her dad.

"That's right," he said. "And if you do get separated from us, do you remember what to do?"

"Stay where I am. If I see a police person, ask them for help."

Her mom nodded. "Right. If you stay by one of the games on the side, Daddy and I will be able to find you easier, okay?"

Kate turned to watch another kid run by ahead of his parents. "Can we go play now?"

Her mom stood. "Yes, we can. What should we do first?"

"I want to ride the horses." Kate took off toward the carousel. She ran ahead of her parents, their warning from moments ago forgotten in her excitement.

"Katherine Lin Barrett!"

Kate barely heard her dad over the rides and people, but she heard him. She skidded to a halt and looked back guiltily as they caught up to her.

"What did we just tell you?" Her dad frowned down at her.

"Sorry, Daddy." She scuffed her toe in the dirt, raised her eyebrows, and looked hopefully up at her parents.

Her dad frowned at her for a moment before he rolled his eyes and looked at her mom. "I can't be mad at her when she makes that face." He shook his head and took her hand in his. Her mom tried to hide her chuckle behind a cough. Kate grinned up at them as her mom took her other hand firmly in hers.

******

As evening came, Kate's dad turned to her. "All righty, Hon. Do you want to go on one last ride or play one last game?"

Kate tilted her head and rested her finger over her mouth as she thought about it. "Can we do that water gun game one more time?"

Her dad nodded and led the way back to the game. The three of them lined up. When the teen in charge of the game gave the signal, they fired at their targets to make their climbers reach the top of the mountain.

"You are both going down!" Kate's dad shouted as his climber took the lead.

"That's what you think," her mom muttered. She corrected her aim with a grin.

"I'm gonna win!" Kate laughed as her dad lost his aim when he looked over at her mom's climber. Kate's climber pulled ahead, but only for a moment. Her mom's climber reached the top first.

"Aww." Kate looked down and pushed out her bottom lip.

"What?!" her dad groaned. "I'm never going to

hear the end of this."

Her mom laughed. "You got that right." She scooped Kate up. "How about you pick the toy, Kit Kat?"

Kate's mood brightened, and she pointed to a small brown teddy. She clutched the bear to her chest as she walked back to the car with her parents.

Kate napped on the long drive home. When they arrived, Kate was full of energy again. "Mom, can I go play outside?"

"Wait until I get dinner started," her mom answered. "Then I will come out with you."

"But mo-" Kate clamped her mouth shut at her mom's warning look and plopped herself down on the kitchen floor to play with the teddy bear while she waited.

HANNAH

Hannah shook her head as she prepared dinner.

"Hannah, I'm going to run to the store." Jim hugged her from behind and kissed her cheek.

Hannah turned and hugged Jim back. "All right. Don't forget the stuff for the church picnic tomorrow."

"I won't. I'll take Emma. Ethan is asleep in the playpen. See you when we get back."

Hannah smiled her goodbye as she turned to finish dinner preparations. Once dinner was in the oven, Hannah grabbed the baby monitor and squatted next to Kate. "What should we play tonight, Kit Kat?"

Kate's eyebrows shot up behind her bangs, and an enormous grin lit her face. She bounced up and down on the balls of her feet. "Can we play hide and seek?"

Hannah rolled her eyes. *I should have known.* She sighed. "Okay, we can play hide and seek."

"Yes!" Kate jumped in the air. "You hide first."

Kate knew not to go past her boundaries, so a few rounds later on Kate's turn to hide, Hannah ran in to check the food and peek in on Ethan. She watched Kate head for the edge of the woods as she went in the back door. She stirred the potatoes, checked the chicken, peeked in on the baby, and went back outside. "Ready or not, here I come!"

Hannah took her time pretending to look for

Kate before she headed to her daughter's favorite hiding places, but she couldn't find her. A knot formed in the pit of her stomach.

"Kate! Kate, I give up. You won. Come out now!" she called. There was no response. Hannah continued to call out as she checked the backyard again. Her chest tightened. She could not quite pull in enough air as she fruitlessly searched the edge of the woods near the yard. Kate still hadn't revealed herself, and that was not like her.

Hannah moved her search to the sides and front of the house. She searched behind bushes and trash cans. Any space that Kate could have squeezed herself into. Still nothing. She felt as if a big iron band was wrapped around her chest. As if she were a bee stuck upside down in a bowl of milk, unable to right herself and fly away. She hurried inside, oblivious to the smoky kitchen and the burning food. She ran through the house calling for Kate, who was nowhere to be found.

Ethan screamed in the living room as Hannah ran down the steps. Tears streamed unheeded down her face.

"What's going on?" Jim asked as he walked in the door. He frowned and set Emma and the grocery bags down.

"We were playing. I checked the food. She's gone." Hannah grabbed Jim's shirt. He held her at arms length by her biceps and studied her.

"What do you mean, she's gone?"

"Kate." She pulled away from him and sniffed in an attempt to pull herself together. "I... I looked everywhere. She isn't answering when I call her. She knows not to go deeper into the woods. It's been almost an hour now, and she hasn't come out."

"She is a kid." Jim wiped Hannah's tears from her cheeks. "Maybe she went deeper into the woods and just couldn't hear you or doesn't realize how long it's been. You know she loses track of time easily. Let's go check." Jim scooped Emma up. "We're going to look for your sister, okay?"

Emma nodded. Hannah lifted Ethan from the playpen and cradled him to her chest as she hurried through the house. She turned off the stovetop and the oven before she followed Jim out the back door.

When it started getting dark, Jim turned to her, his face tight with worry. "I'm calling the police."

Hannah paced the room and shushed the baby while Jim made the call. She met Emma's wide, frightened eyes as she answered Jim's questions. Only one thought raced through her mind. *Where is our daughter?*

KATE

Kate opened her eyes but couldn't see a thing. "Mommy?" she called. She tried to sit up, but slammed her head into something. "Ow!" She rolled around, looking for a way out of the small space, but met walls of some sort on all sides. She reached out and pushed as hard as she could, but the wall over her wouldn't budge.

"Mommy?" her voice trembled. *Where's my mommy and daddy? Where am I?* She suddenly remembered the cold, damp thing that had covered her nose and mouth. She couldn't remember anything after that. Fear gripped her and tears sprang to her eyes. "Daddy! Mommy!" she screamed. "Help!"

She cried, screamed, and kicked, but no one came. It felt like hours passed while she kicked and cried. Finally, she heard a click. The top of the box lifted up and a bright light shone in. She squinted her swollen, tear-filled eyes and blinked a few times, but all she could see was the bright light. Everything else was pitch black.

"She's a pretty little thing, but if you ever act so recklessly again I'll kill you myself."

Kate gasped and shrank away from the voice.

"She's worth a lot, Chaz. I found 'er out at a local fair and followed 'em. Parents left her alone outside. I couldn't pass her up. You know the demand for younger girls now…" The man's voice trailed off.

"You ever pull a stunt like this again…" The man, Chaz, left his threat hanging. "You were right this time, though," he finally conceded.

Kate shrank farther back into the dark space. "I want my dad and mom."

"Yeah, not gonna happen. You give us any problems and my friend here will go back and kill your parents, understand?"

Kate's eyes grew wide and her tears came faster as she stared into the darkness beyond the bright light.

"Quit crying."

Kate bit her lip and tried to choke back her sobs.

"Better. Take her to Juan, JP. She's too young for me to deal with. Don't let him rip us off."

"Right. Watch your head, Kid."

Kate glanced up and saw his hand grab the top of the dark box she was in. "NO! Don't shut me in. Please!" Kate's terror gave her the boldness to beg.

The man reached in and shoved her down before he slammed the lid shut.

Kate kicked at the top again and screamed, "Let me out! I want to go home!" The top remained closed. A moment later, the box rumbled and moved. When the lid stayed shut, and they continued to roll along, Kate's screams turned to whimpers. Exhausted, she let the rumbling, rolling box lull her to sleep.

When she woke, she watched the ground pass underneath her as she thumped against JP's back. She struggled against him and pounded her small fists against his back. "Take me home. Please. I want my Daddy!"

JP readjusted her over his shoulder. "Enough," he growled. "Your parents didn't want you, anyway. You were a burden. Their lives are gonna be easier without you."

"Nuh-uh." Kate sniffled and wiped an arm across her face. "They love me. Take me home!"

"Ha, yeah, that's what all parents say."

Kate continued to squirm and pound on JP's back, to no avail. He finally dropped her and caught the back of her shirt before she collapsed to the ground. He didn't pause, but continued on, dragging her with him. She tried to squirm out of his grasp, but he lifted her off the ground and the front of her shirt choked her until he lowered her to the ground again.

The woods lightened as the sun came up, but he forced her to keep walking. "I'm hungry..." She wiped her face on her sleeve again. Her tired little legs could not keep up with JP's long strides over the uneven ground. "... and tired."

JP ignored her. They walked in silence until they came to a cabin that seemed to appear out of nowhere.

"Ah, finally." JP sighed in relief.

Kate glanced up at him, at the cabin, then back up at him. Her stomach turned. She knew that his relief meant something bad for her. She stopped walking and pushed back against his hand on her shirt. "I want to go home," she said for the millionth time.

JP paused and looked down at her. "Not happening, Kid." He marched her up the stairs and ushered her through the door.

Dread formed a hard pit in her stomach that tightened with each step.

"Francesca?" he called.

A young woman came out of the back room. "Yes?" She glanced at Kate, but quickly concealed her shock.

"Got any food?"

"Yeah. For her, too?"

"Yes." He pushed Kate towards the bedroom the woman had just exited. "Where's Joe?" He asked over his shoulder.

"He's asleep on the back porch."

Kate glanced back and forth between the man and woman. The brief bit of hope she'd felt at the sight of a woman dissipated as she realized that the woman was working with the man.

JP propelled her ahead of him, into the room. Kate looked around. One small window sat high in the wall above the bed. JP pushed her toward a mat in the corner where a crumpled blanket lay. He walked over to a closet and pulled out some ropes. As he walked towards her, Kate backed up until she was against the wall. He knelt down in front of her and held up the ropes.

"You got two choices, Kid," he said. "You sit yourself down on this blanket and don't move until I tell you to; or I can tie you up. It's your choice. If you sit on this blanket like a good little girl, I'll send Fran in with food and water for you, and you can have one of the nice pillows off the bed. But if you try anything-" He broke off as Francesca entered the room. "What?"

"I don't think you need to threaten her, JP." She placed a tentative hand on his shoulder. "Look at her. She's terrified. I'm sure she'll stay there and not cause any trouble. Am I right, Kid?"

Kate nodded vigorously. "I won't move," she squeaked. She pressed herself firmly against the wall to prove she would stay right there.

"See?" Francesca asked with a gesture towards

Kate. "She won't move."

"Hah. Yes, I see." JP grunted. He stood and hung the ropes over the side of the bed, where Kate could see them. "Just remember, you won't like what happens if you get off that mattress." He paused at the door and looked back. Kate stared at him but didn't move a muscle. He chuckled, ushered Francesca out, and pulled the door shut behind them.

******

Kate stood pressed against the wall. She didn't dare move. Silent tears streamed down her face as her exhausted body fought sleep. Every time her head nodded or her legs started to buckle, she jerked herself awake and back against the wall.

The handle turned, and the door opened. Kate stared, terrified. "I didn't move!" she exclaimed. When she saw Francesca and not JP, she felt only slightly relieved.

FRANCESCA

Francesca took in the girl's appearance as she nudged the door partially shut with her foot. She held a plate in one hand and a cup of water in the other. Her heart sank. "You poor thing," she whispered. She hurried across the room and knelt in front of the girl, placing the plate and cup on the floor.

The kid flinched as Francesca reached out to place her hands on her shoulders. "I won't hurt you, Hon." She rubbed the girl's arms. The girl broke down into uncontrollable sobs. Francesca frowned and glanced toward the door. "Shh now, Honey. You don't want JP to come in here."

The girl shook her head frantically and gulped back her sobs. "I w-want m-my mommy a-and d-daddy."

"I wish I could help you, Kid." Francesca sighed. "Listen, things will be easier for you if you don't cause any trouble. They treat you better when you behave. Understand?"

The girl nodded and tried to control her sobs

"That's it," Francesca encouraged her. "Let's see your brave face."

The girl scrubbed at her face, removing tears and spreading dirt. She pressed her trembling lips together and looked up at Francesca with wide, red rimmed-eyes. "Li-like t-this?" she asked.

Francesca nodded and pulled the girl into a hug, wiping her own tears away before the girl could see them. "Just like that, Kid."

"Fran!" JP called.

"Oh." Francesca pulled the girl's arms from around her neck. "Coming!" She quickly rose and grabbed a pillow from the bed. She knelt by the girl again. "You don't have to stand there," she said. "You can lay down and move around on the mat, all right?" She pushed the girl down so she sat against the wall and tucked the thin blanket around her waist. "There you go." She placed the pillow next to the girl, then gestured to the plate and water. "That's for you. I have to go now." She started to walk away when the girl's small voice stopped her.

"Don't leave me."

Francesca turned. "I'm sorry. I have to." She walked backwards. "I'll check on you again later, okay?" When the girl nodded, Francesca spun and ran out of the room.

KATE

Kate huddled under the blanket and stared after Francesca, trying to hold back her tears. She needed to keep her brave face on, like Francesca had said. It was not long before her hunger got the best of her, and she looked at the plate. A peanut butter and jelly sandwich. She leaned over and grabbed the sandwich, careful to not let any part of her body touch the floor, convinced that if just her pinky went off of the mattress, JP would know.

Kate devoured the sandwich. She gulped the water down as soon as she swallowed the last bite. Her hunger abated, she laid down, curled up with the blanket, and fell asleep.

The sound of the door banging open startled her awake. Kate looked around, confused. She spotted JP and Francesca tangled together as they made their way across the room. She watched, horrified, as JP chuckled and pushed Francesca back onto the bed.

Kate ducked her head, pulled the blanket over herself, and curled into a tight ball. She covered her head with the pillow and pressed the sides against her ears to block out the awful noises they made. She lay there trembling and crying as silently as she could until the noises stopped. A few minutes later, snores shook the room. Kate remained curled under the blanket when

K. A. BAUMANN

she heard soft footsteps approach her.

FRANCESCA

Francesca, blanket wrapped around her, knelt next to the girl. She could tell by her silent sobs that she was awake. She wanted to comfort the poor girl. To say something that would make this easier, but she had already told her the only thing that would help. You just had to do what they wanted you to do. She reached out to touch her but paused, her hand hovering over the girl's head. She sighed and pulled her hand back with a shake of her head. The girl would have to get used to this. She bit her lip. There was nothing either of them could do. She rose and walked back to the bed, leaving the girl to comfort herself.

KATE

Nine Months Ago

Desperation spurred Kate on. They were closing in on her. She knew there was no hope of escape, but she wouldn't... couldn't... give up now. Not after she'd come this far. Her mouth was parched, her throat ached, and the world would not stop tilting; but she pushed on.

She yelped as a bullet ripped through her left shoulder. She grabbed her arm as she fell to the ground. The world dimmed and faded in and out of focus. Kate squeezed her eyes shut and groaned through clenched teeth. Her breath came in short, painful gasps, and her heart pounded erratically. She drew in a deep breath before she tilted her head back to search for any sign of her pursuers. She still didn't see anyone, but she could hear them. They were getting closer.

She groaned again, bit her lip, and forced herself up. Her shoulder burned and throbbed. Her stomach roiled, and she swallowed the bile that rose in her throat. Her head felt full of air and her vision blurred. Blood oozed from her wound and dripped down her arm. She didn't dare to look at it.

She crept through the woods and tried not to make a sound. When she came to a deep stream, she felt a spark of hope.

"There's blood. You got her."

She whipped her head around. *Tony.* Her eyes darted back and forth as she searched for the man who hunted her. A twig snapped nearby. Without another thought, she floundered into the water. *So cold!* She bit her lip as she waded as quickly as she could downstream.

Kate stepped forward and slipped on a slimy rock. She gasped as she went down. She tried to catch herself, but landed on her wounded arm and it gave out. The pain sent fire through her body as she dropped into the cold water. She coughed up creek water as she sat up. When she tried to stand, everything around her doubled and faded. She closed her eyes, drew in a deep breath, and pushed herself up.

Later, unsure of how long she had stumbled through the stream, she half crawled, half dragged herself to shore. She made no effort to be quiet. The determination she felt just a short time ago had left her. Exhaustion dragged at her body. She felt more lightheaded with every step. She clung to trees to keep herself upright. Night had fallen, and it was so dark that she could barely see. *I can't do this anymore. God, if you are real, you'll let me die before they find me.*

"AH!" Kate stumbled into a thornbush. She winced as she disentangled herself. It hurt. Everything hurt. Everything in her wanted to stop, but she struggled on. She gasped as she tripped over a large branch and fell to the ground. She groaned, attempted to rise, and sank back to the ground. *I give up. Let them find me… let me die. I don't care… I'm done…* She drifted off into nothingness.

JASON

Jason lay in bed. It was two in the morning and he still couldn't sleep. Usually when this happened, he listened to worship or prayed, but neither of those calmed his restlessness tonight. He had a strange, irresistible desire to take a walk. Finally, he shoved the blankets off with an irritated sigh.

He pulled on a hoodie, grabbed his flashlight from his nightstand, and stalked through the house. He shoved his feet into his sneakers by the front door and headed out.

He loved the path through the woods, so he impulsively walked that way. Jason pushed his hand through his hair in frustration as he walked. He had to be up at five to make it to work. He sped up, walking out his frustration.

As his irritation faded, he paused and looked up at the sky. *Okay, God. I'm out here at two in the morning. TWO in the morning... taking a walk. There has to be a reason?* Jason looked back down and continued walking. He paused when his flashlight beam passed over something strange. He slowly moved the light around until he found it again. It was a leg.

He stared for a moment before he called out, "Hello?" He moved closer and his light revealed the rest of a woman's body. "Hello?"

The woman didn't move.

He knelt next to her and took in her bedraggled appearance. She wore tight, ripped jeans and a baggy blue sweater almost swallowed the upper part of her body. She lay sprawled on her stomach and her tangled, matted hair covered her face. Something dark stained the shoulder of her sweater. *Is that...?* He leaned closer and touched the dark patch on her back. "Blood." He stared at the blood on his finger in the flashlight's beam.

Jason blinked, then frantically patted his pockets in a fruitless search for his phone that was still on his nightstand. *Have to get her to the hospital. Okay, phone's not here... Can't panic.* He took a few deep breaths, then tapped her back. "Hey," he said loudly, hoping for some sort of response. Nothing. He felt her neck for a pulse. It was there, but faint. *My house isn't too far.*

He gingerly turned her over. Despite her dirt covered face, she was a beautiful woman. He brushed her hair from her face, searching for some sign of alertness. When she didn't move, he gently scooped her up, astonished at how light she was. *God, don't let her die.* He prayed as he stood up and started back toward town.

KATE

Tony was kicking her again. Kate tried to move out of the way, but someone held her down. "Please. I didn't do anything," she pleaded, but the kicking didn't stop. He kept kicking her in the same place. Her shoulder. It hurt so much, but something wasn't right. The hands holding her down weren't as rough as they usually were. Kate groaned. *What's going on?*

JASON

Jason couldn't understand her mumblings, but figured he was hurting her. "I'm sorry. Hang on. We're almost there." He tried not to jostle her shoulder as he walked.

She groaned, and Jason looked down. He watched as her eyes fluttered open. He stared into her clouded blue, pain and terror glazed eyes, and his heart skipped a beat. The sudden surge of protectiveness that rose up in him, and the anger at whoever was responsible for her injuries, surprised him. He tightened his hold on her as she struggled against him. Her movements were so feeble. *She is so weak. God, please, let her make it!*

KATE

Kate forced her eyes to open and looked up into a pair of worried brown eyes. *Where...?* Her shoulder pressed into his chest as he carried her, intensifying her pain. Memories flooded back. *Tony!* She didn't need him to shoot her to know how furious he'd been that she had ratted him out.

She struggled to get out of the man's arms. *Where are we? Is he one of Tony's men? That doesn't make sense...* Fear of the unknown overwhelmed her, but her struggle did nothing except bring more pain. The world would not stop spinning. Everything hurt.

Kate squeezed her eyes shut, resigned to the fact that there was nothing she could do except let him carry her to wherever he wanted to take her. She felt herself slipping again. She tried to fight it, clinging to consciousness as best she could, but she lost. Her head dropped back as darkness enveloped her again.

******

Kate faded in and out of consciousness. There were so many people. She had no idea who they were or what they wanted. She caught bits and pieces of the frantic conversations around her, but none of them made any sense. The voices sounded muffled. Like they were far away and under water. The darkness that beckoned every time she started to wake was too wonderful. She gladly fell back into it each time.

When partially conscious, she wanted to ask what was going on. She tried, but her voice wouldn't work. Her throat was parched and her tongue felt thick and dry. She opened her eyes. Everything looked disconnected and blurry. Lights. Lots of bright, bright lights. Too bright. A head loomed above her. A mask covered the lower half of its face. She wanted to back away. She tried to scream for help, but her dry throat wouldn't make a sound. The darkness pulled her down again, and everything faded.

******

Beep! Beep! Beep! *What's that noise?* Kate groaned and rolled over, but stopped as pain shot through her. "Ah!" she gasped, opened her eyes, then squinted at the lights. She blinked a few times as the room came into focus. *A hospital?* She looked down to see a needle taped into her arm. It seemed as if everything else around her faded as she focused on the needle. Fear coursed through her. *No! No drugs.* Her weak and uncooperative fingers fumbled with the needle as she tried to rip it out.

"Hold on there." A nurse grabbed her wrist with a strong, gentle grip. "It's just an I.V. to hydrate you, Dear. We need to leave it in. All right?"

Kate looked from the I.V. to the nurse and back. "I.V.?" she croaked.

The nurse nodded. "You're extremely dehydrated. We need to get fluids in you."

Kate slowly relaxed. She closed her eyes, exhausted by that small effort. The nurse smiled and released Kate's hand. She turned back to check the monitors as Kate fingered the tape that held the I.V. in place.

"Do you know what happened to you?"

Kate eyed the nurse before she blinked and shook her head. *If I can play it off like I don't remember, maybe I'll be safe. Maybe I can get away.*

"Hey, Leese. How is she?"

At the sound of the man's voice, Kate's stomach clenched into a knot. The familiar pang of animosity and apprehension twisted in her gut. She turned toward the voice, and a face came into focus. He stood just inside the door. He looked slightly familiar. As if she had seen him in a dream.

"Hi, Jason. All things considered, she is doing very well," the nurse answered.

Jason smiled at the nurse before he turned to her. "How are you feeling?"

Kate frowned. *How are you feeling? Who asks that question?* She ignored him and turned her face to the ceiling. *They must have given me something for the pain. It doesn't hurt like it did... I've seen what drugs do to people. I don't know how I've avoided getting addicted, but I do NOT plan to start now. I'll refuse whatever it is if they try to give it to me again. I'll... I'll fight them if I have to.* Drugs signified someone else having control over her life. Too many people already had control. She would never allow herself to willfully be subject to another "Master".

"Okay, well, I should probably get to work. I'm glad to see you're awake."

Kate could feel his eyes on her, but she refused to look at him.

"Do you have anyone you'd like me to call... anyone that should know where you are?" When she didn't respond, he said, "Well, I'll come by or send my friend, Jen, to check on you later. Okay?"

Kate kept her face blank and continued to ignore him. She could see him in her periphery as he walked to the door. He looked back with a frown before he shrugged and closed the door softly behind him.

FRANCESCA

Nineteen Years Earlier

Francesca entered the room. The kid bolted upright and watched as she approached.

"C'mon, Hon. time to go." She reached a hand down to her.

The kid shrank against the wall. She looked from Francesca to the door and back with wide, frightened eyes.

"It's okay. He told me to come get you. He won't tie you up. I promise."

The kid hesitantly reached out and took Francesca's hand. Francesca led her out into the main room of the cabin. The kid glanced around and seemed to relax.

"What are we gonna do?"

Francesca led her to the bathroom and grabbed a bag off the counter. She knelt down next to the kid and pulled out an outfit with the price tag still on it. "What do you think of this?"

The kid's eyes widened at the shorts and t-shirt with Belle from Beauty and the Beast. "It's so pretty."

"JP got it for you."

Her eyes widened farther. "Really?"

Francesca nodded and stood up. "Really. Now, let's

get you showered so you can put this on."

The kid pressed a finger over her lips and seemed to be deep in thought. She finally nodded. "Okay."

Francesca helped the kid shower and dress in her new outfit. She smiled when the kid beamed at her reflection in the full body mirror. As she turned this way and that to see the sparkles in Belle's hair, Francesca's smile faltered. She bit her lip. "All right. Let's go. There's some leftover pizza in the fridge."

The kid hummed the music to Belle's theme song as she followed Francesca to the kitchen.

Francesca brushed and braided the kid's hair while she ate. When she finished, Francesca went to the back door. "She's ready for the picture."

"Bring her out."

The kid's head snapped up. She hopped off the stool and backed into a corner.

Francesca hurried over and knelt in front of her. "It's okay. He won't touch you, all right? He's just going to take a picture. I'll be with you."

"A picture?"

"Yeah. Just a picture. Okay? No big deal. We can get some ice cream after. Would you like that?"

The kid's eyes brightened. "I like ice cream."

"Good. Let's go get this picture, then we'll get you some ice cream, okay?"

The kid nodded. "Uh huh." She stuck close to Francesca as she followed her to the back porch.

KATE

Kate sat on the kitchen floor playing with a barbie JP had brought for her. Francesca's and Jackson's muffled voices drifted through the back door. Kate glanced toward the door and frowned. She wasn't sure why Francesca stayed here with Jackson and JP. She could sense her fear of the men, but she seemed attached to them, too.

Kate shrugged and continued to play with the barbie. JP and Jackson both left her alone, and she did her best to stay out of their way. She looked toward the door that JP had disappeared through. JP terrified her. *I hate him.* Guilt pricked at her. He was the one who had brought her here, but he did bring her sweets, clothes, and toys.

Jackson and Francesca walked in, and Kate jerked her head up. She scooted back to the corner of the kitchen to get out of their way.

"Make sure she's ready." Jackson nodded his head at her.

"I will," Francesca responded.

Kate kept silent until Jackson walked out the front door. "Get me ready for what?" she asked.

"We're going on a road trip," Francesca answered. She smiled, but Kate could tell she wasn't happy.

"A road trip?"

"Yeah, doesn't that sound fun? You'll get to see some new places. Isn't that exciting?"

"I've never been on a road trip before." She pursed her lips and placed her finger over them. "Can… can I go home after the road trip?"

Francesca spun away from her and leaned over the table.

Did I say something wrong? Kate wondered. Francesca had been nice to her, and she didn't want to upset her. "I'm sorry," she whispered. Tears sprang to her eyes. She wanted to go home but to make Francesca happy, she wouldn't ask again. She slipped her hand into Francesca's. "I want to go on a road trip. I never did that before."

Francesca's hand trembled as she squeezed her hand, but she wouldn't look down at her. Kate frowned up at Francesca and watched as she took a deep breath.

"Fran?" Kate asked.

Francesca turned to her and smiled brightly. "Okay. Let's go get ready." She hurried off, pulling Kate behind her.

Kate followed, but wondered why Francesca had tears in her eyes.

FRANCESCA

"Let's go!" JP called from the front of the cabin.

Francesca jerked her head up at the sound of his voice. "Coming!" She glanced over at the kid, who sat patiently on the mattress in the corner of the bedroom. She had her arms wrapped around her legs, her chin rested on her knees as she watched her pack.

Francesca's heart contracted yet again. She turned her face away from the kid's searching eyes and shoved her last t-shirt into the bag. *I don't want to do this. Why do I have to do this? This kid's life is over now...* She yanked the zipper shut.

I should've done something. I had time. I could've gotten her outta here. Maybe while we waited for the passports. JP and Jackson would have found them. She had no idea where they actually were or where she could find help. *But I should've tried.* Instead, She'd been a coward. She had done nothing. She had helped end this little girl's life.

She glanced at the girl again. She looked up at her with sad, fear-filled eyes, but there was trust in them, too. Francesca covered her face with her hand and tried to stop the tears. *I can't do this. She deserves a chance.* Her hand shook as she wiped it over her face. She would die, but maybe the kid could make it.

She grabbed the bag and reached out to the kid.

The kid took her hand, and Francesca led her to the kitchen. She knelt down in front of her. "Hey."

The kid looked up at her with wide eyes.

"Listen. I want you to go out this door." Francesca pointed to the back door. "I want you to run. Okay? Run and don't stop, no matter what you hear. Understand?"

The girl's lip trembled, but she nodded.

"That's a good girl." Francesca pulled her into a hug, then turned her toward the door. "Now go. Go and don't stop."

The girl took a step forward, then paused. She turned back. "Are you coming?"

Francesca shook her head. "No. You have to go on your own. Now go, before it's too late."

The girl just stared up at her. Francesca opened the door and shoved her out. "Go!" Her voice came out in a harsh whisper. The girl stumbled out the door, and with one last glance, she ran.

"Where's the kid?"

A knot formed in Francesca's stomach as she turned to find JP's form filling the room.

"I… uh…" Francesca took a step back. All her bravery from moments ago gone. *Why did I tell the kid to run?*

"Where is she, Fran?" He stepped closer.

"JP," she pleaded quietly. She backed against the wall as he approached. Her legs trembled, barely holding her upright.

He grabbed her hair and yanked her head back, forcing her to look up into his face. Tears streamed down her face. "Sh-she's j-just a-a kid," she whispered.

JP scowled and tossed her aside. "Jackson, out back! The kid's running!" He turned back to her and pulled his gun from his waistband. "Against the wall.

Now."

Francesca backed against the wall. She'd had it pretty good compared to some, but she was still only property to JP and Jackson and she knew it. She glanced out the window and saw Jackson sprint past. *He's gonna catch her.* It had all been pointless. *I should've followed the plan.* She stared silently, anxiously, at JP as he paced. He occasionally scowled over at her.

She had seen him angry before, but this? He was furious, but he was holding it in. That scared her more than anything.

KATE

Kate struggled in Jackson's arms as he carried her back into the cabin. She had run as fast as her little legs could carry her, but Jackson had been faster.

"Put me down!" She pounded her tiny fists against his back. "Put me d-OAH!" Jackson dropped her without warning and she landed hard on the kitchen floor. Tears sprang to her eyes, but she held them back as she looked around frantically for Francesca. She found her cowering against the other wall, tears streaming down her face.

Kate felt like the earth dropped out from under her. *Why is Francesca crying?* "Fran?" Kate pushed herself up and started toward her. JP grabbed her arm and yanked her back. "Ow!" she cried out. She looked up at JP's face. She had seen him mad before, but she had never seen that look in his eyes. He glared down at her as his fingers dug into her arm.

She tried to pull away, but his fingers tightened around her arm. "Owww," she whimpered. "You're hurting me."

JP's grasp didn't ease. "Kid."

He gestured toward Francesca, and Kate noticed the gun in his other hand. She stopped squirming and froze, staring at the gun.

"Look at me." JP's voice was hard and sent chills

through Kate's little body.

She tore her gaze from the gun and looked up at him.

"This'll be a lesson for you. You did good until Fran here decided to tell you to do something other than what I said."

"JP, please..." Francesca reached out a hand.

Kate's eyes darted back and forth between the gun, JP's hard face, and Francesca. She couldn't breathe.

JP pointed at his chest with the gun. "You listen to me," he continued, "things will go a lot better for you. Got it?"

Kate stared wide-eyed up at JP and nodded mutely.

"Good." He pulled Kate in front of him and released her arm. She breathed a sigh of relief, but his hand clamped around the back of her neck. She winced and tried to duck away, but he pulled her back. He gestured at Francesca again. "Look at her."

Kate obeyed and turned her frightened eyes to Francesca.

Francesca wiped her face on her sleeve and clenched her jaw as she made eye contact with Kate. "Keep your brave face, Kid," her voice quavered. "I'm sor-"

The gun exploded in Kate's ear. She cried out, squeezed her eyes shut, threw her arms over her head, and tried to drop to the ground.

JP yanked her back up. She gasped and cringed away as the semi-warm metal of the handgun pressed against her neck. She couldn't suppress the whimper that escaped. JP shook her so hard her teeth rattled together. "Open your eyes," he ordered.

Kate shook her head. Tears streamed through her closed eyes. She didn't know what she would see, but she knew she didn't want to see it.

JP shook her again. "I said, open your eyes." His grip on the back of her neck tightened; his fingers digging into her tender flesh.

Kate whimpered again. She didn't want to open her eyes, but she was afraid of what JP might do to her. She was sure if she didn't do as he said, he would shoot her. Her whole body trembled as she blinked her eyes open. It took her a few moments to comprehend what she saw. Her mouth dropped open in horror. She wanted to close her eyes, to turn away, to unsee what she was seeing, but she knew she could never unsee the sight before her.

Francesca lay slumped against the wall, her eyes stared unseeing at JP. Blood darkened her shirt around the hole in her chest. Kate stared at Francesca's body, unable to turn away.

"You ever try to run away again, you'll end up just like her. Got it? And don't forget, I know where your parents are. You want them to end up like this?"

The threat drew Kate's attention from Francesca and she tilted her head up to look at JP. In her shock, her tears had stopped. She clamped her mouth shut. Her eyes widened at the thought of her parents looking like Francesca did at the moment. Fear twisted in her gut. She shook her head so hard it hurt her neck. "I-I-I w-won't ru-un."

"That's smart." JP pulled the gun away from her and shoved it back into his waistband. "Now grab that bag and get in the car." He shoved her toward the bag Francesca had packed.

Kate stumbled over the bag. She quickly righted herself and threw a terrified glance behind her. JP turned to Jackson and ignored her. She could barely hear their voices over the ringing in her ears. This had to be a nightmare. She would wake up and Francesca was going to tell her everything would be okay, if only she kept her brave face on and did what they told her. Fran would get her some cereal from the cabinet and distract her throughout the day, just like she always did.

"What are you waiting for, Kid? Grab the bag and let's go."

Jackson's voice sounded so close to her that Kate flinched. She looked over at Francesca one more time, willing her to get up. Willing herself to wake up.

Jackson's hand connected with the back of her head and knocked Kate forward. No, this was very real. She bit back a quiet whimper, and attempted to listen to Francesca's last warning to keep her brave face and grabbed the bag. Jackson grabbed her arm and propelled her from the room.

******

Kate remained silent for most of the drive. She did not want to draw attention to herself. JP had warned her that he would shoot her if she made noise but had promised to get her ice cream if she behaved. It wasn't a very hard choice.

Every rest stop they came to, JP ordered her to lay on the floor. She dropped to the floor without hesitation, terrified that if she took too long, JP would get angry and shoot her. They would wait silently in the car while Jackson filled the gas tank and bought food and drinks. Every now and then, JP would pull over on deserted side roads for her to use the bathroom.

Kate tried to forget the day they had left the cabin, but it was burned into her memory. *This was supposed to be a fun trip. Fran should be with us.* Instead, she lay covered in blood on the kitchen floor with a hole in her chest.

After about a week on the road, they took an exit to a random back road. They pulled onto the shoulder next to an empty car. Jackson nodded to JP and left her alone in the car with him. She watched as he jumped into the other car and drove off.

JP turned around and held out a bottle of water. "Drink up, Kid," he ordered.

Kate obeyed, her eyes filled with tears she was too afraid to shed. She wanted to ask JP where they were going and why Jackson had left them, but she knew she shouldn't. He hadn't told her it was okay to talk. Her eyes grew heavy, and her body relaxed. She leaned her head back and shut her eyes.

******

Kate woke as JP lifted her out of the car. She blinked a few times to remove the blurriness from her vision. Her head felt stuffed with cotton. He carried her to a small room where five men lounged and set her down. Through the door, she saw a courtyard with a few raised gardens and benches. On the other side of the courtyard stood a large building. The men talked, but she didn't pay much attention to what they said. She hid behind JP, using him to shield her from the other men, and stared out the door.

JP pulled her from behind him as he talked with the men. *Why is he holding me out for the men to see?* She didn't like the way they looked at her. She squirmed and tried to hide behind him again. One of the other men stared at her and nodded. Kate watched, wide-eyed, as he handed JP a heavy duffle-bag. She stared at the bag as it changed hands, then looked at all the men with guns who stood around the room. JP opened the bag. He shuffled the contents around, nodded, and turned to walk out the door.

"No, wait!" Kate yelled.

He looked back at her before he turned and hurried through the door.

"Don't leave me," Kate cried. She tried to follow him. Two men stepped in front of her, blocking the door. Kate backed up. "Where's he going?" she asked. "Is he coming back?"

The men ignored her.

"I want JP," she sniffled. Yes, he terrified her, but she knew him. He gave her stuff when she listened. She didn't know any of these men.

When the men continued to ignore her, she tried to push past them. One of them shoved her back. She flailed her arms to regain her balance. Fear welled up inside her. She looked up at the unfriendly faces of each of the men around her. "I want to go home," she cried.

One of the men turned to her. "You will go home. Maybe. One day. If you listen and do what I tell you. Understand?" His voice sent shivers up Kate's spine. "If you do not listen to us, we will get JP to tell us where your parents are and we will kill them. If you listen, your parents will live. Do you want your parents to live?"

Kate stared up at him as tears streamed down her face. Compared to this man, JP had not been scary at all.

He raised his voice. "Do you want your parents to live?"

JP had told her the same thing. That her parents would die if she didn't listen. Even though he wasn't here, the threat still hung over her. Kate nodded and gulped down her tears. She reminded herself to use her brave face like Francesca had told her to.

"That's right. Be a good little girl then." He patted her cheek, then waved dismissively and spoke in a language she didn't know. "Remember this, Kid," he said as one of the other men picked her up. "No one cares what happens here." He turned away, and the man carried her down a dark staircase to a door with a lock on it. Another man stood right outside the door. He unlocked it and pushed the door open. A terrible smell wafted out. The man put her down and motioned to the dark room that had only one bare, flickering light bulb.

She shook her head. "I don't wanna go in there. Please don't make me." The man huffed, shoved her forward, and pulled the door shut behind her. She spun around and pulled at the door handle as the bolt slammed into place. "Let me out! Let me out!"

Something moved behind her and Kate jerked around. She flattened herself against the door. As her eyes adjusted to the dim light, she made out a woman's form.

"It's okay, Dear," she said gently. "I won't hurt you."

"Who... who are you?" Kate asked. "Where are we?"

The young woman held out her hand. "My name

is Miranda. What's yours?"

Slightly comforted at the sight of a woman, Kate took her hand. "I'm Kate. I want my dad and mom," she whimpered.

Miranda gently drew Kate closer to her. "I know, Hon. I know. I wish I could get you to them. Come on. I'll protect you while you sleep a little."

Kate started to pull back when another woman spoke up. "Don't coddle her, Miranda. Look at her. She's not going to last. She's going to die if they don't end up killi-"

"SHHH!" Miranda interrupted.

Kate's eyes grew wide, and she trembled. "I don't want to die," she whispered.

"Ha. You'll change your mind quick enough," the same woman spat bitterly.

Miranda shook her head. "She's so frightened already. Leave her be."

The other woman huffed and turned over on her blanket bed.

"Come on. Don't listen to what she says," Miranda encouraged as she sat down.

Kate was so worn out and frightened that she didn't resist again when Miranda drew her onto her lap. She laid her head on Miranda's chest as Miranda sang.

"God will take care of you, be not afraid; He is your safeguard through sunshine and shade; Tenderly watching and keeping His own, He will not leave you to wander alone." *

Within seconds, Kate was fast asleep.

JASON

Nine Months Ago

Jason hurried home, showered, and dressed for work. On his way out the door, he grabbed his phone and car keys. He pressed the voice command button as he settled into his car. "Call Jen." When the phone started to ring, he pressed the speakerphone button and pulled out of the driveway.

"Hello."

"Hey Jen, it's me."

"Hey Jay, you sound exhausted. What's up?"

"Had a crazy night. No sleep and now I'm headed to work. But I have a favor to ask."

"Yeah, what is it?"

"I found a woman last night in the woods. Someone shot her."

There was silence on the line.

"Jen?"

"Are you messing with me?"

Jason shook his head. "No. No joke. I took her to the hospital."

"Oh, my gosh."

"Dr. Baker says she's lucky the bullet didn't hit her heart, but she lost a lot of blood and is in bad shape. I'm…" Jason trailed off. *What am I?* "She…" *She what?* He shook his head. "I don't want her to be alone," he finally finished. "She was unconscious when I found her. She woke up just before I left. She had no I.D. and wouldn't say if there was someone we could call. The police were there, but she claims she doesn't remember anything. I feel responsible for her. God led me out there to find her. I'm sure of it. Would you go check on her later today? I'll come by again when I get out of work."

"That's crazy." Jen muttered. "Of course I'll go check on her. Want me to call the others?"

"Yeah, sure, you can tell them. Maybe get a prayer chain going? She was stable when I left but still in really bad shape."

"Okay."

"She's in room 224."

"Room 224. Got it."

"Thanks, Jen."

"Of course. I'll see you later."

"Bye."

Relief flooded him as Jason disconnected the call. He knew Jen would do whatever she could for the woman. He smiled. They, along with John and later, Casey, had grown up in this little town and had been inseparable. They would do anything for each other and they all knew it.

JEN

Jen stared at her phone after Jason disconnected the call. She blinked a few times, still trying to process what Jason had just told her. *God, be with this woman, whoever she is. Heal her, Lord. Show us what you want us to do for her. How to help her. In Jesus' name.* She shook her head and scrolled through her contacts. When she found John's name, she tapped it and stood up to pace her living room.

"Hello?"

"Hey John, I'm calling for Jason."

"Oh, good. I've been wondering where he disappeared to. Haven't seen him at all today. What's up?"

"Well, apparently, he couldn't sleep last night so he went for a walk. He, uh, he found an unconscious woman in the woods."

"What?"

"Yeah, she was shot." She quickly filled him in on the details. "Can you call the prayer chain when you get a minute? I'm going to shower and head over to the hospital."

"Wow. Yes, I'll do that."

"Thanks, John."

"Keep me posted?"

"Yeah." Jen disconnected the call and took her steps two at a time. She paused by the door to her sister's room. *Should I tell her what's going on? She probably won't care much beyond the gossip factor. Nothing like this ever happens here. Still, I should let her know.* She raised her hand to knock on the door. "Ugh." Jen shook her head and left her sister undisturbed. *I'll tell her if I see her when she gets home from work tonight.*

Within a half hour, Jen had showered and was on her way to the hospital. She was glad she had a day off and was free to go check on the woman. *What was she doing out there? Who is she? Where's she from? Where are the people who shot her?* She drummed her fingers on the steering wheel. *This world is crazy.*

She had always loved being from a small town without the insanity of cities. Everyone knew each other and looked out for each other. Crimes were rare. Bored teens egged houses or shoplifted like her sister had done. Drugs and alcoholism were an issue, but, for the most part, the town acted like a large, extended family.

Jen parked and headed right to room 224. She hesitated outside the door. *God, I don't know what to say or do. Guide me please.* She took a deep breath and knocked before she opened the door and walked in. The woman stared at her with such an intense, narrow-eyed gaze that Jen felt like it could burn a hole through her. She forced a smile. "Hi, I'm Jen. Jason told me what happened. I... wanted to come see if you need anything?"

KATE

Kate studied the woman who walked in. She was tall with a sweet, pretty face and long, light-brown hair. Her green eyes had no hardness in them. *Life's been good to her. I might be tempted to trust her, if I could trust anyone. But I can't. Just like I couldn't trust those cops who came to my room earlier.* She had told them nothing. Pretended that she couldn't remember a thing. *Do they know the cops who work with Tony?* She didn't know, but she couldn't take that chance. *Maybe they were good cops like the ones who tried to help me before, but maybe they weren't.*

She focused on the woman again. "I'm fine," she answered tonelessly. *Not that you really care. No one cares. Juan was right.* She turned her eyes back to the ceiling she had memorized every crack of. The pain in her shoulder was something she needed to live with. There was no other way. *Unless... This is a hospital... There's gotta be something here I can use to kill myself.* She let her eyes wander the room searching for something she could use, but found that her gaze strayed back to the other woman. She hadn't said anything else, but stood awkwardly by the door.

Kate frowned and silently held eye contact with the woman for a few minutes. *What does that guy want from me? Why did he send this woman to watch me?* Kate's gaze flickered over the woman, taking in everything about her. Her frown deepened. *She seems so... pure.*

The woman looked at her with eyes so full of concern that Kate fidgeted. She had to be reading that look the wrong way. *Why would this woman be concerned for me?*

The woman finally spoke in a soft voice. "Jason told me you don't remember anything?"

Remember? Kate huffed a breath through her nose. *How could I forget?* "I don't." Her voice came out flat. It conveyed none of the emotions that boiled just below the surface.

"Does it hurt much?" The woman nodded to Kate's shoulder.

"Like Hell."

"I'm sorry."

The look on the woman's face stirred a faint memory that Kate couldn't quite grasp. "Why should you be sorry?" she asked, bothered by the woman's openness and the memory that refused to form. "You didn't shoot me." She couldn't keep the bitterness from her voice.

"No, I didn't." An emotion Kate was not accustomed to seeing flitted over the woman's face. "So," she continued, "I'm guessing you have nowhere to stay when you get out of here?"

Oh. I didn't even think about that. Kate's heart sank. With no money, she'd be out on the street and back where she came from in no time. She only knew how to do one thing. She was a strange woman in a strange town who had been shot and supposedly didn't remember anything. *What can I do? Death is the only option now.*

JEN

Jen noted the defeated look in the woman's eyes and her heart filled with sorrow. "Look, I don't mean this to be weird or anything, but I have a guest room. You are welcome to come stay with me until you can figure things out." The words shocked her even as they left her mouth. *Who did I just invite to live with me? Well, God, if this is you, let me have to convince her. If she accepts too readily, I'll know something's off and will pay for her to stay somewhere else… or something.*

The woman frowned but said nothing for a few minutes. Finally, she spoke. "You don't know me. Why would you do that?"

Jen shrugged.

The woman shook her head. "I have no way to pay you."

"I don't want any money from you." Jen shook her head. *I guess that's my answer, Lord.*

KATE

The offer startled Kate. Money solved everything that sex didn't, but this woman claimed to want nothing of it. *What could life be like? Making friends. Doing whatever I want.* She shook herself back to reality. *What would she want from me?* Kate renewed her study of the woman. *Is it sex that she wants? Maybe I was wrong about her.*

"Look," Jen interrupted her thoughts. "You need a place to stay and I have room. There aren't many other options and I don't want you to end up on the streets." She shrugged again. "Besides, I wouldn't mind the company. My sister works nights and sleeps during the day so I don't get to see her much. If you're worried about money, we can figure that out once you've healed." She smiled. "At least think about it, okay? I'm going to grab something to eat and I'll be back." Jen left the room before Kate could say anything, but quickly poked her head back in. "Would you like anything?"

Yes! Kate thought. *I'm starving.* She couldn't remember the last time she had eaten. It had been days, if not over a week. Kate opened her mouth to say yes, but changed her mind. She didn't want to owe anyone anything. She shook her head.

The woman's gaze seemed to look through Kate's eyes and into her soul for a moment before she disappeared through the door again. Kate stared after her. *Who is this woman? I can't accept this. If she's telling the truth, then this would be perfect. I need a place to stay. But Tony... I could put her in danger. But he knows he shot me. I'm sure he thinks I'm dead. And if she's lying... well, it couldn't get me into anything worse than I've already been in.*

MIRANDA

Nineteen Years Ago

Miranda bit her lip, drew Kate closer, and rocked her back and forth.

In her twenty years, she had seen God do amazing things. Things that people wouldn't believe even if they had seen it. She had seen God heal the blind, lame, and deaf. She had seen the sick recover when all hope was lost. Her life as a missionary kid had firmly established her beliefs in her heart. Her relationship with the Lord meant more to her than her very life. That didn't mean she hadn't ranted at Him or questioned Him about why he had allowed her to be kidnapped and forced to be a sex slave. She abhorred the situation she was in, but never once considered turning her back on God.

It had become clear early in her captivity that she needed to look past her own hurt to minister to the other captives. Being there for them helped her cope with the situation, and she could tell it touched their hearts. They were used to fending for themselves. To have someone show concern for them worked wonders. She spent almost every possible moment in prayer for each of the women. They knew there was something different about her. Slowly but surely, the other women had begun to trust her and to lean on her for strength.

Some of them listened to her when she talked about God, but most of them couldn't understand how she could still follow a God who let her be abused.

Miranda's heart contracted. Silent tears slid down her cheeks as she looked down at the child in her lap, then around the room at the other women who lay on their blankets. They did not understand when she tried to explain that maybe He allowed this to happen to her so they could have hope and the chance of a relationship with Him. *If I could only help them understand! If I could do something. Anything to get them out of here.* She frowned and shook her head, looking back down at the child. *God*, she silently prayed. *Be with this child. Protect her. Show her that you love her. Don't let this life spoil her or harden her heart to you. Have your hand on her and get her out of here, Father. In Jesus' name, I pray.*

The door swung open, and Juan entered. Miranda quickly woke Kate and put a finger to her lips to shush her.

"Where is the kid?" The dim light flickered as Juan headed straight for Miranda.

Miranda stood, put Kate down, and gently pushed her behind her back. "Please, don't do this."

"Girl, do not make me ask again," he warned, his voice laced with frustration. "You are more trouble than you are worth. I thought by now you would have got it in that thick head of yours you have no say what happens here. Move!"

Miranda felt Kate's small hands grab onto the back of her leg and heard her whimper. Her heart felt as if it were being torn to pieces again. "Please." She shook her head and opened her mouth, but the words she wanted to say came out in a gasp as Juan grabbed her hair and twisted his fist.

"I will deal with you later." He shoved her out of the way, grabbed Kate's arm, and dragged her, sobbing, from the room.

Miranda sank to the floor, wrapped her arms around her legs, and rested her head on her knees as tears fell from her eyes.

"I don't know why you keep trying, Miranda. They're going to get so mad with you one day that they kill you. Why do you insist on being so stupid?" one of the other girls asked.

Miranda shook her head against her knees. "They won't kill me. Not soon at least."

"You don't know that."

"I..." Miranda couldn't tell her that God had told her she would not die until she had made a difference. *She wouldn't understand it. I don't even fully understand it.* What that difference could be, or when it would happen, she had no idea. "I don't know. I can't just sit here," she mumbled.

The other girl shook her head. "You had better learn how to."

JASON

Nine Months Ago

Jason walked into the hospital after work. Jen stood scowling at the snack machine. He walked up next to her. "Hungry?"

"No." Jen shook her head. "Just ate."

"Okay... How's our mystery woman doing?"

Jen turned to face him. "She's in pain. There is such a haunted look in her eyes." She hesitated a moment, then added, "I offered to let her stay at my house when she's discharged."

"Oh." Jason tilted his head. "Are you sure you want to do that? We could all pitch in to get her a room."

"No." Jen chewed on her bottom lip. "I really think this is what I'm supposed to do. You know when you get that feeling about something that you just can't ignore?"

"Yes, that's how I found her."

"It'll be nice having someone else around if she agrees. With her job, I rarely see Jemma."

"How is she?"

"Jemma?" Jen frowned. "I don't know exactly. She isn't very open with me except for when she drinks too much."

Jason frowned. "I'm sorry, Jen." He squeezed her

shoulder. "Your parents would be proud of you for taking care of her all these years and trying to be there for her."

Jen gave him a small smile. "Thanks, Jay. I just wish she hadn't turned so far from God when they died. It's hard enough becoming responsible for your twin sister as a teen, but when she totally turns her back on everything she was taught and starts drinking and shoplifting..." Jen sighed and shook her head.

"And you're sure you want to add someone else to that?" Jason asked with a frown. He knew Jemma's lifestyle weighed heavily on Jen and that she felt responsible for her since their parents had died in a car accident five years ago.

Jen's eyes brightened a little. "Yeah. I don't kid myself that it'll be easy, but it seems like that's where God is leading. I just hope that if she does come to live with me, she doesn't join Jemma." She sighed and shrugged with her face. "Anyway, how are you?"

"Tired. Very tired. I-" The James Bond theme interrupted him.

Jen raised an eyebrow. "Bond?"

"That's James Bond to you." Jason grinned before he glanced at the phone. "It's John." He slid the green button to answer the call.

KATE

Fifteen Years Ago

Kate's guard herded her through the back door of the hotel. She barely noticed the people who turned their backs as he directed her to the stairs.

Her guard stopped right outside the door and jutted his chin at it. "You know what to do."

She dipped her head. Her stomach knotted as she knocked on the door. The trembles began, just like they did every time. *Get a grip!* She tried to steel herself for what was coming. *Use your brave face.*

Her brave face had changed from tear-filled eyes and trembling lips to a confident smile. And she did feel confident. She wished she could thank Francesca. Her brave face made it appear like she was in control, and when the men saw that, they seemed to respect her. Yes, she was young. Miranda didn't think she was even a teen yet, but she had learned to act like a woman. She knew what she was doing, after all. She knew what men liked. How to satisfy them. She shook her head to clear it and focused on the task at hand. She knocked again, and her guard moved down the hall towards the stairs.

"He has you for thirty minutes," he said over his shoulder.

She glanced at him and noted the warning in

his eyes. She gave a quick nod of understanding, then turned back to the door as it opened.

She looked up into the face of a slightly older man. Revulsion swirled deep in her gut and she gulped before smiling. "You called for me. Are you going to invite me in?"

The man's face registered surprise before he regained his composure.

"Please." He stepped to the side to make room for her and gestured towards the room. He glanced up and down the hall and nodded at the guard before pushing the door closed. It didn't shut all the way, but the man didn't notice. He watched her run her hand along the edge of the bed. She glanced back at him, unsure. He hadn't moved, but she could see the desire in his eyes. Her look seemed to get him moving.

"Make yourself comfortable," he said as he headed toward the bathroom. "I'll be right back."

She sat on the edge of the bed and swung her feet to keep herself busy. She fought the trembling in her stomach. The hate. The fear. The confusion. They tried to gain control of her, but she pushed them to the farthest reaches of her mind and blocked them there, leaving nothing but emptiness for the moment. She would deal with the emotions later.

She looked around the room, noting how little he had brought. This night, now, was likely the only reason he had come here. Her eyes wandered to the open door. She stood and crept towards it. She knew her guard would be downstairs now, enjoying himself while he kept watch on the time. Kate pulled the door open and took a step out. The hall was empty. *Maybe I could-*

"What are you doing?" the man asked from behind her.

Kate jumped and spun around. She didn't even realize what she had been doing. "I... uh... I..." She stumbled over her words at a loss for an explanation.

"I don't know where you think you're going. I paid for you, you know." He came toward her, determined.

Kate shook her head. "I wasn't going anywhere." She stepped back into the room and pushed the door shut. She remained completely calm on the outside, but inside? Inside, she cringed and suppressed a shudder as the door clicked shut. That was the sound of her moment of freedom snatched away. The sound of a lifetime of torture yet to come.

Kate smiled. "I thought I heard someone at the door." She pushed all the sweetness she could muster into her voice. "I was just checking. It must have been another room." She saw his doubt at her claim. She needed to convince him. It could get ugly if she didn't.

She braced herself, swallowed her revulsion, and stepped towards him. She laid a hand on his arm. "Honest. I wasn't going anywhere. You'll get what you paid for." She trailed her fingers down his arm as she stepped around him and sauntered to the bed. He followed, convinced.

KATE

Nine Months Ago

Kate lay staring at the ceiling again. She felt a little better with the liquids in her, but her shoulder hurt. Hunger and exhaustion fought for attention. Unfortunately, sleep evaded her. Every time she closed her eyes, flashes of her past haunted her. Uncertainty of the future would not let her mind rest. Then there was Jen and that guy who had found her. *Why didn't I just die? If there really is a god, if you really exist, why would you let me live?*

The door opened. The guy who had found her walked in with the woman behind him. Kate forced herself to relax with him so close, but she couldn't quite calm the trembling in her stomach. She didn't understand him, and that made her even more nervous. She understood men who wanted sex and money. This one... this one seemed so different from any man she had ever known and it set her on edge.

The nurses' conversation, when they thought she had been asleep, haunted her thoughts. They had whispered about how he found her and had carried her in from the woods. Apparently, he had refused to leave until they were sure she would live. They had joked about how cute he was and how lucky Kate was to have him save her. Their conversation quickly turned to the cutest guys in the hospital, and Kate had tuned them out. Now, here he was again. *What does he want?*

"Hey, how are you feeling?" he asked.

Kate clenched and unclenched her hand as she studied his face. The kindness there set her on edge. She shrugged her good shoulder and let her face settle into an emotionless mask. "Fine." Her voice came out terse and sharp.

He smiled, though his eyes showed his disbelief. "That's good. Jen told me she said you can stay with her." His voice remained kind, despite her complete lack of civility.

Kate looked from the man to the woman and back again. Her breath came quick and short. It seemed as if the walls were closing in on her. She was sure the panic she felt was clear to see. *So much for my emotionless mask.* "I... I can't..."

"Jay, leave it be," the woman interrupted with a scowl. But she didn't scowl at Kate. She scowled at the man. "She's barely had time to think about it."

The man made a face at the woman, but then shrugged and turned back to Kate. "Okay. But let me tell you... You won't find a better place to stay around here than with Jen. Plus, she's an amazing cook."

The woman, Jen, rolled her eyes. "Get out of here." She shoved him toward the door.

The man chuckled. "It's true." He looked back as he allowed Jen to push him from the room. "Keep that in mind while you're thinking about it." He waved as Jen pushed the door closed, shaking her head with a grin.

"I'm sorry about him," she said.

Kate stared at Jen, everything within her in a turmoil. She'd been sure the man would turn and hit Jen when she pushed him from the room, but he had let it happen without retaliating. The fact that Jen had even dared to do such a thing astonished her. *Is she not afraid of him at all?*

A nurse walked in. "It's time to change your bandage, Hon."

Kate bit her lip and squeezed her eyes shut as the nurse carefully removed the bandage. As hard as she tried to keep it in, a gasp of pain escaped her.

"I'm sorry." Condescension filled the nurse's voice. "It would really help if you took the medi-"

"No!" Kate took a deep breath to steady her voice. "Thank you," she added softly.

Kate squeezed her eyes shut again as the nurse continued to remove her bandage. She needed to distract herself. She opened her eyes and found herself looking right at Jen, who stood off to the side; a slight frown on her face. There was something in this woman's eyes and a strange sense of *welcome? Safety? Something...*

I'll be back out on the street if I don't accept her offer. It can't be worse than that. I'll just stay till my shoulder is better. Yeah. That could work. Kate clenched her teeth and squeezed the bedsheet with her good hand as the nurse cleaned and redressed her wound. *Then I'll repay her somehow and move on.* The nurse finally left. Kate breathed a sigh of relief as the pain in her shoulder lessened.

Jen walked over and sat on the end of the bed. "I got you Cheez-its." She opened the bag and held them out. "I know you said you didn't want anything but-" She broke off as Kate's stomach rumbled.

Kate's cheeks flushed, and she looked away.

Jen leaned over and set the bag down by Kate's hand. "They're here when you want them."

Kate looked up again. Kindness filled the woman's steady gaze and a small smile turned up the corners of her lips. Kate shook her head. It took almost all the energy she had to not grab the bag and dig in, but there were things she needed to know. "Why? Why are you willing to let me stay with you? You don't know me. I can't pay you... Wh-?" She wasn't exactly sure what else she wanted to ask. No matter how hard she tried, she could not comprehend the woman's offer.

Jen shrugged. "Honestly?" She paused and studied Kate for a moment before she continued, "I feel like it's what God told me to do."

"God?" Kate asked. Bitterness laced her voice.

"Yep," Jen answered. "I know it may sound crazy, but I trust Him when He tells me to do things. I know He loves me and, even if it seems completely unusual, He has a reason for the things He does. Who am I to get in the way of that?"

Kate frowned. Miranda had had a faith like that. She had been at peace, well as much peace as she could have been in, in their circumstance. If not for her, Kate would not have made it through those first few years with her sanity... or even at all. *It would be nice to have a faith like that... But I've been through too much. Have done too much. Not even God could love me now. He wouldn't even let me die. That's how much he hates me!*

JEN

Jen watched the emotions flicker through the woman's eyes. It was such a familiar look. She was sure she had seen it somewhere before, but the memory lurked just out of reach. She shook the thought off as her heart broke for this woman. *God, please let her agree to stay with me. Show me how to share your love with her. Give me the right words. Speak to her Father. Fill her with your peace.*

KATE

Warmth filled Kate's heart. It was a wonderful feeling, but so unexpected and unusual that it startled her.

"Look, I know this is probably a strange thought to you, but I don't look at my life as my own. My life is God's. It is to be used to honor Him, love others, serve them, and care for them. If letting you stay with me accomplishes that, then I have done part of what I was made to do. You don't have to decide now if you aren't sure, but the room is ready, and it's yours if you want it."

As confused as she was by this, Kate felt at ease for the first time she could remember. *If she's willing to give me a place to stay, I should just take it and whatever happens, happens.* She hesitated another moment before taking the plunge. "I-I'll stay with you," she said. "But only until I find a job and another place."

"Great." Jen's face lit up. "It will be nice having someone else around." She jumped off the bed and her eyes fell on the Cheez-its next to Kate. "I'm going to go get you some actual food."

"You d-"

Jen interrupted her with a wave of her hand. "I want to. And whether you want to admit it or not, you need some food." She smiled and hurried out of the room.

Kate half expected to never see her again, but she returned a short time later with a tray. Jen laid the tray on Kate's lap and pulled a chair closer to her bed. She sat and folded her legs under her.

"I thought maybe I could share a bit about my life, so you aren't moving in with a complete stranger. What do you think?"

Kate eyed Jen before she picked up the sandwich and took a bite. Did she care about Jen's life or that she would move in with a complete stranger? No, not really. *I've spent my life fulfilling the desires of strangers. Living with another one isn't a big deal. But she just got comfortable and I don't want to offend her in any way. What if she takes back her offer? Besides, if she leaves, I'll be alone with my memories.* Kate suppressed a shudder.

She shrugged and nodded as she chewed her food. *Why not listen to her and get to know her a bit? It won't matter much, anyway. I won't be around long enough for it to matter, but it can't hurt. She'll get nothing out of me if she thinks she can get me talking, though.*

Jen smiled and settled back into the chair. "Okay, well, I have a twin sister. I was born first, though. My parents owned a mechanic shop. I grew up helping my dad work on cars."

Kate listened to Jen's voice more than the things she said. Her voice was soft and clear. Nothing like anyone else's voice she had ever known. She could not hold back a smile at Jen's childhood mischief, but soon she was yawning. She finished her food as Jen continued to talk about her childhood.

Kate rested her head back on the pillows and glanced over at Jen, who was still talking about herself and had asked no questions about her, which was just how Kate had hoped it would go. She wasn't ready to share anything with anyone. She would never be ready to share the horrors she'd lived through. Kate studied Jen's profile as she looked out the window and continued her story. Before she knew it, her eyes drifted closed, and she fell into a deep sleep.

JEN

Jen turned from the window to see the woman had fallen asleep. The strain on her face had lessened, though it was still visible. Affection like what she felt for her sister filled her chest. Jen pulled the blanket up to cover the woman more and smiled. *I should probably leave, but it feels wrong to leave her here alone. What if she needs something during the night? Yes, she has the nurses, but still...*

She grabbed a hospital blanket from the small closet and curled up in the chair again. She yawned, pulled out her phone, opened the Bible app, and scrolled to Isaiah 54, where she had left off the night before. When she got to verses seven and eight, she paused and reread them in a whisper. "For a brief moment I deserted you, but with great compassion I will gather you. In overflowing anger for a moment I hid my face from you, but with everlasting love I will have compassion on you, says the Lord, your Redeemer." She glanced over her phone at the woman asleep on the bed. "God, gather her with your great compassion. Fill her with your everlasting love." She laid her head back and shut her eyes.

******

Jen opened her eyes, not quite sure what had woken her. She frowned and looked around the room.

"No." The woman on the bed pleaded. She tossed her head. Her blanket tangled around her. Her breath came short and fast. Sweat beaded her forehead. "No." She mumbled something Jen couldn't understand, but she understood the fear in her voice.

Jen sat up and tapped her uninjured shoulder. "Hey. Hey, wake up."

The woman didn't react, but continued her frantic tossing.

Jen shook her, trying not to jostle her shoulder. "Hey, wake up," she said louder. Still no reaction. Jen watched her silently, not sure what else to do. She didn't want her to injure her shoulder, tossing and turning like that. "God, give her peace. Calm her fears." After another minute, the woman stopped tossing, but her face was tight and she made a noise that almost sounded like a whine.

Compassion filled Jen's heart, and she leaned over to brush the woman's damp hair out of her face. Worship calmed her when she was afraid. She sang Great is Thy Faithfulness, the first song that came to mind.

KATE

Kate startled awake in a cold sweat, her heart pounding. Her eyes darted back and forth around the room as she tried to place where she was. The shadows that chased her had seemed so real. She was sure she would find them in the corners of the room or lurking next to her bed. As items in the room came into focus and her breathing calmed, she heard a clear, soft voice, and realized someone was brushing her hair back from her face.

Miranda? She wondered. Her heartbeat steadied as she turned her head. A strange woman sat next to her. She blinked blankly a few times before she recognized her. *Jen. The woman who said I could stay with her.*

Jen smiled at her, but continued to sing and stroke her hair.

Kate briefly smiled back and squeezed her eyes shut as tears welled in them. She didn't understand this woman, and yet, she felt so safe around her. *It's probably because she reminds me of Miranda. No, I won't think of Miranda now. I can't!* Kate pushed thoughts of Miranda away as she focused in on Jen's voice. Even though she knew God didn't care for her, the words were comforting and she drifted off to sleep again.

******

Early the next morning, Kate woke as a nurse entered the room. She rubbed the sleep out of her eyes and glanced around. Her terror from the night before was evident by the blanket twisted around her in odd ways. Her eyes landed on Jen's body draped in an awkward position from the chair she was in to a corner of the bed. Her hand was next to Kate's head as if she had fallen asleep while comforting her last night.

Kate felt a stab of confused guilt. This woman didn't know her. Didn't owe her anything, but she had stayed by her side all night. A part of the wall around her heart began to crumble as she again recognized an attitude like Miranda.

A happy tune pierced the quiet room. Kate jolted at the sudden noise, and tingles spread up and down her body. She took a deep, calming breath when she saw Jen's phone glowing on the arm of the chair.

Kate watched Jen grimace as she sat up, rubbed her neck, and stretched. A smile quickly masked her frown when Jen saw she was watching her.

"Good morning." She glanced at the phone. "I'm sorry if this woke you." She tapped the screen, and the ringtone silenced. She put the phone to her ear. "Hey, hang on." She turned back to Kate. "It's my sister. I'll be right back."

Kate nodded as Jen stood and left the room. It wasn't until after she shut the door that Kate realized that she hadn't had time to contemplate her suicide. In fact, the exact opposite had happened. She had decided to live. Against her will, the first stirrings of hope had awoken in her soul. Kate shut her eyes and took a deep breath, steeling herself. *What is wrong with me?* She couldn't let herself hope. That was when you got hurt.

KATE

Eleven Years Ago

Kate stared at the ground in front of her as she plodded along behind her escort. She did NOT want to think about what had just happened. She pushed all thoughts from her mind and focused only on the movement of her legs. *Right. Left. Right. Left. Right.* The man she had just served had not been gentle in any sense of the word. She shivered, rubbed her sore wrists, and forced back the tears that sprang to her eyes. *Left. Right. Left. Crying does nothing.* She reminded herself. Francesca's face came unbidden to her mind as she encouraged her to use her brave face. Kate frowned as an image of Francesca's face just before JP had shot her formed in her mind. The next image was one she'd tried to forget. Francesca crumpled on the ground in a puddle of blood. *That's my future. That's what's going to happen to me.* She walked into something solid and glanced up.

Her guard turned to glare at her. "Watch it," he growled.

"Sorry!" She cringed and scrambled back a few steps before she glanced around. Juan and a few other men were having a very intense discussion. He beckoned her guard over. Her guard took her arm and dragged her past them into the small guard room before joining Juan by the door.

Kate sighed and rolled her shoulders as she prepared to wait however long it would take for this meeting to end. Her eyes flitted about the small guardroom, taking everything in. She paused when her eyes landed on the table. Juan's knife lay there, unsheathed. Her eyes flicked up to the group of men by the door. None of them paid any attention to her.

Inch by inch, she made her way to the table, pausing only to make sure she hadn't drawn attention. She finally reached the table and let out the breath she hadn't realized she'd been holding. She eyed the knife. It was about as long as her forearm. A ragged saw lined the top of the blade. The metal glinted in the dark room, reflecting the dull light from the lamp next to it. Her stomach twisted at the thought of the blade slicing into her throat. She didn't want to die, but if she could escape this life; she was ready.

Kate glanced once more at the men, who still appeared too engrossed in their conversation to notice her. She reached out and gripped the knife, placing the edge against her neck. She hesitated, adjusted her grip on the knife, and tried to gather her courage. The muscles of her arm bunched as she prepared to pull the knife across her throat. She squeezed her eyes shut and pressed harder.

Her eyes popped open as a hand clamped around her wrist. Kate peered up to see her guard glaring at her. She yelped in pain as he twisted her wrist so hard he wrenched her whole body. She tried in vain to cling to the knife as he wrestled it from her fingers. Her guard shoved her toward Juan, who caught her by the throat.

"No!" she cried. Kate gritted her teeth together

as she tried to pull Juan's hand from her throat. He laughed at her and squeezed just hard enough to hurt and block some of her air, but not enough to kill her. *No, they would not want to do that. That would be wasteful.*

She struggled to loosen his hold and draw some air into her burning lungs. Juan lifted her up on her toes, putting even more pressure on her throat. She tried to kick at him, but each movement sent shooting pains through her neck. Desperate, she scratched at his arm.

"Argh!" Juan shoved her hard against the wall.

Her head slammed into the brick. Pain shot through her whole body. She squirmed weakly but couldn't escape his grip.

Juan scowled. He held out his free hand. Her guard placed the knife in it. She froze, her eyes widened as she watched him bring the point up to the corner of her eye. The cold metal sent tremors down her spine. *He is going to cut my eyes out!*

She had been so close to escaping this life! But no. She'd waited too long. She pressed against his arm with both hands, forcing herself more firmly against the wall in an attempt to stop her body from trembling. Death was one thing. Having your eyes cut out? That was a different story.

"Please, no," she croaked. Her eyes flickered from the knife to his face and back again. She tried to tilt her face away, but the knife followed, pressing more firmly into her skin.

Juan leaned close to her ear. "Give me one good reason why I shouldn't," he seethed.

It was useless to try to stop her body from shaking. Kate frantically searched her mind. *What should I say to him?* There was no telling what Juan would do when he was angry. He wouldn't pity her. Crying would only anger him. Begging would do no good. The only thing that he cared for was money, loyalty, and obedience.

Her eyes widened. "Money!" she gasped out.

Juan lowered her until she could stand on her own. His hand shifted slightly on her throat. She felt a split second of relief until his fingers tightened around her jaw, holding her head still. He glared at her but remained silent, his permission to continue.

"Your business," Kate whispered, grasping at the only chance she would get to save her eyes. "I'm one of your best girls. The most requested." She couldn't believe she was using herself as a bargaining chip. *Maybe I should just let him cut my eyes out. Once the men see me without eyes, they won't want me. I'll be useless. They'll kill me then.* But she knew Juan wouldn't let her off that easily. *I need my eyes if I'm ever going to have another chance.*

"They'll lose interest in me," her voice trembled as she pleaded her case. She tried to ignore the knife, searching his face for any hint that what she said made a difference. She felt a glimmer of hope when he frowned. "If men don't request me as much, you will lose a lot of moh-" she cut off in a gasp as his fingers dug into her skin.

"Very well," he said as he looked her over. "You have convinced me to let you keep your eye. This... incident, however, cannot go unpunished." He stood silent for a moment, then nodded as if in response to a suggestion. He nodded again to the other men in the room. "Hold her," he commanded.

Two men took hold of her arms, immobilizing

her between them. They held her still while Juan slowly lit a cigar. He watched the flame of the lighter waver and dance before he snapped it shut.

Kate jumped at the sound and tried to twist away, but the men held her fast. Jaun stared at her as he puffed deeply on his cigar. Kate tried not to squirm under his hard stare. After a few minutes of complete silence, Juan reached out and grabbed the hair at the top of her head. He yanked her head to the side and, before she knew what was happening, pressed the lit end of the cigar to the skin behind her ear.

KATE

Nine Months Ago

Kate shut her eyes and took a deep breath. She fingered the scars behind her ear and stared blankly at the wall. She tried to ignore the pain as the nurses changed her bandage and checked her over one last time. Anxiety twisted her gut. *What was I thinking? Why did I agree to stay with her? This is a really bad idea.* She bit her lip.

She squeezed her eyes shut and groaned as the nurse pressed a new bandage to her wound and taped it on. She drew in a deep breath and pushed it out through her teeth. Kate relaxed, slouching back on the bed as the nurses left the room. She shook her head and pressed her lips together, resting her chin on her hand with a finger over her lips. *What do I do? I can just leave.* She pushed herself up. *But then I will have nowhere to go...* "Ugh!" She sank back onto the bed. *What would Miranda do? Miranda. If she was injured, she would probably accept the invitation, but if she knew she was being searched for... Miranda would never put others in danger.*

Tears sprang to Kate's eyes, and she angrily wiped them away. *I don't have time for this. I don't want to put anyone in danger. But I'm so tired. So sick of being on guard all the time. But that won't change. I will have to be* on guard for the rest of my life. *It's so peaceful when that woman's around. If I could just grasp onto that peace...* She let out a huff. *Not likely. I will never have peace. But maybe, if I am around it for a little, maybe it will give me the strength to keep going. Tony wouldn't find me this quickly anyway... would he? He shot me miles from where that man found me.* She sighed again and ran a hand restlessly through her hair. *He thinks I'm dead. He isn't still looking for me... is he?*

JEN

Jen walked through the hospital doors and headed straight for the elevator. She punched the up button and paced the floor while she waited for the doors to open. When they did, she hurried inside and punched the button for the second floor, tapping her foot impatiently. She was here earlier than she had planned to be. *God, please don't let her be gone. Please let her still be willing to come stay with me. Help me show her your love for her, Lord. Calm her fears and worries.* She had an awful feeling that the woman was going to just up and leave. She had been praying all morning at work and, finally, unable to take it anymore, had talked to Steve. He had insisted he could handle things at the shop, shooed her out the door, and she had driven to the hospital a bit faster than the speed limit allowed.

She tapped her fingers against her thigh and blew out a breath. *What will I do if she left?* She didn't want to think about that. *She didn't have anywhere else to go; I could tell that from her expression the other day.*

The bell dinged, and the door slid open. Jen practically ran to the room. As she hurried down the hall, she thought back to the night before. John and Jason had hosted a worship and prayer night. The woman, Jen hated referring to her as Jane Doe, had been the focus of the prayer time. It had been a full house, which was exciting. The thing that had made the night even better was the fact that everyone who had attended had pitched in to help pay the hospital bill for the woman. Jason had taken care of the bill first thing this morning. Jen was sure God was going to do something amazing in this woman's life if she let Him.

Jen turned the corner and paused mid-step. The woman quietly pulled her door shut.

Jen shook off her concern, relieved to see that the woman was still here. "Hi!" Jen hurried up to her. "It is good to see you up and about."

The woman jumped and spun around with wide, frightened eyes.

Jen grimaced. "I'm sorry. I didn't mean to startle you."

Guilt, fear, anxiety, and relief played across the woman's face before her expression went blank and she dropped her head. She fiddled with the edge of her sling and shrugged. "It's fine," she mumbled.

"Were you headed somewhere? I can walk with you if you want company."

KATE

Kate glanced up at Jen. She looked... hopeful. Kate averted her eyes again. *Should I tell her I changed her mind? That I won't stay with her? That I'll just disappear and she won't ever have to think of me again?*

Kate's chest constricted. For some reason, she didn't want to leave. This woman was offering her a chance. An opportunity she would likely never receive again. *How can I throw that away?*

"Is everything okay?" Jen's soft voice interrupted her thoughts.

Kate knew if she didn't stay, it would crush her. Jen's kindness confused her, but made her feel like perhaps she really did have a chance. And there was something else. She had no idea why, but somehow, she knew that it would crush Jen if she left as well. She didn't want to do that. Jen had been nothing but kind to her.

"Yeah," Kate finally answered. "I... I just took a walk." She gestured down the hall.

Jen drew her eyebrows together for a quick second before her face relaxed, and she nodded.

Kate forced a smile but said nothing else. *Does she know I just lied? Did she see me leave the room just now?* She opened her door again and walked back into the room, leaving the door open behind her. Kate sank onto the edge of the bed and brushed the hair out of her face. She pushed away the memories that tried to fill her mind and focused on the throbbing pain in her shoulder. After a few minutes, Kate felt Jen watching her. She glanced up to see her hovering in the doorway.

"Uh, I know I'm a bit early, but are you ready to get out of here?"

Am I ready? Can I actually take this chance to live on my own terms? Fear swirled in Kate's gut. She hadn't thought about the "what next" when she had seen her opportunity to escape. Now, that was all she could think about. *Can I actually live here? Will staying with Jen actually be living on my own terms, or does she just want to use me like everyone else?* Kate pushed her breath out through her clenched teeth. She didn't know. Regardless of Jen's motives, it would get her out of the hospital and off the streets. She nodded. "Yes."

"All right then, let's go."

Kate rose and followed Jen without a word. She was used to this. Following people wherever they led her. It was a normal thing. One she barely thought about. She couldn't keep from glancing behind her every few steps, though. She was convinced she would find Tony stalking her or that someone had fallen in behind to make sure she wouldn't try to escape.

"Did you have a good night?"

Kate jerked her head up to find Jen had paused and was waiting for her to catch up. That was not normal. "I guess," she mumbled as she caught up to Jen. Jen started again, but slower, matching her pace to Kate's.

They stopped at the desk, and Kate watched the people around them. She paid no attention to the conversation Jen had with the nurse. Her eyes flitted over the people, searching for anyone who seemed familiar.

Anyone who might be a danger. All her muscles tensed. *There's too many people here. It's too open.*

Someone touched her shoulder. Kate yanked herself away from the touch, jolting her injured shoulder in the process, and spun to face whatever danger awaited. Jen stood there, her arm outstretched and her mouth opened in a surprised O.

"I'm sorry." Jen recovered and let her arm drop. "I don't mean to keep startling you. I'll have to work on that."

The sincerity in her face pierced Kate's heart. Once again, she realized how similar Jen was to Miranda. She glanced behind her once more before she relaxed. "I'm sorry." She looked back at Jen. "It's just-" she clamped her mouth shut. No matter how much Jen might remind her of Miranda, she wasn't her. She wouldn't understand. *I'm not even sure I can really trust her. How could I have almost given myself away so easily?* She shook her head and cradled her injured arm to her body.

Jen gave her a tentative smile and tilted her head toward the hall. "Come on."

Kate followed Jen again. *I have to stop reacting that way. I might make her suspicious.* She sighed. *I don't know how I'll manage that...* Her reactions were ingrained into her. They were automatic. An attempt at self-preservation.

"This is us." Jen gestured to a car. She pulled the passenger door open before she headed to the driver's side and got in.

Kate frowned.

Jen leaned over the passenger seat and looked up at Kate. "Everything okay?"

She was just being kind. Kate told herself. Her frown deepened. People weren't kind to her. It just didn't happen.

Jen frowned. "Did you forget something? We can go back in." She moved to unbuckle her seat belt.

Kate shook her head. "No. It's... nothing." She slid into the seat and pulled the door shut. Jen started the car and pulled out of the parking lot. Kate could sense her looking over every few minutes, but she kept her face turned to the window. She focused on blocking her thoughts and fears, going to that place where nothing could touch her. She barely registered the town as they drove through it. The quiet rumble of the engine soothed her, helping her block everything else out.

"So... do you remember your name?" Jen's voice pulled Kate from her safe place.

Kate turned to her and blinked. "Uh..." A memory surfaced so vividly it was like it was happening at the moment.

KATE

Ten Years Ago

"What's your name?" The man asked.

Kate repressed a shiver as his hand slid up and down her arm. He was younger than most of the men she served, but he had that same hunger in his eyes. She stared at a spot over his shoulder and pushed everything from her mind. Only in that place of nothingness could she survive. She plastered a smile on her face and raised an eyebrow. "Most people call me Kid but you can call me whatever you want." She forced a playful tone into her voice.

All the girls went by whatever name the men gave them. They buried their real names, along with their real identities, deep in their hearts to protect them.

Miranda had done her best to make sure they remembered who they were. She had begged them to remember good things from their pasts, asked about their families, their friends, and their lives before captivity, and told them to cling to those things. Most of them doubted they would ever be free, but she had created a safe place for them, even in their circumstances. When they were alone, she would use everyone's real name.

"Kate, Lyubov, Jessica, Hung," Miranda had looked each one of them in the eyes as she said their name, "what is happening to you is NOT who you are. Remember who you are at the core of your being. Deep in your heart." Kate could hear the passion in her voice as if she were speaking the words now. "God created each of you with hopes and dreams. Do not let the evil happening to you snuff those out." Her eyes had been alight with excitement. "I have always wanted to travel the world as a missionary, like my parents. To maybe settle in a village somewhere and help village women raise their children and teach them to read and write. What about you? What do you want to do?"

They had shared their true selves with each other in that dark room.

KATE

Nine Months Ago

Kate's eyes filled with tears as she blinked herself back to the present. Jen's profile came into focus through her watery eyes. She cleared her throat, then bit her lower lip. *Would I remember my name with... what had the doctor called it? Amne... something...?*

Jen glanced over before turning her eyes back to the road. "Hey, if you don't remember, it's okay. No worries. It'll come to you one of these days. Is there something you would like me to call you until you remember?"

Kate breathed a sigh of relief, but then she frowned. Something about Jen seemed familiar. As if she had seen her before somewhere. *But that's impossible.* She shook her head, wiped the tears from her eyes, and focused back on the question at hand. *What would I like to be called?* She wasn't sure after all those years of being called whatever names the men felt like giving her. *Should I use my real name?* Something inside cringed at that thought. It had been so long since anyone had called her that. *Since Miranda had... No.* She shook her head again, willing herself not to go there. *That's too personal. If I'm going to be safe, no one can know anything.* She wracked her brain, going over the different names she'd been called. She couldn't come up with anything she wanted to use. *Why is this so difficult? You would think I'd be able to pick a name for myself!* Finally, she gave up with a shrug and went with a variation of her normal answer. "I don't know. What do you want to call me?"

Jen was silent for so long that Kate mentally kicked herself. *I should have just picked any stupid name. What is wrong with me?* She glanced at Jen out of the corners of her eyes. She was looking out the windshield with a frown. Kate fingered her scars behind her ear again. It was an old nervous habit. *Should I take it back? Just pick a name?*

JEN

What do I want to call her? Jen frowned out the windshield. She hadn't expected that. The light up ahead turned yellow. She slowed and stopped at the light, then peered over at the woman through the corner of her eyes. She looked nervous, anxious even, as she bit her lip and stared straight ahead. *Why does she look so familiar?*

Jen reached up to adjust the rearview mirror to give herself more time to think. The woman flinched away from her arm. Jen sighed.

God, what do I say? I want to believe that she is telling the truth and can't remember anything, but I just have this feeling that she's lying. And her expressions. She looks so haunted... so... hurt. But I don't want to press her for the truth. Do I just let it slide? What can I do to make her feel more at ease? Should I encourage her to choose a name or should I just pick a name and leave it be?

Dawn. Katherine.

Both names passed through her mind like a whisper. Jen focused forward again, and her frown deepened. The light turned green, and she pressed on the gas. *Dawn? Katherine? Are they from you, God?*

The names repeated in her mind again. They were nice names. Katherine was a pretty name, but Dawn? It represented a new day. New things to come. A new beginning. Maybe that's what this woman needed. "What do you think of Dawn or Katherine?" she asked.

In her periphery, Jen saw the woman turn quickly towards her. Her eyes were wide. All color drained from her face as it became a mask of horror and astonishment. Concern filled Jen. *Is she going to pass out?* She turned toward the woman. After a few silent moments, during which Jen was sure the woman was not even breathing, she blinked. All emotion disappeared from her face. "Uh... Dawn. Is fine," she muttered. She turned back to stare blankly out the window.

What was that about? One second she's terrified. The next she seems like she doesn't care at all. Jen could not understand how someone could seem so indifferent to something as important as a name. The woman, Dawn, seemed as if she didn't care at all. *Does she really forget everything, Lord?* Jen wondered again. *I guess her reactions could be because she forgets... but that look in her eyes...*

Dawn sat in silence. Jen couldn't read her expression, but she sensed how uncomfortable she felt. She wanted to ease the tension that rolled off of her. "I can't imagine what you have been through." Jen shook her head and blew out a breath. "What you are going through. But if you ever want to talk, I'm here for you." She turned into her driveway and shifted into park.

Dawn said nothing as Jen reached in the back to retrieve her pocketbook. As she straightened, Jen caught Dawn wipe at her cheek. She thought about asking what was wrong, but so far, Dawn had not seemed to want to talk about anything. Instead, she reached into her purse and pulled out the extra key she'd had made. She held it out to Dawn. "This is for you. I figured you'd probably want a key so you don't have to worry if you want to go out or anything."

Dawn didn't flinch this time, but she stared at the key. Her tear-filled eyes flicked up to Jen's before they returned to the key. Jen watched the muscle in her jaw work as Dawn scowled at the key.

"Um, if you ever forget it, I have a hidden key under the frog by the window."

Dawn clenched her hands into fists on her lap. Jen continued to hold the key out. She wracked her brain for anything else she could say to put Dawn at ease, but came up with nothing. She took a deep breath. *God, give me wisdom. Put her at ease.* She let her breath out and opened her car door. "Well, let's get you settled in." She slid the key into Dawn's fist and moved to climb out of the car.

"Thank you."

Dawn spoke the words so quietly that Jen wasn't sure she had actually heard them. She glanced back to see Dawn staring at her. Jen smiled. "You're welcome." She tilted her head toward the house. "Let's go."

KATE

"This is your room." Jen pushed the door open and stepped back.

Kate could feel Jen's eyes on her, but she focused on the room. Her eyes widened. She took a tentative step forward, then hesitated. *This is a mistake.* A voice in the back of her mind taunted her. *Who are you to think you can live here, in this house, with someone like Jen? You'll taint her. You'll endanger her and her sister. You can never fit in here.* Her heart sank. *It's true...*

"Go ahead," Jen's light, welcoming voice broke through her thoughts.

Kate shifted her weight from one foot to the other, then glanced over at Jen. Jen's eyes lit up with her smile. Kate took a deep breath. She would figure her thoughts out later, but for now... She stepped forward.

"What do you think?"

Kate let her eyes rove over the room. The first thing she noticed was the color. The room was full of it. She couldn't remember ever seeing a room so colorful. It was so unlike the peeling plaster on the cinderblock walls of the room the men kept her in as a child and the dirty, yellowed walls of Tony's apartment.

Three of the walls were a deep purple. The fourth was dark grey. The blanket on the bed to her right had grey and purple circles and a plain grey pillowcase. A night table sat next to the bed with a small lamp.

Against the far wall, across from the bed, a small table sat against the wall with a t.v. and remote. A knot formed in the pit of her stomach when she noticed it. *Why is there a t.v. in here?* Scenes from the porn movies Tony liked to watch in bed flashed through her mind. An involuntary shiver shook her body. The longer she stared at the t.v. the sicker she felt.

She swallowed and turned to the closet set into the grey wall. A few items of clothing hung there, including a robe on a hook on the door and a pair of slippers on the floor.

A tall dresser sat against the wall next to the closet with a single candle on top and a book of matches next to it. *I never would have been allowed to have matches with Tony.*

Finally, Kate turned back to the windows. The shades were halfway down the two windows. Grey curtains tied off to the sides framed the windows. Sheer, dark purple curtains hung down to the windowsill. It was so much prettier than Tony's dirty, broken blinds. But that material. It looked like the night clothes Tony provided for her when she would entertain his guests. *Does it feel the same?*

Kate stepped farther into the room. Her foot sank into something soft and thick. She yanked her foot back and glanced down. A rug with thick grey circles interwoven with thin purple circles covered a section of the floor.

"Well?" Anticipation filled Jen's voice and something else.

Is she nervous? Kate tore her gaze from the rug and turned to face Jen. Yes. Kate could see the nervousness in her eyes, though she contained it well. If she wasn't so used to reading the negative emotions in people, she might not have noticed. The thought shook Kate from her own mind. *What is it like for her, opening her home like this? Inviting a stranger in. Yeah, living with strangers is normal for me, but... is it normal?*

Kate fingered her sling. *I should say something, but what?* She glanced at the room again, then back at Jen. She forced a small smile. "I... it's beautiful."

Jen's shoulders relaxed. The nervousness seemed to disappear. "Oh, I'm so glad you like it. I wasn't sure... I don't mind repainting if you don't like purple."

"No, I... I like it." *Most of it.* It wasn't another lie. She just didn't tell the full truth. *I can deal with what I don't like.*

Jen stepped into the room and gestured to the closet. "I went out last night and bought you some clothes. I guessed your size. There's more in the dresser. Just a few changes of everything you might need. I figured we could go out together another time so you can pick some stuff out for yourself."

Another part of the wall around Kate's heart crumbled. She couldn't understand why she had trouble keeping her shield up around Jen. She wanted to shut down completely and totally shut Jen out, but she was so kind. It seemed impossible.

Kate eyed the clothes. Not one of the items even remotely resembled any of the other clothes the men had provided her with during her life. Kate stared at the closet with longing before she walked over and hesitantly reached out with her good arm. She turned back to Jen, who nodded. Kate touched the edge of a deep blue sweater. The material was soft and thick. Nothing like the silk and lace she was used to. Everything in this closet would cover her completely. Something she had only experienced when going outside with Tony during the winter months and even then, she was just barely covered.

She forced her thoughts back to the sweater in her hand and gently rubbed the material between her fingertips, relishing the feel of it. "These are for me?" she asked, her voice barely a whisper. She bit her lower lip and stared at the clothes. How could she accept these things? *I'm lying to this woman and she's gone out of her way to....* Kate shook her head and forced herself to release the fabric. She avoided Jen's gaze. "You didn't have to do that. I... I can't accept these."

"Yes, you can. They're a gift."

The walls seemed to close in on her. She ran a hand through her hair and stopped by her ear to finger her scars. "But.. y... you don't under-"

"It's okay. I don't *need* to understand."

Kate finally made herself meet Jen's gaze. Her eyes were calm and clear. *Does she... she knows I'm lying.* Fear spiked through Kate, and she took a step back. "Y... you know...?" her voice trembled. She paused and swallowed, but couldn't make herself finish the question.

"I figured you haven't lost your memory. You seem too... haunted." Jen smiled, her compassion radiated from her. "Dawn, I meant what I said in the car. If you ever want to talk, I am here for you. But, if not, that's fine too. I fully intend to be here for you in other ways. You need clothes and food and all. I want to provide those things for you. Besides." Jen shrugged. "A group of us were praying for you the other night and we gathered some donations to help provide you with the stuff you need."

Kate opened her mouth to object, but Jen held up a hand, silencing her.

"Please, let me do this for you. It's what God is calling me to do."

Kate pressed her lips together and averted her eyes again. *She knows I'm lying, but she still wants to do this?* It made no sense at all. When Juan or Tony had caught her lying... She shuddered. She didn't even want to think about it. *If she's okay with this, I should just accept it. She's not asking any questions... But what if she tells someone?* Kate drew in a deep breath. *I'll just have to take that chance.* She nodded slowly.

"Great." Jen's voice sounded light and relieved, but Kate couldn't bring herself to look up at her again. "Well, make yourself at home. I'll be downstairs if you need anything, okay?"

Kate nodded again. She kept her eyes on the floor until she heard the door click shut. She stood there a moment, fully expecting to hear a bolt slam into place. After a minute with no other sounds, she crept to the door. She hesitated, afraid her fear would turn out to be true. Finally, she reached out and turned the handle. The door opened easily. She eyed both the door and the frame. No bolts or locks of any kind on the outside.

She eased the door shut and stared about the room. Her eyes fell on the blue sweater. She glanced at the door, then walked over to the closet. She fingered the sweater again. *Jen said it's for me...* She bit her lip and pulled the sweater off the hanger. She awkwardly pulled it over her head, only pushing her good arm through the sleeve. It was so soft. She smiled briefly and sank onto the bed.

She rolled onto her good side, wincing at the pull on her wound, and curled into a ball. She stared at the wall. All of her emotions in a tangled mess. Her stomach knotted and her chest constricted as she pictured the compassion on Jen's face. *I don't deserve her compassion. She doesn't deserve my lies...* but she couldn't bring herself to tell her the truth. *Maybe it's enough that she knows I'm lying?*

Kate groaned. *Why am I worried about being honest with this woman I just met? I need to worry about survival... and only survival.* She pulled her knees in tighter to her body. She squeezed her eyes shut, pushed all her thoughts to the corners of her mind, and formed her safe place.

The room was in shadows when voices finally broke through Kate's barrier. She forced herself up and opened the door a crack. Men's voices. Her stomach twisted. Kate carefully pulled her door open and crept down the steps until she could peek over the railing towards the dining room. She could hear them now. She didn't recognize the one's voice, but the other? *Is that...?* Tingles shot through her body. It was that man. The one who had saved her. Their voices came even clearer as they stepped out of the kitchen and into her line of sight.

"Don't burn it this time, though." A man she didn't recognize said.

"Get out of here." Jen scowled, but a smile quickly replaced it. She threw a dish towel at him, and it covered his head. "That was your fault and you know it."

The three of them laughed. It was a pure, joy filled laugh. Kate frowned as she studied them. Something was different about this group. There didn't seem to be that tension of fear or hatred that she was so accustomed to. There was a mutual respect between the men... even Jen. She didn't understand it, and that scared her. Yes, she hated the situation she had been in, but at least she had understood it. She had known where she fit in. Here, she was lost.

She blinked, then focused on the guy who had saved her. *Why would he carry a dying stranger miles to his home to call the ambulance? Why didn't he just leave me?*

JASON

"She's got a point," Jason grinned. John was like an older brother. Their mothers had known each other before they were born. Jen's family had moved into the area when they were young. She had quickly become a close friend to them both.

"Who's side are you on?" John yanked the dish towel from his head, revealing his mock scowl.

Jason pointed to Jen. "Her side. Always her side."

Jen nodded. "You are a wise man." She patted him on the back, then turned to John. "Unlike someone over here who is insulting the women cooking for him. Maybe I'll burn it on purpose."

"You wouldn't."

"Wouldn't I?" She raised her eyebrows. The timer went off in the kitchen, but she remained where she stood and folded her arms. A grin tugged at her lips.

John threw his arms up. "Okay, okay. It was my fault you burned the food last time."

Jason's heart warmed. He laughed as Jen smiled triumphantly and turned back into the kitchen. John whipped the dish towel at him, but he jumped back out of reach.

"Always on her side?" John asked. "What happened to that bond of brotherhood we've had since birth?"

"Hey." Jason shrugged. "You heard her. I'm a wise man."

John rolled his eyes and smiled. "Yeah, sure."

The back of Jason's neck tingled. He rubbed it and turned to scan the living room. His eyes landed on the woman he had found. Dawn, Jen called her. She was leaning over the railing and watching them. Her eyes widened. Even across the room, he could see the fear on her face. Before he could do or say anything, she yanked her head back out of sight.

Jason stared at the spot where she had been. *Why is she so afraid?* He turned to John.

John shrugged. "Who knows what she's been through? We just need to keep praying for her."

Jason nodded.

"She's still recovering from being shot, too. I'm sure there are fears she has to work through with that."

"That's true," Jason agreed. Still, he couldn't help feeling that it went a lot deeper than that.

"All right." Jen came out of the kitchen with two paper plates wrapped in tinfoil. She handed one to each of them. "Here you are."

"You are my hero." John grinned and took his plate. "Chicken Pot Pie is my favorite."

Jen smiled. "Yeah, I know."

"Thank you, Jen."

"Yep, now I need to kick you guys out. I want to go check on Dawn and see if she's hungry."

"What smells so fabulous?"

Jason cringed at the voice.

"Hey, Jemma." John nodded at the newcomer as she walked toward them.

"Hey John. Jason." Jemma nodded at them and

smiled.

It wasn't a sweet smile. It reminded Jason more of a predator. He forced a smile and nodded to her.

"There's chicken pot pie on the stove, Jem. You should eat before work." Jen gestured to the kitchen.

"Yes, Mom." Jemma rolled her eyes and strolled past their group, resting her hand on Jason's arm as she passed.

Jason took a deep, slow breath through his nose and held it for a moment before he released it. No matter how uninterested he acted, she would not leave him be. Only recently had she begun to pursue him in earnest, but he just wasn't interested. If she kept this up, he would tell her straight out to leave him alone. She wanted something completely different in life than he did, and she didn't follow the Lord. That was a must for him. He turned to John and Jen.

"I'm sorry," Jen mouthed.

Jason rolled his eyes and shrugged. It wasn't Jen's fault. "Well, it was good to see you again. We'll head out now."

"Right. Thanks for bringing the groceries, guys. I appreciate it." Jen waved her hand in the air. "With everything else, I forgot to make sure I had food in the house."

They walked to the door. "No problem. I'm glad we can help." John gave Jen a quick hug and pulled the door open.

Jemma hurried from the kitchen. "Leaving already? I just came down." Her voice sounded petulant. Like a sulky child.

"Yeah, we have some of our own shopping to do and," John held up his plate. "This delicious food to eat."

"Oh. Well, I need to head to work anyways. I have off tomorrow. You should come by!" Jemma perked up at her own suggestion.

"We'll see," Jason answered, careful to keep his tone even. "We don't want to get in the way while Dawn settles in." Too late, he saw Jen shaking her head.

Jemma cocked her head. "While Dawn settles in? Who's Dawn?"

"Oh. Umm… We… we gotta go." Jason turned to Jen. "Sorry about that."

Jen sighed. "It's fine. I'll see you at church?"

Jason nodded. "Yep." He pulled Jen into a quick hug and hurried to follow John out the door. When they got to the car, he turned to glance at the house. The curtain in the guest room swung across the window. Jason frowned. *What happened to her?* He shook his head and pulled the car door open. Standing here on the sidewalk wouldn't solve anything.

JEN

God, give me wisdom! Jen prayed. She leaned her forehead against the door and sighed before turning back to her sister.

Jemma crossed her arms and raised a perfectly shaped eyebrow. "Who's Dawn and why does she need to settle in?"

Jen gave her half-hearted smile. She couldn't get over how much her sister looked like her, a more made up version of her, but still. It amazed her how alike two people could look, but how different they could be. "I wanted to tell you earlier, but you were asleep. It was only just decided last night. We, um, we have a new housemate. Dawn is not from around here, but she was injured and needed a place to stay while she heals. I invited her to stay with us."

"You didn't think to ask me first?" Jemma's voice sharpened with indignation.

Jen shrugged. "I'm sorry. I guess I figured it didn't really matter since you aren't around all that much."

"Didn't matter? I may not be around, but I do still live here! Is she at least going to help with the bills?"

Jen winced. "I'm sorry, Jem. Really. I didn't think it through. But I couldn't just let her be put out on the street. She had nowhere to go, and it's what I felt like God was leading me to do. And no. I will handle the bills."

Jemma rolled her eyes. "Do you know anything about her? It's not normal to just invite some stranger to live with us. It's weird and not safe. What if she's like a murderess, or something?"

"She's not a murderess, Jem."

"How do you know?"

"Jem, come on."

Jemma pursed her lips, but then shook her head. "Whatever. How was she injured?"

"She was shot."

"Shot?! Shot by who? Where?"

"Shh!" Jen pressed a finger to her lips. "I think she's asleep."

Jemma lowered her voice, but just barely. "Well?"

"She was shot in her shoulder. I don't know who shot her. I didn't ask, and she didn't say." Jen knew Jemma would ask Dawn a lot of questions; she was just that kind of person. She liked to know things to the point of prying into people's lives. Jen wanted Dawn to feel safe and comfortable here. From Dawn's previous reactions, she figured questions would do just the opposite. "The doctor said she likely has amnesia from hitting her head when she fell, so we shouldn't ask questions right now. We just need to be here for her and help her heal. Okay?"

Jemma frowned, her disappointment obvious. "Has amnesia, huh? Likely story," she muttered. "How long will she be here?"

Jen closed her eyes and took a deep breath. While she knew Dawn was lying, if Jemma truly suspected that was a fake story, it could cause issues. *God, please blind Jemma's eyes to the truth of Dawn's situation. Protect*

Dawn from Jem, Lord. It feels weird asking you to protect her from my sister… but still… "I don't know. I told her she is welcome to stay as long as she needs to."

"Hm. I guess that was kind of you." Jemma frowned and glanced at her phone. "I need to go get ready for work. Give me a heads up next time you're planning to bring a stray home." She jogged up the steps, paused by Dawn's door, then continued to her room.

Well, that went better than I expected. Thanks, God. Jen sighed and headed to the kitchen to make a plate for Dawn.

KATE

Kate silently pushed her door closed as Jen's sister hurried up the steps. Her heart still pounded erratically at having almost been caught watching the guys through the window. She backed away from the door and sank onto the bed. She could not figure out how to process what she had seen and heard today. Jen knew she had her memory, but she had just told her sister that the doctor said she had amnesia. *Why would she do that?* Kate shook her head. Jen had actually stood up for her. *And that guy, he caught me eavesdropping, but he didn't do anything about it.* She rubbed her side as she remembered the last beating she had received from Tony when he had only thought she had been eavesdropping on him.

Her eyes landed on the key that lay on the end table. *Who trusts a complete stranger with the key to their house?* Her stomach clenched. *Why would she leave a key outside for anyone to find?* She felt as if she were in a dream. None of what she had experienced since waking up in the hospital made any sense. If not for the pain in her shoulder, she would be convinced it wasn't real.

A light knock sounded at the door. Kate jumped up off the bed.

"Dawn, can I come in?"

Jen's voice. "Yeah."

The door opened and Jen edged in, a plate and cup in her hands. She smiled. "Oh, that sweater fits perfectly. It's a great color on you. Do you like it?"

She had forgotten she had it on. Kate fidgeted with the edge of her sweater. She had never received a compliment that didn't make her feel degraded or dirty. But she actually felt like Jen saw *her*, not just what she looked like. She ducked her head. "Yeah. It's nice."

"Good. I'm so glad. I brought some dinner up for you. I wasn't sure if you'd feel up to coming down tonight." Jen handed the plate to her and placed the cup on the end table. "Do you need anything else?"

Kate shook her head, then looked down at her plate again. She had never seen food like this before. It looked like a pile of slop with vegetables in it. She frowned. "What is it?" As soon as the question left her mouth, she glanced up at Jen, horrified with herself. "I'm sorry, I didn't mean..." she trailed off as Jen chuckled.

"Don't worry about it." Jen waved a hand in the air. "It's chicken pot pie. Have you never had it before?"

Kate shook her head.

"It's one of my favorites. John's and Jason's too. We grew up eating it. If you don't like it, I can order pizza or something. Just let me know."

Kate nodded. "Okay."

After a moment of silence, Jen spoke again. "So, we are going to church in the morning." She hesitated. "You are welcome to come if you want. Or you can stay here. It's up to you."

It's my choice? I never thought I would hear someone say that. It's my choice... I'm free to do what I want. Just as quickly as her excitement came, fear replaced it. *What do I do? Will she kick me out if I don't go? I have nothing I could wear if I did go...* Her eyes flitted over to the closet. *Okay, that isn't true, but still... I can't go! With the things I've done. If God exists, he must hate me.*

"Actually," Jen interrupted her thoughts. "Why don't you just stay here and rest? You can stay in bed and watch t.v. or go downstairs or whatever. And help yourself to anything you want to eat or drink. How does that sound?"

"Yeah." Kate nodded in relief.

Jen smiled. "Great. I'll come back up in a little while to help you change your bandage. And let me know if you don't like that." She pointed at Kate's plate as she left the room.

Kate sat back down. It was all so overwhelming. She didn't want to think about what it all meant. She picked up the fork and moved the food around on her plate before she scooped some up and took a bite. The flavor exploded in her mouth. "Mmmmmm." She sighed with pleasure and shoveled the rest of the food into her mouth. When she finished, she placed the plate next to her and stared at the clothes in the closet. There wasn't much to do while she waited for Jen to come back, but she was used to sitting in silence.

******

Kate woke the next morning to the scent of bacon. Her mouth watered as she thought of yet another day she would eat only what she could scrounge up. *One day, I'll have my own life.* She reluctantly opened her eyes, frowned, and scanned the room. *Where am I?* She tried to sit up, but a searing pain shot through her shoulder. She groaned and slowly leaned back to rest her head against the wall. She scanned the room again before she realized where she was. Jen's house. *I do have my own life now. At least, I think I do.*

The stairs creaked. "Dawn?" Jen's voice came quietly from outside her door. "Can I come in for a minute?"

Kate clenched her jaw against the pain in her shoulder and pushed herself away from the wall. "Yeah." Jen pushed the door open and entered with a tray. Kate frowned at it before she looked up at Jen.

Jen smiled. "Good morning. I made you breakfast. There's coffee, cream, and sugar. And juice here, too. I didn't know which one you like more with breakfast." She placed the tray on Kate's legs.

Kate stared down at it, speechless. Eggs, bacon, and toast. A napkin folded with silverware, and the drinks in the corners of the tray. No one had ever done anything like this for her. "This… is for me?"

Jen nodded, still smiling. "I hope you like it. I'm headed out to church now. If you don't want to go downstairs, that's fine. Just leave the tray here and I'll get it when I get home. Do you need anything else?"

Kate shook her head. "No," she answered quietly.

Jen nodded. "There's shampoo, soap, towels, and anything else you might need in the bathroom. Be careful not to get your shoulder wet. I can help you with your hair when I get home if you want. I'll see you later."

"Thank…" The door clicked shut and Kate tore her gaze from the food. She realized she was too late, but she still whispered, "you."

JEN

Jen smiled to herself as she left the house. Joy bubbled up within her. It was such a blessing to serve this woman who was obviously not used to kindness. *God, thank you for this opportunity.* She glanced at her car and shook her head. *I'll walk. It's such a beautiful day!*

She took a deep breath of the crisp fall air and sighed. She could not wait to talk with the guys. She wanted to tell them about her talk with Jemma and how Dawn was settling in. *Plus, Casey is back in town!* She felt a little apprehensive about seeing her other friends, though. Not everyone understood her willingness to do whatever she felt God called her to do, regardless of the risk to herself. *There are times I wish news didn't travel so fast in small towns. There's going to be so many questions... Questions I can't answer. All I know is that God told me to let Dawn stay with me, and that is what I will do.*

As she turned the corner, Jen paused and studied the church on the other end of the street. She drew in a deep breath and steeled herself for the bombardment of questions and unasked for advice. *God, give me grace for this and show me what to say.*

She let out a relieved sigh when she saw John and Jason waiting for her by the door. She smiled and waved. Jason had been like a brother since her family had moved into the area. She used to view John as a brother too, but lately... She shook her head, feeling a slight blush rise to her cheeks as she took the steps two at a time. "Hey, guys."

"Hey, Jen." Jason greeted her with a slight frown.

"Hey." John smiled, but Jen knew by the look in his eyes that he was irritated.

Jen grimaced. "Questions already?"

John sighed and nodded.

"How is she?" Jason asked.

"She's fine." Jen smiled, her joy from this morning chasing away the worry of what others might say. "She was still in bed when I left, but I took her breakfast. She is always-" Jen broke off as a few others joined their circle.

A little girl tugged on Jen's skirt. "Is it true you let the lady who was shot stay with you?"

Jen looked down and smiled. She couldn't help it. That face staring back up at her with wide, curious eyes was so cute. "Yes, Beth. She is staying with me."

"Did she tell you what happened?" an older woman asked.

Jen shook her head. "I didn't ask. The doctor says she has amnesia. She really just needs a place to heal."

"What if it wasn't an accident? What if the person who shot her is still after her?"

Jen glanced up at the man who had just approached. Fear swirled her chest. She had mostly avoided that thought. *What if that is the case? I honestly don't know.* It was a legitimate fear, but God had led her to open her home to Dawn. "I don't-"

John stepped forward and rested a firm, warm hand on her shoulder. "If that's the case, we will deal with it when we need to." His voice was calm, confident, and reassuring. "Jen knows what God has called her to do. He will take care of her and Dawn."

Jen smiled up at him.

"Besides," Jason added. "She isn't alone. Jemma is there and John and I will be around."

The man made a face, but he nodded. "I'll be praying for you." He turned and headed into the church.

Jen let out a breath. *God, thank you for John and Jason.* She saw Casey, her best friend, making a beeline for them. *And for Casey, God.* She chuckled as her friend approached, slightly out of breath.

"Jen!" Casey threw her arms around her and squeezed her tight before releasing her.

"Casey! How are you?"

"Me?" Casey brushed her blond bangs from her eyes and shook her head. "How are you?" She looked around. "How is everyone reacting?"

Jen glanced at the others who were arriving. Most of them looked at her curiously but didn't say anything. She shrugged. "Pretty well, I guess having the prayer and worship night deflected some of the curiosity. They've had a few days to adjust to a stranger in town. There are still a few who don't think I should have Dawn staying with me though."

"Psh!" Casey waved the idea away. "God told you to do this, right?"

"Yes."

"Well, that's that then. And I'm doing great. Really glad to be home. I've missed this place and everyone in it."

"Good." Jen smiled. "We've missed you too."

"You're home from... Antartica, this time?" Jason asked.

"Ha! You're funny. It was Morocco." Casey slapped him on the shoulder and turned to enter the church. "Let's go. Worship is starting."

Jason laughed and followed her.

John held his arm out to Jen and smiled down at her. "Shall we?"

Jen grinned. "We shall." She looped her arm through his, and they walked into the church together.

JASON

Jason glanced at his friends as they walked back to Jen's house. *Jen handled herself well after the service. I'm so proud of her. Most people were encouraging, but a few...* he shook his head.

"So, what do we want to do about the possibility of someone coming after Dawn?" he asked.

John shrugged. "Well, if Jen thinks it's needed, we could always get a few other guys and take shifts on her couch until Dawn leaves."

There was silence for a few moments.

"That would be comforting..." Jen hesitated.

"But?" John prodded.

"But I don't think Dawn would be comfortable with that. I also wouldn't want there to be any issues with Jemma. She works nights and gets home really late and you know what she's like."

"That's what I was thinking." Jason nodded.

"That's true," John agreed.

Jen pursed her lips. "I don't think it will be necessary. I mean, no one came while she was in the hospital or last night. That would have been their best time to come if they knew where she was, right?"

"I would think so," Casey agreed. "Besides, God already knows what's going to happen, and He still called you to do this."

"So we stay on call," John said. "Just like always, but even at night, we-," he gestured to Jason and himself, "keep our phones on and with us. If you need anything, or feel unsafe, or anything at all, you call us."

Jen nodded. "Thanks, guys."

"Of course." Jason looked up at Jen's house as they approached. Dawn wasn't in the window today.

"Maybe you guys should wait out here while I go let Dawn know you are coming in."

"As you wish," John grinned.

"I am *not* Buttercup and you are certainly not Wesley." Jen scowled at him before she rolled her eyes and entered the house.

Jason shook his head and smiled as he walked over to the porch swing and sat down. He pictured Dawn's face when he caught her listening to them over the railing. He frowned. She had looked terrified.

"Hey guys?" Jen's voice came from around the side of the house.

John leaned over the porch and looked around.

"Up here."

He tilted his head up and smiled. "Hey, Buttercup."

Jen grumbled something that Jason could not make out. "You guys can head in. I'll be down in a few minutes."

John laughed. "Okay."

"And tell Casey the ingredients she mentioned are in a bag on the counter. The meat's in the fridge."

"As you- will do."

"Thanks."

John turned to him and Casey. "If looks could murder, I'd be dead." He laughed and opened the door.

"You heard the lady."

Casey laughed and pushed off the railing. She rubbed her hands together. "Harira, here we come!"

John grinned and turned to Jason. His grin disappeared. "You okay?"

Jason sighed. "Yeah. I'm fine. Just thinking."

"About Dawn?"

"Yeah," Jason nodded. A small smile formed on his lips. John could read him like a book. He certainly had the gift of discernment. It was annoying sometimes, but it also made it easier to talk with him.

"You want to talk about it?"

Jason shook his head. They had already gone over the shock of finding her in the woods. They had talked multiple times about the reasons she could have been out there and what might have happened. "Nah. That's okay. It's just the same stuff."

"All right." John nodded. "You know where to find me if you change your mind."

"Thanks, John."

John nodded and headed into the house.

Jason leaned back on the swing. "God," he breathed quietly. "Whatever has gone on in her life, whatever she's been through, be with Dawn. Heal her, Lord. Take away the fear that she has. Give her your peace." He shut his eyes, leaned forward, and rested his elbows on his knees. "Be with Jen. Show her the best way to help Dawn. Show me, John, Casey, and the others how to support Jen and Dawn." He started to push himself up, but paused. "And God, please reveal yourself to Jemma. Let her see you at work here. Also… Please help her to understand that I'm just not interested. In Jesus' name." *Time to help with this dinner.* His stomach rumbled as he stood and headed into the house.

KATE

Kate clenched and unclenched her hands as she paced the room. Jen had come up a few hours ago and helped her with her bandage. She had told her that the guys and another friend were there and that they were making a special dinner. She had invited her down, but Kate had declined. Now her room smelled of the spices they had used. Kate's heart pounded. She wiped the sweat from her forehead. Her entire body felt hot and clammy. Her stomach twisted in knots, and the room tilted.

Kate groaned. She gripped her bad arm against her middle and walked to the corner. She sank down against the wall and pulled her knees up against her chest. A burst of joyous laughter from downstairs reached her ears, a complete contrast to the emotions raging within her. She squeezed her eyes shut and leaned her head back against the wall. The room was different. The people were different. But that smell. That smell sent her back to the hotel.

Images formed behind her eyelids and her eyes popped open. "No," she whimpered. She shook her head and rocked back and forth. "No, please, no." Even with her eyes open, a memory materialized as if she were living it again.

KATE

Ten Years Ago

A guard opened the door to their room, disturbing the safety they felt when they were left alone. He strode in, yanked Kate from Miranda's side, and shoved her through the door. Dread filled her as he marched her across the compound to the hotel. That distinct scent drifted in the air. They walked through the back door of the hotel. The smell of that spice filled the hall. Kate glanced down the hall toward the kitchen, hoping someone would see. That someone would care. Maids and servers turned their heads away from her. The guard marched her up the stairs to serve yet another man.

JEN

Nine Months Ago

"That smells so good." Jen took a deep breath, savoring the strong scent of cumin. "I cannot wait to try this Harira. And I'm so glad I didn't have to cook today." She grinned at Casey.

"I'm sure you are. Don't these guys ever take a turn with cooking?" Casey waved the spoon at John and Jason.

"Hey, we cook." Jason made a wounded face at them.

Jen smiled. "They do. Maybe not as often as they should. But they do."

"Our food never turns out as good as yours," John said. "Why should we bother when you are more than willing to cook for us?" He winked and grinned.

Jen rolled her eyes, but her smile grew wider as she made eye contact with him. His dark brown eyes shone with admiration.

"So, John," Casey's voice broke the moment and Jen flushed. "When are you going to propose to this girl?"

"Casey!" Jen spun on her friend.

Jason burst out laughing. "You don't beat around the bush."

Casey shook her head, a satisfied smirk lighting her face. "Nope." She raised an eyebrow and turned to John. "Well?"

"Um..." John's eyes flickered over the group before resting on Jen. "Well, I really can't say with her here, now can I?"

Jen's cheeks felt like they were on fire. "Case, we only recently started going out in that way..."

"So? You've sure known each other long enough." She turned to John. "But I guess you make a valid point." She pointed her spoon at him. "We will talk later."

John grinned. "Can't wait."

"John!" Jen turned to Jason. "Would you do someth-" She frowned. The feeling that she should check on Dawn overwhelmed her.

"Jen?"

Jen blinked and looked up at her friends. She shook her head. *I was just up there a short time ago. I don't want to bother her again.* She pushed the feeling aside. "Would you do something with them?" She waved her hand at John and Casey.

"They're hopeless." Jason shrugged.

Jen rolled her eyes. "Thanks for nothing."

"Hm. Well, dinner is almost ready," Casey announced. "Do you think Jemma will come down?"

Jen shrugged. "I think so. I'm surprised she hasn't come down yet." The need to check on Dawn came back stronger than before. "I'll be right back, guys." She didn't wait for a response, but hurried from the room. At the top of the stairs, she knocked lightly on Dawn's door. She waited a moment, but there was no response. "Dawn?" she called. She knocked a little louder. Still nothing. *I don't want to wake her if she fell asleep.* Jen bit her lip. *What do I do?* She didn't know why she had this need to see Dawn. To make sure she was okay. She had just seen her after church. She had helped her with her bandage and told her she'd bring her some food because she had said she didn't want to come down. Jen leaned toward the door. "Dawn?" she called again. No answer. Jen shrugged, took a step down the stairs, then paused. She knew this feeling was from God. *God, what do I do? I don't want to just walk in there. That's Dawn's room now. I don't want to invade her space. What if she's sleeping and I'm just worrying over nothing?*

The feeling grew stronger until it seemed to fill Jen's whole being. She shook her arms out, trying to ease some of the anxiety building within her. "Okay, I'll go in," she whispered. She cracked the door open and peeked in. Dawn wasn't on the bed. Jen let out a relieved breath. *I'm not waking her up.* She opened the door farther and stepped in. She froze when she saw Dawn in the corner, rocking back and forth.

"Dawn?" Jen hurried over and dropped to her knees in front of Dawn.

Dawn's face was pale and drawn. Her eyes, filled with tears, seemed to look through her. Her breaths came short and ragged. *God, what do I do? Show me what to do!* "Hey." Jen placed her hand on Dawn's knee.

Dawn blinked, sending tears streaming down her face.

"What's wrong?"

Dawn blinked again, and her eyes seemed to focus on Jen's face. Recognition sparked in her eyes.

"What is it, Dawn?"

"I... c... can't...."

"Can't what?" Jen searched Dawn's face. *What do I*

do?!

"Can't b... brea... the."

"Can't breathe? Do you have asthma? Do you need an inhaler? I'll call nine-one-one." *Did I wait too long to check on her? What if she dies because I ignored God?* She started to push herself up, but Dawn reached out and grabbed onto her arm.

"No! Don't.... l... leave me." She looked up at Jen with wide, pleading eyes.

"But, you need help." *God?*

Dawn frantically shook her head, not breaking eye contact.

Jen held eye contact with Dawn for a moment before tearing her gaze away to search the room for something that might help. Her gaze fell on the window. She leaned over and yanked the window up and the screen after it. Cool, fall air with a hint of rain blew into the room. Jen sank down next to Dawn. "Can I pray for you?"

Dawn nodded.

Jen put an arm around Dawn's shoulders, resting her hand lightly on her injured side. "God, I pray for Dawn right now. I ask that you would touch her, Lord. Whatever is going on. Help her breathe normally." As she prayed, Jen could feel Dawn's breathing change from short hurried breaths to longer, deeper breaths. She breathed out a sigh of relief as she continued. "Give her your peace. I ask that you would heal her, Father. From her inner wounds, to her breathing, to her shoulder. I ask that you would make her whole and complete, lacking nothing. I ask that you would reveal yourself to her, too. That she would see how awesome you are in the things you do in her life. Thank you, God. In Jesus' name, amen."

Dawn laid her head on her shoulder. She gripped Jen's sweater sleeve in her good hand like a child would cling to her mother's sleeve. Jen tilted her head and looked down at Dawn. She breathed normally now. The color had come back to her face. Tears still trailed down her face, but she seemed to be doing better than she had been moments before. Jen couldn't help feeling like she was comforting a panicking child. *God, heal her, please. Show me how to help her.*

KATE

Kate drew in a long breath. She could breathe normally again now that the wind had mostly cleared her room of the smell of that spice. Her body had stopped trembling. She felt calmer now. Almost peaceful. *Does it have anything to do with Jen's prayer, or did I just calm down?*

She peeked up at Jen. The shoulder of Jen's sweater was soaked. She swallowed, then forced herself up off of Jen's shoulder. She released Jen's sleeve and clutched her hands together. Jen adjusted her arm around her shoulders but didn't remove her arm. She would never admit it, but she didn't want Jen to move her arm. She couldn't remember the last time someone had comforted her like this.

It had felt nice to trust someone for those few minutes. Her face warmed, and she blinked, shocked. She had trusted Jen. Completely trusted her in that moment of panic. She rubbed her eyes with her hand, removing the last of the tears. "I'm sorry," she mumbled. She fingered the scars behind her ear. "I… I don't know what's wrong with me."

"There's nothing to be sorry about." Jen smiled. Kindness radiated from her. "Are you all right now?"

Kate turned her face away and nodded. She tried to build her wall up again, but it didn't seem to be half as strong as it used to be. Jen had broken through it somehow. Fear swirled within her. She curled into herself again and rested her forehead on her knees. *What do I do now?*

Jen rubbed her hand in circles on her back. "Hey, it's gonna be okay. Whatever's going on, we'll figure it out. We'll work through this."

We? Kate lifted her head and looked over at her. She wanted Jen to be right, but was it possible? *How can she sound so sure?*

Concern shone in her eyes, but she smiled. "With God's help, we'll get through it, okay?"

Kate chewed on the inside of her cheek. With God's help? Bitterness rose within her, but she pushed it aside. Miranda had often said something very similar to that. "With God's help, we can get through this. Don't give up! He is always there for you, even when you don't feel it." Kate could see the passion in her eyes. Could hear it in her voice even now. A lump formed in her throat, but she swallowed it down. *I won't cry again. Not now. Not after I just stopped.*

"Okay." she nodded again. Her voice sounded hoarse, but she couldn't do much about that.

"Okay." Jen smiled. She sat up on her knees. "Do you have any idea what caused your... uh... panic attack?"

Kate recoiled from the question. She started to shake her head, but stopped herself. *I at least owe Jen the answer to that. Don't I? After all she's done for me...* She sighed. "Maybe. I... I think it was the smell."

Jen frowned. "The smell?"

"Whatever you're cooking." She wrinkled her nose. "The whole room smells like it."

"Oh." Jen's eyes opened wide. "I am so sorry. I didn't think…" she trailed off, looking deep in thought. She pushed herself up, hurried over to the door, pulled it open, and leaned over the railing. "Hey guys!"

Kate sucked in her breath and pressed herself back into the wall. She ignored the pain in her shoulder, in her fear. *Why is she calling the guys?*

"Yeah?" One of the guys called back.

"Can you open the windows down there? I have some fans in the basement. Maybe get one blowing into the house and another blowing out?"

There was silence, then a questioning. "Sure?"

"Thanks!" Jen turned back into the room. "That should air the house out and take away the smell. I won't cook here with cumin anymore."

Kate closed her eyes and relaxed. She let out the breath she had held. Her fear dissipated. Jen had given her nothing to worry about so far. *I should be safe… right?*

Kate avoided Jen's gaze as she stood with her hands on her hips, studying her with worried eyes. After a few moments, she approached Kate and held out her hand. Kate hesitated a moment before she reached out and let Jen pull her to her feet.

"Will you come downstairs? I don't want to leave you up here alone after that. You don't have to sit with us or anything if you aren't comfortable with that."

Go downstairs with Jen? Be around those men and Jen's friend? Kate didn't want to stay up here alone after those memories, but would she be able to handle being around other people? Would the men want anything from her? *They don't seem to want anything from Jen. Why would they want something from me?* A small voice in the back of her mind taunted her. *Because you're not like Jen. You're a whore and they can tell.* She bit her lip. *It's true.*

"Please?" Jen pleaded.

I should go down with her if that's what she wants. She's done so much for me already. If something happens, at least I'll have paid her back. "Okay."

JASON

Jason set the pot of soup in the middle of the table before pulling his hoodie on. With the windows open and the fan on, it had gotten chilly in the house pretty quickly.

"Why do you think Jen wanted the fans on?" Casey asked as she set the last cup on the table.

Jason shrugged. "No idea." He turned toward the kitchen. "John, grab the soda and water on your way in?"

"Sure thing," John called back.

"Oh, good! Here she comes." Casey grinned. "We can- oh. Hi. You must be Dawn."

Jason spun around to face the living room. There, hiding just behind Jen, stood Dawn. She made eye contact with him for a brief second before she looked down. His breath caught in his throat.

Casey swept past him. "I'm Casey. You can call me Case or Cass. All my friends do." She stuck out her hand.

Dawn flinched, glanced at Jen, then slowly reached out to shake Casey's hand. "Hi." Her voice was so quiet he barely heard her.

"You remember Jason?" Jen gestured to him.

Dawn nodded.

Jason smiled and nodded back at her. His heartbeat quickened and he closed his eyes. *Get a grip. You barely know her.*

"And that's John." Jen gestured behind him. He glanced back to see John placing the drinks on the table.

John turned and smiled. "Hi. It's nice to meet you. I'll grab another place setting." He hurried back into the kitchen.

Jason turned back to Jen and Dawn. Jen whispered something to Dawn and gestured to the couch. Dawn shook her head, and Jen smiled, looking thrilled. They headed to the table, and Jason stepped aside to let them pass first. Dawn glanced up at him as she passed. There was such a mixture of emotions in her eyes that he couldn't quite get a read on any of them except her fear.

"Here we go." John came back into the dining room with a full place setting.

"I'll grab a stool." Jason headed to the kitchen. When he returned with the stool, Dawn sat hunched down in her chair between Jen and Casey, staring at the table. He set the stool down, perched on top, and gestured John to the last chair.

"John, would you pray for us, please?" Jen asked.

Dawn's head jerked up. She pressed her lips together and frowned.

What is that about?

"Sure."

Jason closed his eyes and lowered his head. He had to force his thoughts to focus on the Lord and not the woman sitting across from him.

"God, we thank you for this day. We thank you for Dawn being here. Please, heal her shoulder quickly and help her to settle in."

Jason couldn't help himself. He opened his eyes and looked over at Dawn. She straightened and stared with brows drawn together at John's bowed head. She must have sensed him looking at her because she glanced over. Jason smiled, then forced himself to shut his eyes again.

John continued, unaware of the confusion he had caused. "We thank you for Casey making it home safe and for sharing some new food with us. Please bless this food to our bodies and may our conversation be pleasing to you. In Jesus' name, amen." John rubbed his hands together. "Let's eat!"

Jason chuckled and leaned over the table. "Pass your bowls." Jen and Casey pushed their bowls over to him. Jen glanced at Dawn, who sat unmoving. *Maybe she didn't hear me?* Jen whispered to Dawn, who shook her head. Jen shrugged, took Dawn's bowl, and handed it to him. He filled the bowl and set it back down in front of Dawn before filling the rest of the bowls.

"Mmmmmmm, Case, this is delicious! How did you make it?" Jen asked.

"Thanks." Casey smiled and tossed her hair. "Basically, just throw all the stuff together. It's pretty simple." She waved her hand. "I can write the recipe down for you later if you want."

"That would be fantastic."

"How long were you in Morocco?" John asked.

"About a year."

Jason glanced at Dawn as his friends continued their chatter. Her eyes darted back and forth between them. She seemed perplexed. She stirred her spoon around in her bowl, pushing the soup in circles. She looked down at her bowl and made a strange face before she slowly lifted a spoonful out. Her hand trembled as she raised the spoon to her lips.

Jason frowned. *What did she live through to make her so afraid? What is she so afraid of? Who-*

"Earth to Jason." Casey waved her spoon at him.

"Huh?" He blinked and turned to her.

Casey raised an eyebrow and cleared her throat. "When is the next church trip?"

"Oh, uh..." Jason thought back to the last ministry meeting he'd had. "June."

"And where will it be to this time?"

"M-" He broke off as something thumped against the front door.

Dawn jumped with a gasp and dropped her spoon into her bowl, spilling soup over the side. She stared wide-eyed at the door, her eyes full of terror.

John looked at Jen with a slight frown. "Were you expecting someone else?"

She shook her head.

John grabbed his glass and moved toward the door. He motioned for Jason to stay back with the women. Jason nodded as he stood and hefted the stool. He glanced at the women. Casey had stood and brandished a vase from the small table by the window. Dawn cowered on her chair. Jen had an arm wrapped protectively around her. He looked back at the door. John was almost there when the door swung open.

Jemma stumbled into the house, then froze when she saw them all. "Woah. Just me guys. What'd you espect? Stormtroopers?" Her words slurred together, and she laughed at her own joke.

Most of the tension eased from the room. Jason set the stool down and sighed. John relaxed. Casey put the vase back on the table and returned to her seat.

Jemma's laughter died away when she realized no

one else was laughing. "Sheesh, lighten up guys."

Jen rose and walked toward Jemma. Jason rested a hand on her shoulder as she passed. She looked back at him gratefully.

"This is going to be awkward," Casey mumbled.

Jason smiled wryly at her. "That's an understatement."

"Jemma, I thought you were still in bed. Where were you?"

Jason could see how irritated she was. *Lord, give Jen wisdom. Be with her. Calm her, Lord.*

"I was out." Jemma drew herself to her full height, which was about equal with Jen's five feet six inches.

Jen drew in a deep breath. She opened her mouth to say something but, before she could say it, Jemma looked past her.

"Is that th' one who's stayin' with us?" Jemma asked. She pushed past Jen, leaned both hands on the table, and studied Dawn. "Y'know, you should get some seep. You don' look so great. I'm Jemma. Wha' was your name again? Daisy? Darlin'?"

Jen followed Jemma and planted herself next to Dawn. She scowled at Jemma. "Her name is Dawn." Jen's voice was harder than Jason had heard it in a long time.

Jemma chuckled. "Dawn. Right. Soun's like a stripper na- ey!"

Jen grabbed Jemma by the shoulders and propelled her backward. "That's enough!"

Jason blinked, horrified. *How could Jemma say something like that? Dawn's been through more than enough.* He drew in a deep breath and glanced over at Dawn. She sat in her chair, her back straight, her face blank. She stared straight ahead. It seemed like she didn't even hear Jemma. Her hands clenched in her lap. Aside from her short, quick breaths, she sat still as a statue.

"Get off me!" Jemma demanded.

Jen turned her around, but Jemma tripped over her own feet. Jen caught her, waited till she got her balance again and half led, half supported her to the steps. "It's only four in the afternoon, Jemma." The distaste in Jen's voice was obvious. "I told you I don't want you here when you're drunk."

"Ugh. You are so like Mom and Dad. They never wanned me t' have any fun." There was a loud thump on the stairs.

Jason heard Jen's voice again, but couldn't hear what she said.

"Fine!" Jemma's loud, slurred voice was easy to hear. "I jus' wanned to see th' guys. Le' go! I'm fine."

John came back over to the table and sat in his chair. He shook his head.

"Yeah," Jason agreed.

John frowned toward Dawn. "Are you all right?"

Jason turned back to look at her again. She hadn't moved, but tears trailed down her cheek.

"What is it?" Jason asked. He couldn't keep the depth of his concern from his voice. He leaned forward to search Dawn's face. Seeing Jemma had set something off. *Or is it what Jemma said?*

She turned her head and looked between John and Jason with that same perplexed look from earlier in her tear-filled eyes.

"Don't worry about Jemma," Casey said. "Jen can handle her. Has been since their parents died years ago. Don't let her bother you."

Dawn frowned.

"What is it?" Jason repeated.

Dawn closed her eyes and took a deep breath. "Nothing," she mumbled.

Jason sat back, but he still studied Dawn. *Did she tell Jen anything?* A grin tugged at the corner of his lips. Jen had looked so protective when Jemma had bumped into the door. Come to think of it, they probably all had. *It must have been a startling sight for Jemma to walk in and see everyone ready to clobber her.*

JEN

Jen crossed her arms and stared down at her sister. She had barely gotten Jemma into the bed before she fell asleep. She looked so like the little girl she used to be. Adventuring past her limits, always asking questions, so curious. Jen's heart ached as love for her sister welled up within her.

She would do anything for her sister. Anything but the thing Jemma wanted her to do. Accept her lifestyle. Tears sprang to Jen's eyes. She leaned down and pulled the blanket over Jemma. "I love you, Jemma. I do. You were made for so much more than drunkenness. If only you knew. If only you could let go of your hurt and anger enough to see."

Jemma had tested her boundaries since she was a young girl. As a young teen, their parents had been pretty strict with her. They hadn't allowed her to go to certain parties because they knew what would happen there. Jen sighed and shook her head. When their parents had died in the crash, Jemma had gone off the deep end.

Jen wiped her tears away, but more took their place. *God, what do I do? Jem won't listen to me... She just doesn't seem to care. Protect her, Lord. Soften her heart to you.* She brushed Jemma's hair from her face.

Yes, she was Jemma's sister, but since their parents had died, she had taken care of her. *We were only sixteen. Too young to lose our parents. Jem blamed you, Lord.* Jen shook her head. *Thank you for your grace in helping me to turn to you during that time instead of running from you.*

With a sigh, she left Jemma's room and closed the door softly behind her. She went to the bathroom and splashed her face a few times with cold water to wash away the signs of her tears. She stared at herself in the mirror for a minute. A reflection of both her mother and father stared back at her.

The memory of Dawn's face when Jemma came into the house got her moving. *I hope she's okay.* She hurried down the steps but paused when she heard laughter. She peeked over the railing to see Casey running in place and waving her arms.

"Come back here!" she mock shouted. "But the rascal didn't even pause. He dodged this way and that." Casey ducked her head sideways, emphasizing her words. "I chased him as fast as I could, but let me tell you, if you didn't grow up running through a Moroccan market, it is NOT the easiest thing to do. And he was so small too! He was ducking around people, under low tables, dodging around stalls, and through materials hanging up. Ugh." Casey shook her head. "It was a nightmare."

John and Jason chuckled. Dawn wore a small, uncertain smile. She seemed to be enjoying the story, but not quite sure if she wanted to let it show. Jen smiled. *Leave it to Casey to boost the mood after something awkward.*

"What happened?" Jason asked.

"What happened?" Casey repeated. "The kid got

away with my bag and I was lost for three hours, just wandering around the Moroccan marketplace! The team sent a search party out after me." Casey laughed.
"They were not very happy."
"I'm sure they weren't." John shook his head.
"Do you never think before you run off on your crazy adventures?" Jen asked as she joined her friends.
Casey whirled around, a sheepish look on her face. "Uh..."
"I'll take that as a no." Jason grinned.
Casey shrugged. "What can I say? I've always been a bit more on the impulsive side."
"Yes, you have." Jen smiled. "It's part of the joy of knowing you."
"Well, thank you." Casey bowed.
Jen's face sobered. "I'm so sorry about that whole episode."

KATE

Kate rubbed at her scars and tried to push away the fear, hurt, and confusion that assailed her. When Jen's eyes met hers, Kate looked away. *Why would Jen apologize for something her sister did? Her sister.* Kate grit her teeth. She knew people like Jen's sister. She didn't like it, but that was what she was used to.

"It's fine, Jen." Casey waved at everyone. "No worries. We know Jemma."

"Yeah, it's no problem." John walked over and side hugged Jen.

Kate watched the interaction between the friends. *What is this? This can't be real life. No one is really like this.* But the throbbing pain in her shoulder told a different story. *This is real.* She rubbed her arm below the wound.

"And are you okay?" Jen turned worried eyes back to her. "I'm so sorry for what Jemma said. It was *not* right."

When Jen had left the room, Kate had been relieved that she had pushed Jemma away from her but terrified to be left alone with the others. Casey had jumped right into telling stories about her trip and the guys had acted the same towards her and Casey while Jen was gone as they had with her in the room.

No one had done anything to make her uncomfortable once Jemma had left. Except Jason. He kept glancing at her. Her eyes flicked up in his direction. He was watching her again. They all were. But none of them looked at her like she was a thing to be used or like they wanted to devour her. All she could see in their eyes was concern.

She looked down again. "Yeah, I'm fine." She couldn't figure out why she seemed to matter to these people. *I'm just a stranger living here until I'm healed... Right? But why are they so kind and concerned then?*

"Okay." Jen nodded, then turned to Casey. "Do you have any other stories you want to tell?"

Casey scoffed. "Do I have any other stories? Of course, I have other stories."

******

Kate stood outside her door. Jen and her friends still sat downstairs talking. She had stayed with them for as long as she could bear it. She had even found herself enjoying Casey's stories, but she couldn't get Jemma's words out of her mind. *Sounds like a stripper name. Is that who I'm always going to be? Did Jemma say that because she could somehow tell? Can Jen tell? Is that why she chose that name?* A thought popped into her mind as if placed there by someone else. *If that were the case, why would she have suggested Katherine as well?* Kate leaned her forehead on the doorway and heaved a deep sigh. She tilted her head and eyed Jemma's door. Part of her wanted to go in and ask her straight out.

Jemma seemed like the kind of person she was used to dealing with. You put on a mask and dealt with what you needed to deal with. Jen, on the other hand, seemed able to see through the mask. *How can two sisters be so completely different?*

Kate closed her eyes and stood for another minute, exhaustion and shame weighing down on her, before she turned her doorknob and entered her room. She didn't bother to change. She curled up on her bed and stared at the wall until she drifted off.

******

"Ah!" Kate gasped as Tony tightened his grip on her arm. He was drunk. Again. He and his two closest men were extra vulgar tonight. She knew it would be bad when they got home and half-heartedly pulled away. She didn't exactly want to get out of his grasp. She knew she wouldn't be able to. But she still wanted to show him that she didn't appreciate his roughness. Not that he cared.

Her arm burned where his fingers dug into her skin as he yanked her back to his side. She would have another bruise in the morning. She hung her head.

"Hey Babe, you wanna come home with me tonight? I'll show you a good time!"

Kate jerked her head up. A young woman walked past them. Kate watched her. *What is she doing around here?* She looked younger than Kate by a few years. A knot formed in Kate's stomach. *She shouldn't be out here!*

The young woman turned and stared Tony down before she glanced at Kate. The compassionate look on her face burned into Kate's consciousness. She looked down in shame. The woman ignored the calls and jeers of the men and walked on.

Why is she out here alone? Doesn't she know better?

It was dark and Kate knew how dangerous the streets were for a lone woman.

When the woman disappeared around the corner, Tony shoved Kate after her. "Follow her and keep her busy. We'll be there in a minute." He didn't even wait to see if she obeyed, but turned and walked into the bar on the corner.

She knew the consequences for disobedience; he had made sure of that. Still, she paused. *This could be my chance. I could run away now. I know these streets like the back of my hand... But so does he. And he has people who will help him hunt me down. No. I can't run. What about the girl?* Reluctantly, Kate followed her.

As Kate approached the corner, she pressed herself against the building and poked her head around the side of the wall. About halfway down the block stood a large, old church building. The girl stood at the bottom of the church steps talking to an older woman by the door at the top of the steps. Huge bushes stood on either side of the door, and a railing ran down the middle of the steps.

Kate leaned against the wall and bit her lip. *I don't want to do this.* She glanced back at the bar. *If I don't, I'll be in big trouble...* She forced herself off the wall and cautiously approached the two.

When the girl saw her, she turned and smiled. "Hello."

The older woman came down the steps, a warm smile on her slightly wrinkled face. "Hello, I'm-"

Kate looked back over her shoulder. "You have to leave!" she said, her voice low and urgent. *Where did that come from?* An image of Miranda floated in Kate's mind. *She would have done anything to get these women out of here before Tony comes back.* Kate shrugged off the warning in her mind that told her she would regret this. *I won't let Tony have this girl.*

The women didn't move. "He's not far behind. You have to go. Hurry!"

The women looked at each other. "What do you mean?" the younger one asked.

The older woman seemed to understand the warning. She searched through her purse as she took a few steps back. "C'mon, Hon," she said quietly. "Let's go."

The young woman glanced between the two and nodded. "Okay. But... come with us?"

Kate hesitated. Tony's drunken laughter boomed from around the corner. She quickly shook her head. "Get out of here."

The older woman found her keys but dropped them in her rush to single out the car key.

Kate cast a terrified glance back again. *There's not enough time. I'll be just as horrible as Tony if I let him do anything to these women... I promised Miranda I'd try to protect other girls if I could... He's going to kill me.* She grabbed the two women, pulled them between some parked cars, and pushed them down. "Just stay here!"

"Stay with us." The older woman grabbed Kate's arm as she stood. "We can help you."

Tony cursed loudly as he rounded the corner.

"Not if he finds you." Kate pulled her arm from the woman's gentle hold and looked away from the concern on both women's faces. She took a deep breath and tried to calm her pounding heart. When he found out she hadn't done as he'd asked, it would be bad, but if she could make it seem like they had just left without listening to her... maybe he wouldn't be as angry.

"What're you doing over there?"

She eyed the woman's keys on the ground before she tore her gaze away from them. Hopefully, he wouldn't notice them. "I was just... uh..."

"Where's that girl? I told you to stall her till we got here!"

She walked over to him. "I tried. She didn't wanna talk. Jumped in her car and drove off."

"You useless piece of-" A sharp SLAP! cut off the rest of Tony's sentence as his hand connected with her face.

Kate stumbled back into one of Tony's men, who caught her by the shoulders.

Tony laughed. "Don't look so angry. It's your own fault," he grabbed her by the chin. "But you're not really useless, are you?" He kissed her roughly, then patted her cheek. "Let's get back." He turned and walked away. His friend shoved her after him.

She didn't dare look back at the cars, but kept her eyes on the ground as she took one step after another behind Tony.

******

Kate woke with a start. The early morning sun shone through her window. Her heart pounded. The dream had been so real. Almost like the day it had happened. She bolted up, oblivious to the pain in her shoulder in her terror. *Jen! That's why I knew her. She was that girl Tony wanted... I have to get out of here! What will she do if she remembers? I'll have to pay her back somehow... someday.* She hurried to make the bed with her good arm.

She dressed in her old, torn clothes and ran downstairs. Her shoulder jolted with each step, but she gritted her teeth and ignored it. With one last look around, she left and locked the door behind her.

She stood on the porch and stared down at the key in her hand. *What do I do with this?* She turned to study the door. *There.* Kate slipped the key through the mail slot and walked down the steps. She had no idea where she would go, but was determined to be far away when Jen got home from work. *She would have kicked me out once she remembered who I was, anyway.* Kate bit her lip. *This was nice, but I knew it was too good to be true.*

She removed the sling as she walked. She didn't need to draw more attention to herself. With a deep sigh, Kate blocked off the emotions that threatened to overwhelm her and took the tree-lined road that led out of town.

JEN

Jen jogged up the steps and didn't pause to sit on her swing like she normally would have done. She had been anxious about Dawn all day to the point she'd had trouble focusing on her work. *I wonder if this is how my parents felt when they left me and Jem home alone.*

She unlocked the door, pushed it open, and looked inside. No sign of Dawn. Jen sighed. *I hoped she would be down here.* She checked the dining room and kitchen, just to be sure. When she was positive Dawn was not on the first floor, she took the steps two at a time and knocked on her door. No answer. She knocked again, louder. "Dawn, can I come in?" She waited. No response. *Is she having another panic attack?*

Jen opened the door and scanned the empty room. "That's odd," she muttered. She glanced at the bathroom door. It was open. Jem would have left for work already. *Maybe she took a walk? Yes, that has to be it. But what if whoever shot her came for her?* The thought sent her heart skittering. "No." She shook her head. "That can't be it." *I'll just take a shower and wait an hour or so. She should be home by then.* She nodded and headed to her room.

Forty minutes later, Jen paced in front of her t.v., a towel still wrapped around her hair. She glanced at the clock for the hundredth time and blew out an irritated breath. *One minute? How did only one minute go by? God, I know I'm just being silly. Dawn is fine… right? Please let her be fine. Be with her. Bring her h-*

Her gaze fell on a key on the floor. *That's weird.* She walked over and frowned down at it before she picked it up. She tried it in her door. As the lock turned, she felt as if a rock dropped into her stomach. *Dawn's key.* She pulled her phone out, tapped John's name, and paced as the phone rang.

"Hello?"

"John, can you get Jason and come over? Dawn's been gone since I got home and I'm worried."

"Yeah, hang on. We will be there soon."

"Thanks." She disconnected the call and pulled the towel off her hair, then scanned the living room. "Ugh." She paced to the couch and sat down. A minute later, she pushed herself up again. *God, please let everything be okay with Dawn. Let her be safe. Even if she doesn't want to stay here anymore. I just want to know she's okay.* She padded into the kitchen, turned the burner on under the kettle, then grabbed a broom and headed out front to sweep her porch.

JASON

Jason sighed and looked back at the top of the page for the fifth time. It was impossible to focus.

"Jay, we have to go over to Jen's."

Jason looked up from his book. "Is everything okay?"

John's brows pulled together. "Jen says Dawn is missing."

"Missing?" Jason's heart felt like it skipped a beat and nausea swirled in his stomach. He clapped his book closed and jumped up. "I'm ready. Let's go." He fidgeted with his seatbelt the whole way to Jen's. The three minute drive felt like an hour.

"It'll be okay. God will watch over her." John glanced at him from the corner of his eyes.

Jason sighed and rolled his eyes. "Yes, I know. But knowing and resting in that knowledge with peace are two different things... and I'm not quite there right now."

John nodded. "I get that."

As they pulled into the drive, Jen ran down the porch steps, broom in hand.

"I am so glad you guys are here. I've been going crazy."

John opened his arms and Jen melted into him. A pang of jealousy shot through Jason's chest even as he grinned. He was glad John and Jen had each other, but he longed for someone to share that kind of relationship with.

When they pulled away from each other, John kept an arm around Jen's shoulders and led the way back to her porch.

"So, tell us what's going on." John and Jen sat on the swing and Jason pushed himself up onto the railing.

He irritably shook his foot as he turned to Jen. *God, let her be okay. I just want to know where she is. God, I don't know why I'm so attracted to her... She doesn't follow you and that is that. I know she's off limits but... Help me to only see her as someone you love and who needs you.*

Jen frowned. "Well, I got home from work and Dawn wasn't here. I thought maybe she just took a walk or something. I showered, but she still hadn't returned. Then, I prayed and paced for twenty minutes, but she still didn't come back. Just before I called you, I looked over and saw this on the floor under the mail slot." She held out the key.

Jason frowned at it. "Your house key?"

"Yeah, I had a copy made for Dawn."

They were all silent for a moment as they stared at the key.

"You don't think whoever..." Jen trailed off.

"You know that's not the case," John said, his voice gentle. "You didn't say anything about signs of a struggle. Plus, what kidnapper would lock your door and put the key back through the mail slot?"

Jen sighed. "True." Her frown finally disappeared.

"Let's pray, then we will decide what to do," John suggested.

Jen nodded.

"Jay?"

"Yeah." Jason took a deep breath and set his heart and mind on the Lord. "God, I thank you for this day. I thank you for Jen and her willingness to do whatever you call her to. I ask right now that you would give her your peace, Lord. Give all of us your peace. I pray for Dawn. Wherever she is, I ask that you would be with her. I ask that she would feel your presence. Protect her, Lord. I ask that you would bring her back safely. Give us wisdom as we decide what to do. Guide us. Thank you, that we can rely on you and help us to do so. In Jesus' name."

"Amen." John smiled. "Okay, so why don't we wait a little longer. If she doesn't show up by," he glanced at his watch, "six, we will go out looking for her. Jen, you can stay here in case she does show up. Jay and I will search town. If she isn't there, Jay can take your car and head east. I'll head west. We will follow the Lord's leading on how long we search."

Jason frowned. *I don't want to just sit here!* He sighed as he looked at his friends. *But it isn't for long and is probably wise.* He shrugged. "Sounds like a plan. If she doesn't show up, we should take some food when we go look for her."

"Good plan." Jen hopped up. "I have some turkey and cheese." Jen froze in the doorway and turned back to them with a frown. "Does she like turkey and cheese? What if she prefers ham? Or only cheese?"

"Why don't we make a few different sandwiches and we will have the others for us if she doesn't want them?" John suggested.

"Okay."

A high-pitched whistle sounded from the kitchen. "Oh! Tea. You should take some tea with you, too. It's getting cooler."

"That would be good." Jason nodded.

******

Six o'clock came and passed and there was still no sign of Dawn.

Jason stood up. "You ready to head out?"

John nodded. "Let's do this."

Jen hopped up and hurried to the kitchen. She returned a minute later with bags of food, water, and some thermoses of tea. She handed a bag to each of them. "Be careful, guys."

John kissed her forehead. "We will."

Jason wrapped Jen in a hug. "We'll find her, Jen. Don't worry." He knew he sounded way more confident than he felt, but he didn't want Jen to worry more than she already did.

She nodded, but the concern didn't leave her eyes.

Jason turned to John. "Let's go." He grabbed Jen's car keys from the hook by the door on his way out. Jason's hope waned with each stop he made through town. Dawn didn't seem to be anywhere, and no one had seen her. He finally met John by the courthouse.

"Anything?" he asked.

John shook his head. "No."

Jason sighed. *Where could she be? Did something happen to make her run off?* "Okay, so we head out. Hopefully, we find her soon." He frowned. "I don't want her to be wandering around, alone, at night. It's not safe."

John nodded. "I hear you. I'll just send Jen a quick update before I head out."

Jason nodded and hurried to Jen's car. "See you."

KATE

Kate paused and leaned against the road sign. Her stomach rumbled. She hadn't eaten since the night before and had had nothing to drink. Her limbs trembled, and the world seemed to tilt. *Did I already forget what it is like to be hungry? I've only had a few days with three meals...* She took a deep breath. *It was getting colder, too. This is a bad place to stop. Anyone could be on this road.*

She looked back the way she had come. Something like regret stirred in her chest. She blinked and refused to allow tears to fill her eyes. She looked in the direction she was headed. The road stretched on till it curved out of sight through hills covered in trees. Shadows covered the area. The sun had dipped down behind the hills a while ago. She sighed, pushed herself off of the post, and trudged on.

Headlights illuminated her from behind. Her heart felt as if it skipped a beat. She gripped her injured arm against her body and ran toward the woods.

Tires crunched on gravel as the car pulled off the road. Kate's stomach knotted. She clenched her teeth against the fear and pain as she pushed herself faster. She stared at the ground in front of her, watching for anything that might trip her.

A car door slammed. "Dawn! Wait! It's me, John!"

John? Kate slowed and heaved in deep breaths of

air. That short sprint had drained her. She frowned and looked back. *What is he doing out here?* She could barely make him out in the dim light. His brown skin blended with the shadows, but she recognized his voice and build.

He waved. "Can we talk?"

Part of her wanted to ignore him and take cover in the trees just a few feet away. Another part of her wanted to crumble to the ground in relief. *It's only John. Not Tony or one of his men. What should I do?* She slowly turned around to face him.

He took a hesitant step toward her, then stopped again. He studied her silently for a moment then asked, "How's your arm?"

Kate shrugged. She appreciated how he kept his distance, but she still took a step back. "It's been better."

"We've all been worried about you."

Kate hunched her shoulders. *They were all worried... About me?* She didn't know what to say, so she stood there. She swayed, her weariness threatening to overtake her.

"Hold on." John jogged back to the car. When he returned, he held a hoodie, a bottle of water, and a sandwich. He held the water out to her. "Here. Take this."

Kate studied him. There was nothing about him that gave her that feeling she always had around men. His eyes were clear and honest. His expression, kind. Not once had he acted in lust, anger, or greed like she was used to.

She licked her dry lips and eyed the water he held out to her. *I think I can trust him.* Fear churned in her gut. *Is that just my exhaustion and thirst that make me think that?* She frowned and rubbed at the scars behind her ear. *I'll trust him. If that's the wrong choice, I'll find out soon enough.* Slowly, hesitantly, she closed the distance between them and took the water. "Thank you."

John seemed relieved. "You're welcome." He handed her the hoodie and, when she looked up at him, he nodded assurance. She carefully pulled it over her head, leaving the left arm to hang empty, then took the sandwich he offered. He sat down, rested an arm over his knees, and patted the ground next to him.

Kate sank to the ground without a second thought and devoured the sandwich. She took a long drink of water to wash it down, then looked over at John. "Why're you out here?"

"We've been looking for you for a few hours now. You're hurt and not in any condition to travel… but… if you are going to leave, can I at least drive you somewhere? Or, I can walk with you wherever you're going." John looked over at her. "I hope you know you are more than welcome back at Jen's. She freaked out when you were gone wondering if whoever… well, wondering if you were safe."

Kate couldn't speak. She searched his face for any trace of malice or humor, but saw only sincerity. *When was the last time someone said they were worried about me?* Guilt worked its way into her heart. *Jen opened her home to me, and this is how I repay her?* "I… I'm sorry. I didn't think… I didn't know…"

"Don't worry about it." John shook his head and smiled. "You're safe. That's what matters." He paused and his face turned serious again. He opened his mouth, shut it, then frowned. "This may seem strange to you since we just met, but I feel like…" He shrugged, "like an older brother to you. I want to look out for you. I know

Jason, Jen, and Case feel the same way. Whatever you need. We *are* here for you."

Tears sprang to Kate's eyes, and she roughly wiped them away. She pressed her lips together and stared at the hills.

"So... what would you like to do?"

Kate looked back the way she'd come, then at the curve ahead. "I have nowhere to go."

"Will you go back to Jen's? She would really love to have you stay with her. She gets kind of lonely being the only girl in our group when Case isn't around."

If there was anything Kate understood, being lonely was it. If she could provide Jen with company, she wouldn't feel like such a burden. *But what about when she remembers who I am?* She chewed on the inside of her cheek. *What about it? She'll kick me out, but maybe I'll have a plan by then. At least I'll have a purpose. I'll do anything she asks. I can keep her house clean... or... anything.* "Okay."

"Okay? Okay, good." John smiled, stood, and held out his hand.

Kate bit her lip and looked at the ground, then slowly reached out and let John help her up. It was the first time she'd let a man touch her since running away. His hand was strong and supportive as he pulled her to her feet. Nothing about him or his touch gave her that sick feeling in her gut. He released her hand as soon as she was on her feet and led the way back to the car. He opened the passenger door for her and smiled again. She studied him a moment before she finalized her decision by getting in.

JEN

Seven Months Ago

Jen looked over at Dawn and frowned. Since John had brought her back, she had been different and started to clean everything. She watched as Dawn scrubbed the spotless counter with her good arm. Jen could tell Dawn's shoulder hurt by the way she cradled her arm to her body, but she didn't complain. *She never complains.* Jen figured she'd wait to see how things played out, even though she knew Dawn should rest. *Maybe I should stop her. This is getting ridiculous. She's cleaned that counter like fifty times today.*

Jen sighed and Dawn glanced up. Shame flashed in her eyes, and she quickly looked down again. Jen caught her breath and stared. *I've seen that look before. Why do I... It can't be!*

She could remember it as if it had happened yesterday. She had been sixteen and in New York on a mission trip with her mom just months before the accident that killed her parents.

She had walked some kids home after an event at their host church. On her way back, she had passed some men. The thought of them still sent shivers through her. There had been a woman with them who had followed her and warned her and her mom that the men were coming. The woman had hidden them, then left with the men.

The memory was so stark. She could see Dawn as she had been that night. She had looked so ashamed. So dejected. Kind of like she had looked since Jason had found her. *How did I not realize this before now?*

She remembered peeking out from behind the car with her mom as the man cursed at Dawn for letting them get away. When the man had hit Dawn, then pulled her back and kissed her, she had lost it.

She'd started to rise, but her mom had pulled her back down.

"Stay! What can we do? She knows those men and didn't want them to find us."

"We have to do something, Mom. Anything. We can't just let her go with them!" They had watched helplessly as Dawn had walked away with the men.

Jen shook her head and stared at Dawn. *It's her. That same woman. The same one I've prayed so many times for. She is living in my house! How does that even...? God... only you could do this. Thank you!*

She opened her mouth to share her memory with Dawn, but something stopped her. She closed her mouth and frowned. *I promised not to ask about her past. She must have so much she needs to unburden. How did she get involved with those men? Are they the ones who shot her? Are they looking for her?* Jen swallowed. *If those... men... are looking for Dawn and find her here... that could be bad.*

She put a hand to her stomach as queasiness and fear overtook her. *No.* She shook her head. *I won't worry. God, you brought this about. You know what you're doing. Help me to trust you. I pray for your protection over myself and Dawn. Whoever shot her, Lord, I ask that they wouldn't find her. I pray your peace over Dawn. Please bring her to you! Show me how to share your love with her.*

KATE

Kate wiped the last spot on the counter and glanced over at Jen. Jen stared at her drink wide-eyed, her mouth slightly open as if she wanted to say something.

Kate frowned, but turned her attention back to her task. She grabbed the cleaner, sprayed the sink, and ripped off another paper towel. She winced and slowly rolled her shoulder. The doctor was happy with how her shoulder was healing, but it still really hurt.

She glanced back at Jen, who hadn't moved. Jen had been reluctant to let her clean, but it gave her something to do. She wasn't used to not being used. All this time and freedom was disconcerting. She didn't know what to do with herself. *At least cleaning can be considered some sort of payment for Jen allowing me to stay here.*

A small smile crept over her face as she thought back over the last few weeks. All of Jen's friends had accepted her into their group. They included her in conversation. Never once had they done anything to make her feel inferior. *No one except for Jemma, that is.* The smile left Kate's face.

She knows my situation is strange, but she's the only one who seems to care that my story doesn't make sense. I see the way Jemma looks at me when no one else is paying attention. Other people in town do it too. Look at me funny when they see me on the porch. Never in front of Jen or her friends, though.

Kate shrugged it off. *Why does it matter? Let them think what they want. It's probably all true, anyway.* But that only made it seem worse. *Why don't Jen, John, Casey, or Jason seem to notice what everyone else does? That I don't belong here? Do they just not care?* She thought about it. *No, it's not that they don't care...it's.. it's that they do care... about me. Not about what I've done.*

The thought sent a shiver through her. It was so strange. She found herself growing more and more comfortable with them despite her attempts to keep them at a distance. It just didn't seem to work. They refused to be swayed by her lack of communication or the way she pulled away. They were so kind and never seemed put off by her. They gave her her space, but they also invited and encouraged her to hang out with them. She constantly found herself responding to their kindness. Like the plants in the neighbors' gardens responded to the care given them. She found herself trusting them. All of them. The guys included. It was hard not to when everything they did and said lined up with what they claimed to believe.

When they argued, they apologized sincerely. Not just to the person they argued with, but to those who had witnessed it as well. They never took advantage of each other, except for when they did and joked about it. It wasn't like she was used to, though. The guys joked about taking advantage of Jen and Casey for their cooking. Jen and Casey joked about taking advantage of the guys for their strength and called them errand boys. It was a good-natured, mutual thing. *Why? Why are they so different?*

A dull ache started behind her eyes and spread to the back of her head. She closed her eyes, leaned on the counter, and rubbed her forehead. Trying to understand them made her head hurt.

"I'm just going to make a call real fast, then I'll be back in, okay?"

Kate jerked herself upright. She had forgotten Jen was there. She turned in time to see Jen hurry from the kitchen.

She sighed and went back to scrubbing the sink. When she finished, she went into the living room and straightened the already straight couch pillows and folded the throw blanket. She didn't intend to eavesdrop, but the window to the porch was cracked open and she couldn't help but overhear Jen.

"You remember I told you about that girl who hid me and mom from those men in New York?"

Kate's blood ran cold. *She knows it's me! What is she going to do now?* She'd known it could only be a matter of time before Jen figured it out. *Now what? She'll hate me now. I can't blame her. She's so... good. How can she continue to let someone like me live here? Someone so dirty from all those sins they talk about? Is she just going to kick me out tonight? Where will I go?*

Kate sank onto the couch. She didn't mean to continue to listen, but as her panic calmed to deep regret, she could hear Jen again.

"No, I haven't told her. I don't want her to freak out or run away again. I'm just so happy that she's here. Case, you don't even know! God has finally answered those prayers and I'm able to care for her and make sure she IS okay."

There was silence, then, "I promised I wouldn't ask about her past and if I mention this, I don't want her to feel like I'm questioning her. I should tell her? I just don't know. Mhmm. Yes, that's true. You think that's okay? All right. Yes, well, I should go now. Thanks for-"

Kate bolted up and took the steps two at a time to her room.

"Hey, watch it!" Jemma twisted on the stairs to avoid her.

Kate ducked around Jemma and mumbled an apology without pausing. Jemma harrumphed and continued down the steps.

Kate shoved her door closed and leaned back against it as she tried to process what she'd just heard. *Jen prayed for me? Some random woman she didn't even know? Is that why I got out? Why things worked out how they did and I could get away? She's told me God doesn't always answer prayer in the way we want or think. Is she really happy that I'm here? She doesn't want me to feel like she's breaking her promise by asking me about this.* Kate shook her head, unable to wrap her mind around what this all meant.

The front door banged shut. *Should I just tell her? She's been so open with me.* Her stomach knotted. The thought of telling Jen anything about her past made her feel sick. *Maybe tomorrow...* Kate got ready for bed but lay awake all night, tormented by images from her past. She tossed and turned as she wrestled with her thoughts. *Am I really okay with telling Jen everything? With her knowing who... what I am?*

By four thirty, Kate gave up on sleep. She pulled her hair back into a ponytail, padded downstairs, grabbed the cleaning supplies, and scrubbed the oven, glad of the pain in her shoulder that distracted her from her thoughts. When she finished the oven, she pulled everything out of the fridge and scrubbed that, then organized everything as she put it back. She sat back on her heels and ran a hand over her face with a deep sigh. She craned her neck to look at the time on the stove. *Six-thirty. Jen will be up soon.*

She had watched Jen make coffee more than enough times. *I should be able to figure this out.* She stifled a groan as she pushed herself up. She fumbled with the coffee maker until it looked right, added the coffee and water, then turned it on.

As the coffee maker started to gurgle, Kate pulled a stool over to the counter and sank onto it. She folded her arms on the counter and rested her head on them. *Do I tell her? Do I just leave? I can be out of here before she comes down. She won't know I'm gone till later.*

Everything in her wanted to run. It was the easiest thing she could think to do. *I won't have to tell Jen or the others anything. I can just disappear from their lives.* Jen's face came to mind when she had walked back through the door with John after the last time she had run. Then John and Jason's faces. *They were all so worried about me... and so kind. So happy to have me back. I don't want to do that to them again. I don't deserve them. They don't deserve my cowardice. God, if you are there, if you do care like Jen says, help me have the guts to tell her. And if at all possible, please don't let her kick me out. I'll do anything... but don't make me have to go back out on the streets again.* Kate sighed. *I'm not this person. I don't have a normal life. I'm sure she'll come to her senses soon enough and kick me out. I might as well just get it over with...*

JEN

"That coffee smells delicious!" Jen drew in a deep breath as she walked into the kitchen. Dawn had never made the coffee before. *This is a good sign, right?* "Thanks f-" Jen broke off and frowned.

Dawn leaned on the counter like it was the only thing that held her on the stool. She lifted her grease smudged face. The depth of pain in her eyes when she looked up pierced Jen's heart. Dawn winced and looked down, but Jen had seen the dark circles under her eyes. Had noticed her puffy face.

"Dawn?" Jen stooped down next to her and placed a hand on her good shoulder. "Are you all right?"

Dawn remained silent, but just when Jen thought she wasn't going to answer, her eyes flicked up to meet hers again. "I didn't sleep well," she said. She straightened and tried to smile. "How are you?"

Jen frowned. "I'm fine, but what's wrong? Did something happen last night?"

Dawn shook her head. "I'm fine, really."

Jen didn't say anything, but she studied Dawn. *She probably overworked herself. It's my fault. I should have stopped her from using all her energy to clean rather than heal. But not today. Today she will rest.*

Jen pulled out her cell phone, scrolled through her contacts, found her manager's number, and hit call.

"Hello?"

"Hey Lainy, how are you?"

"I'm fine. Is everything okay? It's still early."

"That's good. Yeah, things are okay, but, listen. I can't come in today. I need to take a personal day. Sorry it's such short notice."

"Oh, Steve and I can handle the shop. Do you need anything?"

"I know you can. I'll see if I can get any paperwork done from home. No. There's just something that came up that I really need to do."

"Okay. Give me a call if there's anything I can help with."

"Yes, for sure. Thank you so much. Call if you have any questions, all right? I'll have my phone on me."

"I will. We should be fine, though."

"Great. Have a great day, Lainey. Thanks again. Bye." Jen disconnected the call and frowned at it. She turned to face Dawn, who watched her with her eyebrows drawn together.

Jen gave her a small smile. "I'm fine," she answered Dawn's silent question. "You, on the other hand." Jen shook her head. "Not so much. You've been working too hard and I won't let you do it anymore. Where's your sling?"

Dawn opened her mouth to object, but Jen raised her hand. "Don't say it. I know. You're fine. You can take care of yourself. I should just go to work and leave you here to scrub everything for the millionth time and make it harder for your shoulder to heal and ignore the pain you are in and so on, but I'm not having it anymore."

Dawn closed her mouth and stared blankly at her.

Jen rested a hand on Dawn's back and pressed lightly. "Come on." She led Dawn into the living room. "Sit down."

Dawn pressed her lips together and sat without a word. Jen hurried to the kitchen. She leaned on the counter and whispered. "God, give me wisdom to know how to help her and what to say to her... or what not to say." She took a deep breath and focused on the Lord. *Listen.* The word resounded in her mind. Just that one word. After a few moments of silence, she pushed off the counter. "Listen. Right."

She grabbed a glass, filled it with orange juice, and popped a frozen breakfast burrito in the microwave. When the microwave dinged, she grabbed the plate and headed back to Dawn. She placed the plate and cup on the end table within easy reach for Dawn, then sat on the chair. "So the rules for today. You need anything, you ask, and I will get it for you. Sleep all day if you want. Watch t.v. Read. I don't care, but I do not want to see you up and doing anything at all today. All right?"

Dawn nodded and leaned back. She stared at Jen as if trying to figure her out. Within seconds her eyes drifted closed and she took deep, even breaths.

Jen smiled. *Good, she needs sleep. I'll listen to her when she wakes up.* She leaned back in her own chair and closed her eyes.

KATE

Tony, Juan, JP, and a few nameless, faceless men surrounded Kate. She crouched in the middle of the room, covered her head with her arms, and waited for the beating she knew would come. Suddenly, she was outside of the circle, tied up on a blanket in a corner of the room. She looked around, confused, and realized they were now in the cabin where she had been taken when she was first kidnapped. She heard footsteps on the front porch. Tony and Juan both turned and sneered at her.

"She's here," Tony announced in a gravelly voice. The men stepped back.

Kate whipped her head toward the door and watched anxiously as the door opened. Who was she? She strained to see through the dim room as a shadow appeared in the doorway. The men laughed with an eerie echo as someone dragged Jen, kicking and screaming, into the room.

"No," Kate whispered. She shook her head.

"Dawn." Jen stopped struggling and looked right at her. "Why didn't you tell me?" she asked.

"NO!" Kate struggled desperately against her bonds as the group of men split up. Half encircled her and half encircled Jen.

"We are going to have fun tonight!" Juan shouted.

"Don't do this, Tony... Juan, you can't do this!" Kate could feel the ropes cut into her wrists as she struggled, but she didn't care.

"No one cares what happens here, Kid. No one cares." Juan reminded her of this fact, as he had reminded her so many times before.

"NO!" Kate shouted again. The men ignored her cries and descended on both her... and Jen.

******

Kate bolted up. She blinked, trying to clear the sleep from her eyes, as she looked frantically around the dark room. She jerked her arms in front of her and stared at her free wrists. Scarred, but free. Her heart pounded as if trying to break free of her chest. Kate rubbed her wrists, still able to feel the sting of the rope as it cut into her flesh. She frowned as her eyes adjusted to the dim light. She wasn't in the cabin. *Where...?* As different objects came into focus. She blew out a breath of relief and sank back into the couch. It was only a dream.

She looked across the room. Jen still sat in the chair. She had dozed off as well. Tears filled her eyes, and she turned from Jen. *She's fine. She's not in any danger. It's okay.*

"Do you need anything?"

Kate jumped at the sound of Jen's voice. She bit her lip and shook her head. "No, thank you." She had the sudden, irresistible urge to just get the conversation over with. They would have to talk, eventually. It was inevitable. But for some reason, she couldn't bear to wait any longer.

"Why do you care?" she asked. Her voice came out harder than she intended and she winced.

Jen cocked her head and frowned. "What do you mean?"

"You remembered me." Kate bit her lip again and rubbed her wrist scars. Her insides trembled. She didn't want to do this. *Why did I start this?* She wanted to back out. To take back what she had just said, but it was out now. There was nothing to do but push forward. "I... I didn't mean to listen to your conversation last night..." Shame and fear fought for prominence. Her dream still fresh in her mind, she continued. "No one ever really cares." She looked down, unable to make herself meet Jen's eyes, and fidgeted with her hands in her lap.

"No one... Oh, Dawn."

Kate couldn't help it. She glanced up to see Jen watching her with sad, kind eyes. She looked down again and squirmed under Jen's gaze. "I..." *She needs to know.* She gulped and fingered the scars behind her ear. "I'm a... I'm a whore." She'd been called that more times than she could count and had come to believe it. She shook her head. "Why would you care for someone like me? Why would you let me stay if I'm not doing something... being useful in some way?" She scooted to the edge of the couch, agitated and ready to bolt.

Jen was silent for so long that Kate thought she would ignore her. *Great. Now I've done it.*

JEN

Jen's heart broke at the pain, confusion, and loneliness in Dawn's voice. *God, help her to see your truth! Give me the right words to use. Speak through me, God.* "You're not... Dawn, you... ahh." Jen paused, searching for the words to use. "Yes, I remembered you. You saved me and my mother. You seemed like you wanted to get out of the situation you were in but, to protect total strangers, you went right back into that life. Willingly. Without looking back. You made me wonder if I could ever be that selfless."

Dawn let out a harsh half laugh, half sob. She shook her head. Her lips twisted, and she lowered her head farther and turned away.

Jen stared at Dawn's lowered head and wished she could make her understand. *God, soften her heart to you.* She searched the living room and spotted her Bible on top of the entertainment center. She jumped up and grabbed it before she sank into the chair again. "Do you mind if I read you something from the Bible?"

Dawn seemed to draw into herself even more, if that were possible, but she didn't object.

"This is Psalm one thirty-nine. It is one of my favorites." As she came to verse thirteen, she emphasized the verses. "For you formed my inward parts; you knitted me together in my mother's womb. I praise you, for I am fearfully and wonderfully made. Wonderful are your works; my soul knows it very well. My frame was not hidden from you, when I was being made in secret, intricately woven in the depths of the earth. Your eyes saw my unformed substance; in your book were written, every one of them, the days that were formed for me, when as yet there was none of them."

When she finished the chapter, Jen glanced up to catch Dawn's reaction. She sat still as a statue but, as Jen watched, a tear landed on her leg. Jen wanted to wrap her arms around Dawn and take all her pain away, but she had a feeling Dawn needed her space. And, as much as she wished she could, taking Dawn's pain away was not her job. Her job was to point her to the One who *could* take it away, *if* she would let Him. *I wish I could make her understand!* She took a deep breath and continued. "I know you have heard me and the guys talk about this before, but I want to make sure you get this. When I say God loves you, I don't say it just to say it. I believe it with all of my heart. He loves you no matter who you are... or were. No matter what you've done. He created each of us, Dawn. He paid special attention to every detail of our lives. Of your life. And He didn't just create us and leave us. He is with us always."

Dawn gave a derisive snort. "If God does exist, He doesn't care for me." Her voice was tight, as if it would snap.

Jen almost felt as if she'd been punched in the gut at the depth of emotion in Dawn's tear-filled voice. *God? How do I combat such lies? It doesn't surprise me that she believes that, but it isn't true. What do I say? Only you can reveal the truth to her. Please do it.* Peace filled her and her next words seemed to come from somewhere else. "Do you really believe that's true? Has there been nothing in your life that was good? No one you can look back on and say that God put that person in your life?"

Dawn started to shake her head, but stopped. Tears trailed down her face, and she frowned. She wiped at her face and dropped her head again. "Maybe."

Ask her if you can break your promise, Jen.

Jen recoiled from the thought. *But God. I can't break my word. Not now!*

Just ask her. You won't break your word if she doesn't give you permission.

Okay then… Here goes nothing. "Dawn, can I ask you a question? …about… your past? If you don't want me to, please, just tell me and I'll drop it."

KATE

Tingles shot through Kate. Her heart began to harden as she grabbed onto the anger that flared within her. *She's asking about my past when she said she wou-* She did not break her promise. She only asked if she could. The thought came almost as a suggestion in her mind. She didn't know where it had come from, but she knew it was true. She glanced up and saw the kindness in Jen's face.

Her anger melted away, and she felt the loneliness deep in her soul. *I need to talk to someone. I can't keep going like this. Being afraid to talk in case something slips out and gives me away. Putting on an act for the people who took me in. Lying to them. Worse, endangering them. They need to know.* Kate clenched her teeth together and nodded again.

"Okay." Jen sat back. She closed her eyes and took a deep breath before she spoke again. "What's your story? Why were you with those men in New York? How did you end up there?"

Kate pressed her lips together and took a few deep breaths to steady her nerves. She swallowed, but the lump that formed in her throat remained. She wiped at her eyes to remove the new tears that gathered. "M... my story?" Kate thought back as far as she could remember. She had long since forgotten her parents' faces, but she remembered playing in her backyard as a kid. She remembered telling her parents she wanted to be a ballerina, then changing her mind and saying she wanted to be a police-woman because they actually helped people.

Her parents had laughed and told her she had plenty of time to decide. She puffed air through her nose in a self-deprecating snort. *My parents were supposed to protect me, but I had to protect them. JP or Juan would have gone back and killed them if I didn't obey them. They threatened to. Often.* She had learned to close up her longing for her parents deep in her heart.

Normally, she blocked those memories from her mind. It was easier to only let herself remember from the time she started going with men willingly, so they didn't beat her. She shook her head. *How much should I share?* She wanted to keep her experiences locked away. People knowing these things gave them power over her. Another part of her didn't care. She was dying for someone to know what she'd been through. To know that someone cared about what had happened to her.

"I was... taken from my family... when I was a kid." She almost stopped there, but something inside pushed her to continue. "They sold me to someone who... If I didn't do what he said... he beat me." She swallowed the lump in her throat and continued on, her voice sounding detached and mechanical, even to her own ears. "One day I realized it was easier to just go along with it instead of fighting. They treated me better, then. Kind of. Eventually, I was sold to Tony. He's the one you saw me with." The words seemed to pour out of her now that she had started. "He gave me more freedom than I'd ever really had. Me and this other girl... we um... served him... and the others. Sometimes, they let us choose who we wanted. It was like a game for them. See who the girls pick. But it wasn't a real choice." Kate shook her head. "We knew who owned us and what would happen if we disappointed them. They took us to drug deals sometimes. That's how I got this." Kate nodded to her shoulder. "I don't know what I was thinking. I got hold of a phone and called the police. I told them when and where the deal was going down. It was stupid."

"What... what happened?" Jen's voice was low and gentle, but it trembled.

Kate was too afraid to look up. She kept her head down and rubbed her scars. She thought back to the morning of the deal. "He found out. I wasn't supposed to go with him that time..."

KATE

Nine Months Ago

"Babe, you're coming with us."

Kate jerked her head up and stared at Tony. *He's joking, right? The deal isn't even supposed to happen for another few hours.* But no. His tone was anything but joking. His face was completely serious. Her body tensed and her stomach quavered. She swallowed.

"Aw, c'mon, Man. We were havin' a nice time."

"Do I care?" Tony turned toward the door but glanced back. "What're ya still sitting there for? Go change. I left something nice for you."

Kate turned to the man who held her. She couldn't remember his name. It didn't matter either way. "Sorry." She gave him an apologetic smile that was anything but sincere and pushed herself up off his lap.

He grabbed her arm and pulled her back down for another kiss.

"Babe!"

Kate pulled away. "I gotta go."

The guy groaned but released her. She guessed he didn't want to risk Tony's wrath any more than she did. She rubbed her arm as she hurried after Tony. *Of all the deals he could take me to, why this one? Why so early? What happened to Blondie? She was supposed to go this time.*

Kate hurried down to the basement. Strewn across the futon, that doubled as her bed when she had a rare night alone, was a blue dress. A backpack sat next to it. Kate quickly changed into the dress. She barely noticed how tight or short it was. She had learned long ago to ignore that. She wasn't sure why, but she stuffed her jeans, tank top, and sweater into the backpack. It was the same bag she had used countless times before to transport drugs for Tony.

Kate glanced around as she hurried to catch up with Tony. The railing was missing posts. Stairs were missing pieces. The front door was missing a hinge and some glass where a bullet had knocked it out. Dirt and litter were strewn about the floor. Holes peppered the smoke-yellowed walls. Some were bullet holes, some holes were from fists; others? She paused and stared at one hole in particular. That hole happened when Tony had shoved her into the wall. He'd been drunk and rough. She had tried to fight him off, but had failed miserably. Like always. She rubbed the back of her head as she remembered the pain as her head had hit the wall. She pulled her gaze from the hole and hurried on. *I hate this place. But it's the closest thing to a home I've ever had.*

If Tony finds out what I did, I'm dead. What on earth made me think it was a good idea to leave that tip? He has men on the freaking police force! Is that why he wants to bring me? Fear gnawed at her insides, but she tried not to let it show. If Tony didn't know, then she couldn't give him any reason to doubt her.

She grinned at him as she slid into the front seat of his car. "Where are we going this time?" she asked. She already knew. He had talked about this for days now, but what did that matter? She was just an ornament. She wasn't supposed to listen to his plans unless he specifically included her. That didn't mean she didn't hear them, though.

Tony ignored her, and she bit her lip.

Is this what it was like for Francesca? Always on edge? Trying to guess the moods of the men around you and having to figure out what they wanted before they asked? Always putting on the brave face? If you messed up, you lost the little freedom you had or were punished in some other way?

Tony's second in command, Joey, and another of his men got into the back of the car. A car with four other guys pulled up behind them and honked. Tony pulled away from the curb, his face tight. Kate kept up the charade. She asked questions and got him to talk about himself, but inside she trembled. Tony's answers were short, and he seemed distracted.

Tony pulled off the road into the parking lot of an abandoned building. Kate searched everywhere. *Why are we here so early? Are the police here? Did they even believe my message? Did Tony's men find out and tell him?* She couldn't see anyone. Her heart pounded. The place looked just as abandoned as it had the last time she was here.

Kate glanced down the street. Rows of low-income homes lined the streets on either side of the property. *I hope everything goes well. I don't want any kids to get hurt.* The guys in the back of the car got out and stood ready.

They don't normally act this way. He knows. He is going to-

Joey knocked on the window. Kate jumped.

Tony scowled at her and rolled down his window.

"They're here," Joey announced.

Kate gulped. She tried to swallow her fear. *If Tony knew, there's no way he would be this calm.*

"Right. Let's go." Tony got out of the car.

Kate put a hand on the door handle and paused. She took a deep breath.

"Babe!"

She slid out of the car, slipped the backpack on, and sauntered up next to Tony. She put on her best brave face as they approached the new vehicle parked in the middle of the lot and slipped an arm around Tony's waist. He remained stiff as a statue. Her smile faltered, but she quickly pasted it back on.

Two cops exited the car. All the breath left Kate's lungs. She had seen them before. They worked with Tony. She tried to stay calm, but couldn't stop her limbs from trembling. Tony knew.

"This her?" The older cop asked. He turned his dark eyes to her and looked her up and down with hungry eyes.

Kate took a step back, but her legs almost gave out.

Tony grabbed her arm so hard she yelped.

"What's going on?" she asked.

"You betrayed me."

"What? No." Kate shook her head. *I'm dead. Dirty cops got my message. Not the good ones.*

"Don't play with me." Tony tightened his grip even more.

Tears sprang to her eyes. She tried to pull away, but Tony yanked her arm back and twisted it behind her.

"Ah!"

"I treated you nice. How could you betray me like that?"

Nice? Kate didn't dare to argue with him. She sucked in a breath and bit her lip until she tasted blood. "I'm sorry."

"Sorry?" Tony shook his head. His voice was hard when he spoke. "I trusted you, but you betrayed me. You know what happens to traitors."

"No, Tony, please!"

He ignored her plea and faced the policemen. "You sure you got the message before others found out about it?"

Kate's breath came short and fast. This was it. She would die now. No one would know or care. No one would mourn her death. *Maybe it'll happen quickly. Maybe they'll just kill me and be done with it.* One look at the older cop destroyed that hope. It would not be a quick, painless death. She couldn't hold back the whimper that escaped.

"I'm sure. The officer who took the tip is on our payroll."

"Good." Tony handed the older cop a large envelope.

The cop opened it and studied what was inside for a minute before he nodded. "This should cover it."

"It better." Tony scowled. "Here."

Kate stumbled as Tony shoved her toward the two cops. The younger one caught her by the shoulders. He didn't hold her very tightly. She wrenched out of his grasp, but only took two steps before the older cop grabbed her arm and pulled her to his side.

"Augh!" She gasped as he twisted a hand in her hair and pressed his face into it. Fear gripped her, and

Kate's stomach heaved with revulsion. Her body trembled. Tears spilled down her cheeks unheeded.

"Do what you want with her, then get rid of her. Just make sure her body can't be connected with us."

"You got it. No one will ever find her."

Kate's stomach dropped. *No.* She tried to pull away from the cop, but his grip in her hair kept her by his side. Kate reached for Tony. She knew it was pointless. He would do nothing for her. She had betrayed him. But she had to try one last time. She couldn't keep the crazed fear out of her voice.

"Tony, no, please! I'm sorry. I don't know what I was thinking. Please!"

Tony grimaced at her. "Worthless whore. I should have killed you that first time you gave me trouble. I won't make the same mistake. Get her out of my sight."

"No!" Kate twisted and tried to free herself from the cop who held her. He shoved her at the younger cop, who twisted her arms behind her as she struggled.

"Get her in the car."

The younger cop nodded and yanked her over to the car. He pulled the door open and shoved her into the back seat. She threw a wild glance around. They had removed the handles. Bars and thick glass separated the front from the back of the car. She couldn't get out.

The cop leaned into the car. Kate backed up against the farthest door. She couldn't keep the tears from falling down her face. The cop's expression softened. He glanced behind him, then turned back to her.

"I'm sorry if I hurt you. I'm undercover," he whispered.

Kate stared at him in disbelief. *Is it possible?*

"There are police waiting around the corner. This

will all be over soon. These sorry excuses for men will be behind bars thanks to that tip you called in. I knew something was happening but they wouldn't tell me what until you called and they wanted us to come... take care of you... I've got to go but stay low in case shots are fired, okay?"

Kate blinked at him before she gave him a nod. She was almost too afraid to believe him. Too afraid to hope. He straightened and slammed the door shut. She was trapped. *Is he really undercover? Will I actually survive?* Kate huddled in the backseat for what felt like hours.

Finally, she heard more car doors slam. She twisted onto her knees and peeked through the window. The two cops, Tony, Joey, and another four men, stood around the new car. Tony gestured at the car, and one of the men opened the trunk. Tony and his men gathered around the trunk and looked in. She noticed the younger cop inch his hand to his gun. Two cop cars sped into the lot. Shouts erupted from the men around the car. The young cop drew his gun at the same time as Joey. Kate's eyes widened. She dropped down and pressed herself against the backseat as shots rang out.

The door opened. Kate stared wide-eyed as another cop looked in. He crouched next to the car.

"We have to get you out of here. Let's go. Stay low."

Kate wasn't sure if this cop was good or bad, but she really didn't care. She did not want to be trapped in there anymore. She scrambled out of the car. "What hap-" She broke off as her eyes landed on the undercover cop sprawled on the ground. She gasped and froze.

The cop pulled on her arm. "Keep moving. We need you to stay alive."

Kate had seen dead people before. Had even seen people killed, but never had it been someone who had tried to help her. She couldn't move.

"Hey." the cop shook her lightly.

Kate tore her gaze from the cop on the ground to the one crouched next to her.

"We'll get you out of here, okay?" He pointed to the back fence. "See that break in the fence?"

Kate looked to where he pointed and nodded.

"Good. When I tell you to, I want you to run for that spot. Got it? Find somewhere to hide. We will come find you when this is over."

Kate's chest heaved as she tried to breathe normally. *This is all too crazy. I must be dreaming.* More shots were fired. Kate ducked and covered her head.

The cop nudged her. "When I say run, you make for that spot and don't stop for any reason."

Kate gulped. *This won't work. I'm gonna get shot. I always knew that, though. But what if there is a chance I survive?* She slowly lowered her arms and raised her head.

"Okay." The cop carefully raised his head and peeked over the edge of the car. "And... go. Go!" He stood and fired over the trunk of the car.

Kate stared across the lot at the hole in the fence. She didn't give herself time to think about it. She pushed up and ran toward the hole in a desperate attempt to get away. She fully expected to be plowed down by a bullet, or one of the men, but she made it to the fence without issue. She glanced back once and saw Joey crumple to the ground.

She dropped to her hands and knees and crawled through the hole. Once on the other side, she paused and took a few deep breaths before she forced herself up and ran. *Forget about hiding nearby. I'm out.*

KATE

Seven Months Ago

Kate paused her story and sighed. "I thought I was safe. I walked till I couldn't anymore. A few days later, I was on the highway. Tony and two other men pulled over in front of me. Tony told me Joey'd been killed. He claimed he only wanted to talk, but I knew better than to believe that." Kate blew out a breath. "He was gonna kill me. I ran again. They chased me into the woods and shot me. I must have passed out. The next thing I knew, I was in the hospital." Kate bit her lip. "That's it, I guess." she lightly massaged above her wound and sat there awkwardly. She didn't know what else to say.

JEN

Jen stared at Dawn's bowed head. *What do I even say to that?? What can I say?* She opened her mouth multiple times, but nothing came out. She closed her eyes, rubbed her hands over her face, and drew in a deep breath. *God, use me. Speak through me. I don't even know what to say. What does she need to hear?* A lump formed in her throat. Tears stung her eyes, but she blinked them away. She didn't want Dawn to think she couldn't handle what she'd shared.

"I... can understand why you feel the way you do... about God," she started. "But you are still alive. And you are here now. You aren't with them anymore," Jen's voice cracked. She stopped and swallowed, then tried to make eye contact with Dawn, but she refused to look up at her.

"I... I can lea-" Dawn clamped her mouth shut.

Jen watched as her jaw muscles worked, but Dawn didn't seem able to finish her sentence. *She thinks I want her to leave.* Jen rose, sat next to Dawn, and put her hand on Dawn's good shoulder. She tilted her own head to look into Dawn's face. "Dawn, this is your home now. I don't want you to leave." She hesitated a moment, then continued. "If nothing else, maybe meeting me all those years ago was God moving in your life. I don't know if you heard this part of my conversation last night, but I prayed for you, Dawn. Whenever I remembered you, I prayed that God would be with you and that He would help you through whatever you were going through. I prayed that if you were still with that guy, that you would be able to get away from him. You being here right now is an answer to prayer."

When Dawn finally looked up at her, Jen gave her what she hoped was an encouraging smile. The disbelief and hope that fought for prominence in her eyes encouraged Jen. *She's listening!* Suddenly, a thought struck her. "Dawn, did you say you were taken from your family?"

Pain flashed in Dawn's eyes. She raised her hand to rub behind her ear like she always seemed to do and nodded.

"Did.... does anyone know you're still alive? Did you tell the police what happened?"

Dawn's eyes filled with terror. "The tip I left was stupid enough. With all the cops Tony's got on his payroll, he'd find me again."

"You have to tell someone, Dawn. What about your parents? They probably think you're dead."

Dawn shook her head frantically, her hair flying out around her face. "No! I don't want them to know... It's better they think I'm dead."

Jen remained silent. She did not want to push Dawn. *There has to be something we can do to get word to her parents, though. I'll bring it up again another time.*

"Jen, I... I want to tell the others."

"You want to tell them? Are you sure?"

Dawn nodded slowly. "I don't want to keep hiding it. You all have been so kind and honest. They should know. They should be able to decide if they still want to..." Dawn swallowed audibly. "If they still want me around. I could be putting you all in danger. I don't... I don't know where Tony is. He might still be looking for me. They need to know."

Jen bit her lip. *So she's thought about that too... But that doesn't matter. Dawn does.* She nodded. "I'm sure they would appreciate knowing. When do you want to tell them?"

Dawn pressed her lips together and drew in a deep breath through her nose. Jen could see the fear in her eyes and hear the tremble in her voice as she answered. "I... I should just do it tonight. They are coming over for a movie still?"

"That was the plan. Are you still okay with that?"

Dawn drew in a deep breath and nodded.

"Okay. If you are sure?"

"Yeah."

"Okay. We can have them come earlier if you want?"

"No. Please. I've interrupted your life enough. Don't change your plans for me. You were supposed to go out with John before the movie."

"Dawn, I can't-"

"I won't do anything. I'll stay on the couch like you told me to. Please. Go out with him."

Jen sighed. "Okay, we will go out. But we'll be quick. And you have not interrupted my life. You've become a part of it. There's a difference."

A smile turned up the corner of Dawn's lips even as more tears filled her eyes. She shook her head and turned away from her. "Thank you," she whispered.

******

Jen ran a hand through her hair and sighed. She stared into her coffee as she thought over the day. "What do I do?" she whispered.

"You okay?" John asked.

Jen sighed again and glanced up. John's dark brown eyes searched her own, his brows drawn together in concern. "Yes. I'm just worried."

"I don't think the coffee is going to give you the answers you're looking for."

Jen looked down at her coffee, then back up at John. She chuckled and shook her head. "I guess not." She glanced around the coffee shop. It was a quiet day. Only a few people sat at the other tables. She glanced out the window. No one was outside. The clouds hung dark and heavy over the town. Kind of like her emotions over her life. *How does Dawn do it?*

"Earth to Jen."

"Huh?" Jen turned back to John. "I'm sorry, what'd you say?"

"I'm worried about you."

"What do you mean?"

"It seems like you've got that Eyore storm cloud hanging over your head. It's not like you. Did something happen?"

"Um..." Jen curled her fingers around her mug and savored the warmth of the coffee. "Dawn shared some stuff about her past with me. She wants to tell you guys tonight," she hesitated. "It's bad, John. It's really bad. And she doesn't want to go to the authorities." Dawn's empty expression as she'd shared her life story hovered in her mind. The hopelessness in her voice. The terror when Jen had suggested they talk to the police.

"I don't know how she…" Her voice cracked, and she stopped again and shook her head. Tears stung her eyes. "How can such evil exist? I know God is sovereign, but when you hear things like that…"

John frowned. "Jen, are you in danger? Does she need to move out? We can find her another place."

"No." Jen shook her head vehemently. "I mean, danger is a good possibility, but I will NOT kick her out. I can't. Especially after what she told me."

John nodded and his hands covered hers. "Why don't we pray?"

Warmth flooded Jen's heart. She smiled up at him gratefully and nodded as a tear slid down her cheek. She wiped it away with her shoulder as John turned his hands over. She laid her hands in his and smiled at the contrast of his dark skin against her light skin as she bowed her head.

"God, I thank you for Jen," John's voice was quiet but sure. "I thank you for her kind, loving heart. I thank you for the things you are teaching her. I thank you for her trust in you. Lord, we know you reign over all. That nothing can happen without you allowing it to happen." John gently squeezed her hands as he continued. "Sometimes, though, it is just so hard for us to trust. We hear of great evils in the world and we wonder how a good, loving God can allow such things. But God, we know you have our best interest at heart. That you see the big picture. That you know the past, present, and future. That you do know best. I ask that you would help us to trust your goodness in our times of feeling unsure about it. That you would reveal your goodness and that you would strengthen our faith. Lord, we ask that you would be with Dawn. Father, please draw her to yourself. Reveal your goodness, kindness, and great mercy to Dawn. Free her from her dark, hurtful past." John's voice filled with passion as he prayed. "And I also pray for Jen. That you would help her to bear the burdens that Dawn has shared with her. Help her to lay those at your feet and not try to carry them herself. I ask that you would strengthen her, Lord. Give her your joy and your peace as she wrestles with her confusion right now. I ask that you would clear her mind and help her to rest in who you are. In Jesus' name, amen."

Jen swallowed. "Amen." She looked up and met John's gaze. "Thank you."

John smiled and nodded, but his eyes remained serious. "You know I am always here for you, right?"

Jen nodded. "Yes, I know."

"Will you be all right?"

Jen took a deep breath and held it. *Will I be all right?* She released her breath as she felt the presence of God surround her. She smiled. "Yeah. I'll be fine. I'm just a little overwhelmed at the moment. It will be good to talk again after she has shared with you guys."

"Okay," John nodded. He glanced at his wristwatch. "You ready to go? Case and Jay will be at your place soon."

Jen glanced at her phone. "Is it that time already? I told Dawn we wouldn't be long." She took another sip of her coffee and stood. John held the door open for her as they left the coffee shop.

KATE

Kate sat at the dining room table. She bounced her leg up and down as she watched Casey and Jason. Even after everything she had shared about her life, Jen still treated her with kindness. Still wanted her to join them for the movie tonight. She shook her head. *I don't understand it.* Kate bit her lip. *Jen might be okay with me, but will the others be?*

Kate blinked and focused on the two in the living room again. Casey sat on one end of the couch and Jason sat on the other.

"Are you kidding me?" Casey asked. She threw her arms out to the side. "It's only the best movie ever."

Jason raised an eyebrow. "The best movie ever?"

"Okay, fine. *One* of the best movies ever."

"I don't know, Case." Jason shook his head.

"Ugh. You just don't appreciate good movies." Casey sadly shook her head.

Nothing had happened to make Kate feel uncomfortable, but her past refused to leave her in peace. Her stomach knotted. *I should have stayed upstairs until Jen got back. Why didn't I?* Kate sighed. Jason glanced over at her. Her cheeks flushed, and she averted her gaze.

"Everything okay? Do you need something?"

At the sound of Jason's voice, Kate made herself look up. His kind eyes searched her face. Her flush deepened and she rubbed at the scars behind her ear. "I'm fine," she answered, her voice almost too soft for even her to hear. *Will he still look at me that way after I tell him what I am? Why does it hurt to think that he probably won't? Why does it even matter?*

"I'm going to go put some tea water on." Casey stood and headed towards the kitchen. "Come with me?"

Kate looked at Casey, turned to Jason, then back to Casey, and nodded. She followed her to the kitchen.

"I hope you know you can trust these guys." Casey grabbed the teakettle off the stove and filled it up. She glanced over before she turned her attention back to the kettle. "They really care about you. We all do."

Kate shifted her weight from one foot to the other. *What should I say?* She drew her brows together and studied Casey. She spoke with kindness. She seemed to fit right in with Jen, John, and Jason. She was a bit more energetic than them, but no one seemed to mind. She seemed so sure and confident about everything, even when she said she wasn't. She knew Casey spoke the truth about her friends, though. *Somehow, maybe it was God like Jen suggested, I ended up with these people. They do care. I can tell. I've never met anyone like them... except Miranda.* She rubbed her shoulder. "I think... I know..."

Casey placed the kettle on the stove and turned the burner on before she looked up. She smiled and rested a hand on Kate's uninjured shoulder. "Good. I'm glad you know that. I get that old habits die hard, but I pray you will be freed from them and from your past, whatever it is. Life's too short to let the past hold us back. God is a God of healing. It's not always easy to do, but if we let Him, God can heal us and help us move forward in life instead of running from or clinging to our past." She squeezed Kate's shoulder. "Now, what kind of tea should we give Jason?" She turned and pulled open the drawer of tea bags. "Hmmm. Do you know what you want?"

Kate opened her mouth, but nothing came out. She blinked. *How does she do that?* She'd had whiplash many times. This felt the same, but with her emotions instead of her neck. *God is a God of healing. If we let Him, God can heal us and help us move forward...* The words played in her mind again. *Can He do that for me? Can I let Him? What would that mean?*

"Hey, Jay, how do you feel about Lemon Ginger tea?" Casey called into the other room.

"Uh, I prefer Earl Grey if there is any."

Casey ruffled through the drawer. "Ah ha! You're in luck. Looks like it's the last one."

"I can drink something else if one of you wants that."

Kate jumped and spun around. Jason leaned in the doorway, his arms crossed over his chest. She took a step back. How had she not sensed his approach? She could always tell when a man was close to her. She stared up at him, dumbfounded.

"Sorry. I didn't mean to sneak up on you." He smiled apologetically.

"I don't want Earl Grey. Dawn, did you want it?"

Kate looked at Casey, shook her head, then looked back up at Jason. He seemed to fill the doorway with his one leg crossed lazily over the other as he rested his shoulder against the doorframe. His dark brown hair was tousled, as if he had run a hand through it too many times. His brown eyes shone with kindness and concern as they looked deep into hers. Stubble covered his jaw. Laugh lines creased his face. His forehead was smooth. He didn't have that permanent line between his brows like the other men she knew.

Kate's stomach flipped, but it wasn't with fear. This was a completely new sensation. One she had never experienced before. Kate pressed a hand to her middle and gulped. *What's wrong with me? What's happening?*

Casey cleared her throat.

Kate tore her gaze from Jason's as heat rushed up her neck. She fought the urge to look back up and stepped farther away from him.

JASON

Jason watched Dawn as she stared at him. Her lips parted slightly, as if she might be about to say something. Her eyes widened as she stared. *She didn't run from the room or turn into herself when she realized I was here. She's actually staring at me instead of avoiding me.* He searched her face. Once again, he was struck by the sadness in her eyes. *I wonder what she's thinking.*

Everything in him wanted to wrap her in his arms. To tell her it was okay. That she didn't have to be sad anymore. That he would protect her from whatever... whoever she was afraid of. Instead, he silently watched her as she watched him. He took in the way her brown, wavy hair framed her face. The way her round blue eyes stared into his.

Casey cleared her throat. Jason blinked and jerked himself upright. Dawn blanched and turned away. He turned to Casey. "Yeah?"

Casey raised an eyebrow, not even trying to hide her amused grin. "I asked if Dawn wanted to look at the tea selection, but I don't think either of you heard me."

Jason shrugged sheepishly. "Sorry, Case." He glanced at Dawn again. She held a hand against her stomach and one against her mouth as if she were about to be sick. He frowned. Casey must have noticed because she turned as well, all signs of amusement gone from her face.

"Dawn?"

Dawn shook her head and, after another few moments, she swallowed and lowered her hand from her mouth. She wrapped her arms around her middle and looked over at Casey. She looked so much like a lost, wounded puppy. Jason's heart melted.

"If you're feeling sick, a lemon or ginger tea is really good for you. The Ginger settles your stomach."

Dawn nodded. "That'd be good," she whispered.

Thank you, Casey, for always being practical. Jason shook his head. *Why do I feel so attracted to her? She doesn't follow you, Lord. Help me stay focused on you! Or... bring her to you! That would be great.*

Half an hour later, Jason sat back in his corner seat on the couch and rested his mug on his knee. Casey sat across from him on the other corner seat. Dawn curled into the chair farthest from him. She had not looked at him since that moment they'd had in the kitchen, but she had stayed down with them. That was a good sign. It both surprised and thrilled him. He liked having her around. He enjoyed the way she watched his friends, like she had never seen anything or anyone like them.

Casey prattled on about something or other. He wasn't really listening, but it didn't seem like she expected him to. She was talented that way. She could talk and talk and talk and not need anyone else to participate in the conversation. She didn't do it all the time, but he was thankful for it right now. It seemed to put Dawn at ease.

John's laughter sounded from outside, and Jen pushed the door open. Jason glanced over at Dawn. The relief on her face was evident. He smiled, glad that she felt more at ease. *I wonder if she will ever feel that comfortable with other people when Jen isn't around.*

"Dawn." Jen made a beeline for Dawn and plopped into the chair next to her. She wrapped an arm around her shoulders. "How are you?"

Dawn leaned into Jen's embrace. "I'm fine."

"Hey guys." John closed the door and took a seat on the floor next to Jason. He slapped Jason's leg in greeting as he leaned back against the couch.

"We waited for you guys to pick the movie." Casey piped up from the corner. "What should we watch? I'm always down for a musical."

Jason's attention was drawn to Jen and Dawn, who whispered together. Jen seemed really intent. Dawn looked… terrified. Again, he felt the desire to hold her close and keep her safe. He shook the feeling off as she nodded to Jen. Jen hesitated a moment, then turned to the room.

"Actually, guys, Dawn would like to share something with you. We may need to postpone the movie."

KATE

Kate shoved her hands under her thighs. She trembled as she finished her story. She couldn't bring herself to meet any of the other's gazes. Her eyes skirted around the room, not staying long on any one thing. "I should have told you before. I'm sorry." She lowered her head. Shame filled her. Heat crept up her neck and over her face. "I... I know I should leave... But Jen asked me to stay. I don't want to keep putting you in danger. I understand if you... if you don't want me around anymore." She lifted a shoulder in a helpless shrug. "Tony is still out there. If he even thinks I might still be alive, he will look for me until he finds me. If he... if he finds me here...." She trailed off and squeezed her eyes shut. She didn't want to even consider that possibility.

There was complete silence for a few terrible moments. Kate refused to lift her head. She did NOT want to see the look in the other's eyes that she had seen in so many other people's. She bit her lip and rubbed the scars behind her ear. The familiar motion brought an odd sense of comfort. She had come to care for these people and, though telling them the truth of her past had been harder than anything she could remember doing, she felt a strange sense of peace and relief. *It doesn't matter what happens, as long as I'm not lying to them anymore.*

"Dawn," Casey's voice sounded hesitant.

"Hey, Dawn," John's voice came more confidently, but without a touch of anger or judgment.

Still, Kate refused to look up.

"Dawn," John said again. "I've told you this before and I will say it again. You are a part of our family now and our family sticks together. We are not going to abandon you."

"We most certainly will not," Casey added. Her voice back to its normal tone. "Especially not due to some…. Ugh!" She suddenly went quiet, but Kate heard her rise and pace the room. Casey's voice came again, full of emotion but no anger. No disappointment. "I can't even. How did you… How…" she trailed off again.

Is it possible? Do they, like Jen, not care about what I've done? Does the danger not bother them?

"Wow. Casey is speechless. That's a first." There was a smile in Jason's voice.

Casey snorted.

Kate couldn't suppress a small grin at the jab. She finally dared to glance up. Casey was glaring at Jason, but her eyes filled with laughter despite the tears in them. John was shaking his head. Jen had not left her side. Her eyes connected with Jason's as he watched her. Her breath caught in her throat at the emotion she saw there.

"Dawn, thank you for trusting us with your story."

The others nodded.

Casey dropped to her knees next to her and wrapped her in a hug.

Kate stiffened, but then she relaxed and returned Casey's hug.

"I'm so sorry you went through all that." Casey

pulled back and cocked her head. "It does explain a lot though."

A spark of guilt shot through Kate. "I'm sorry, I should hav-" Kate cut off as Casey waved her hand dismissively.

"Don't even. You should have done what you felt was the right thing to do to stay safe."

"So, it... it doesn't bother you that I've been hiding this? That... that I'm a-"

"An amazing woman?" Jason interrupted. "You had good reason to keep it from us. No one can blame you for protecting yourself. I'm just glad you trust us enough to tell us the truth. That cannot have been an easy thing to do. You are..." Jason paused and pressed his lips together for a moment before he shook his head. "You are very brave."

Kate stared at him, speechless. *Brave? Me?* She wanted to laugh. *I'm the farthest thing from brave.* Even now, her body still trembled with fear and anxiety. She couldn't stop the worry that Tony would find her. It was a constant thought in the back of her head. She couldn't step outside without looking over her shoulder. She opened her mouth to say so, but then noticed the others nodding their heads in agreement. "Brave?" she asked.

"It's true." Jen smiled. "You have been through so much, but still you can smile. You are sitting here with us. You are a survivor, Dawn."

Tears filled Kate's eyes. *This can't be happening. These things they're saying... they're just words meant to make me feel better. Right?* But as she looked into the eyes of the group and saw the respect, the kindness, the care, the truth in their eyes, her heart felt too full for words. She wrapped her arms around herself as a tear trailed down her cheek.

"Can we pray for you?" Jen asked.

Kate nodded.

"Is... is it okay if we all lay a hand on you?" Casey asked.

Kate's eyes skimmed over the group before she nodded again. She didn't exactly want to be touched, but she did not want to do anything to ruin this moment. She tensed as they all gathered to her side, and each one laid a hand on her shoulder or back. She expected fear, anger, or disgust to fill her when the guys touched her. Instead, warmth radiated on her back where they laid their hands. She felt comfortable and safe under their touch. It made no sense to her. Even though she couldn't understand it fully, Kate knew this was how it was supposed to be. She knew she was safe with John and Jason. That they would never do anything to harm her.

As each of them prayed, the feeling of comfort and warmth in her heart grew. Peace filled her. Her fear melted away. *Is this what Miranda tried to tell me about? I feel... free.* Kate hung her head as tears fell, but the tears did not feel like a burden. They were a release. As her tears fell, the hardness in her heart softened. It both terrified and thrilled her.

JASON

They had just finished praying and regained their seats when the door swung open. Jason glanced up. *It's only Jemma.* Relief warred with irritation. *God, forgive me. I know I shouldn't be irritated at just the sight of her. It's better her than those men Dawn told us about, though.* The knowledge that that man was still out there, possibly looking for Dawn, put him on edge. They had speculated about it, but hearing it confirmed by her made it much more real.

Jemma eyed them all curiously. "What's going on?"

Jason glanced around. *We do look like a pretty solemn group.* Dawn, had seemed completely relaxed for the first time he could remember, until Jemma walked in. She sat stiff and straight in the chair next to Jen, her head down. *Trusting us is one thing, but trusting Jemma? That's quite another story. I don't blame Dawn for shutting down again.*

"We've been here for hours and we haven't decided on a movie. I think we should watch Fiddler on the Roof."

Jason turned to Casey, and she raised her eyebrows. "What?" She took a sip of her tea as her eyes darted to Jemma.

"Nothing." Jason grinned. *Quick thinking, Casey.*

As usual. "I'm down for Fiddler. We're going to need some popcorn or something though." He glanced back at Dawn. She raised her head, a confused look on her face. Relief shone in her eyes when she met his gaze, but she quickly looked away. Jason smiled again. This time, it had nothing to do with Casey's brilliance.

"I'll order some pizza." John pulled out his phone. "Supreme and veggie okay with you guys?"

"That sounds fantastic." Casey sighed happily.

"Sounds good to me. As long as I don't have to cook tonight, I'll be happy," Jen added.

"You know I will eat just about anything." Jason picked up the remote and turned the t.v. on. He scrolled through the video options and found Fiddler on the Roof.

"Are you okay with those options, Dawn?" John asked.

Dawn glanced over. The gratitude in her face and voice filled Jason with satisfaction and assurance that they had done the right thing in changing the subject as they had. "That's fine." She gave them a brief smile before she averted her gaze again.

"Jem? Are you going to eat and watch the movie with us?"

Everyone looked at Jemma. She eyed them suspiciously. "Yes," she drew the word out as if she could not make up her mind. Her gaze flickered between Jason and Dawn. "I'm going to shower first. Don't wait for me." She ran up the stairs.

There was a collective sigh as a door closed upstairs.

"Nice cover there, Case," John nodded at her.

"Thank you."

Jason turned to Dawn. "Do you still want to watch the movie?" *Please say yes!*

Dawn met his gaze for a moment, eyed the stairs, then looked over the others. "I think... yes. If you're okay with... me...?"

"We most certainly are." Jason nodded. Dawn drew her brows together, but Jason could see the confused joy in her eyes. He grinned. "All right, ready?" When his friends nodded, he hit play.

As the opening music started, Casey grinned. "I hope you all know I am going to sing with every song."

Jason chuckled as his friends laughed. He glanced over and saw that even Dawn smiled.

KATE

Five Months Ago

"What do you think?"

Kate studied herself in the mirror. She followed the lines of her face. She had gained a little weight. Her face didn't look as sharp as it used to and her eyes actually seemed to have some life to them rather than the dull, guarded orbs she used to have. Her hair even seemed to be more alive, if that were possible. She pulled at some hair and stared down at the dark brown strands. When she released it, it twisted back into its naturally wavy form.

She glanced back up at herself. *I don't even recognize myself... I'm looking at a stranger.* For the first time she could remember, she didn't have dark circles under her eyes or bruises anywhere on her body. *Nothing hurts. I feel... safe.* Yeah, she still wasn't exactly comfortable around people, but it wasn't the same as before. She still checked behind her, even if she only went out on the porch.

Her eyes wandered to her reflection's shoulder. She stretched her arm out and twisted it this way and that with barely a pinch of pain. A smile pulled at her lips. The doctor had prescribed physical therapy but told her she wouldn't need to come back.

She focused on her reflection again. A deep green dress draped her body and hung to just below her knees. Aside from pants, it was the longest thing she'd ever worn. The dress showed her form, but it didn't cling to her body. The neckline came to just below her collar-bone and half sleeves covered her shoulders. A large pink flower decorated the left side with pale green vines curling out from it. Small, intermittent, pink flowers decorated the vines. She glanced up and made eye contact with Jen's reflection.

Jen raised her eyebrows and smiled. "Do you like it?"

Kate nodded. "It's beautiful."

"Good." Jen patted her shoulder before she turned away. "We should get going. Come on."

Kate didn't have to see Jen's face to know she was excited. She bit her lip before she turned to follow Jen. "Are you sure this is a good idea?"

Jen turned back to her with a grin. "Yes. I'm sure." She frowned. "But, if you still aren't ready, you can stay home. You can always come some other time."

Kate ran a hand through her hair and paused by her scars. She ran a finger over them. *I already told her I would go. I don't want to disappoint her.* She shook her head. "No. It's okay. If you're sure." She flattened the wrinkle-free dress and swallowed. *What was I thinking telling her I would go to church? I'm going to be struck down.*

Jen grinned. "Great." She turned and hurried down the steps.

Kate followed. *At least I'll die doing what I said I would.*

Jen stayed close to Kate's side as they walked. Jen

still baffled her. She didn't understand how Jen, or the others, could treat her the same as anyone else while knowing the things she'd done, but she was getting used to it.

As they approached the church, Kate paused and stared up at the building.

Jen slipped her arm through Kate's. "It's going to be fine," she said.

Kate nodded and forced her feet to move. *I don't belong in places like this. Everyone will know I don't belong. I'm going to drop dead because I'm stupid enough to step in the place.* She winced as she stepped through the door. She fully expected a lightning bolt to come flying down at her from the sky. Nothing happened. She breathed a sigh of relief and looked around.

The service hadn't started yet. People milled around the entry in groups. The double doors into the sanctuary stood open. People sat in pews waiting for the service to start. Sunlight streamed through stained glass windows that lined the upper parts of the walls. A podium stood front and center on the same level as the pews. A man stood behind it and rifled through some papers.

Kate felt eyes on her and turned from the front of the room to see everyone in the entry staring at her. Some more covertly than others, but they still stared.

Kate pulled back. *God didn't strike me down, but I'm NOT ready for this. Maybe Jen and the guys don't care about my past, but these people?* Her eyes darted back and forth as she took in the stares of the people who surrounded her.

Jen had not released her arm when they walked into the church. As Kate pulled back, Jen tightened her hold on her.

Kate pulled back harder. "I... I can't..." She couldn't breathe. The walls seemed to grow taller and close in on her.

"Hey, Dawn," Jen's gentle voice broke through her panic. Jen turned to face her and placed both hands on her shoulders.

Kate reached up and clutched Jen's wrists. She clung to her as if she were an anchor.

"It's okay. Just breathe. Deep breaths. In. And out. In."

Kate focused on Jen's face. The kindness and concern in her eyes. Her confidence. She swallowed and drew in a deep breath.

"That's it. And out."

Kate released her breath.

"One more time. In."

Kate drew in another deep breath.

"Good. And out."

As Kate released her breath, her tension slowly eased.

"Better?"

"A... a little. T... they're all staring at me."

"They are just curious. They haven't seen you around much. Don't worry, you don't have to talk to anyone if you don't want to."

Kate nodded and released Jen's wrists. "Sorry."

Jen smiled. "You're fine."

"Is everything okay?" John's upbeat voice sounded from behind.

Kate turned to see John, Jason, and Casey had joined them. Relief washed through her. Whether they meant to or not, the group created a type of shield around her. She felt safe. Protected. Even with the guys. Especially because of them. *Is it normal to feel this way around men?*

"Yeah, I think we're good now." Jen raised an eyebrow in question.

Kate nodded. "Yeah." She glanced up and made eye contact with Jason. Her stomach did that weird flip thing it had been doing lately. Jason smiled.

Heat crept up her neck, and Kate quickly looked away.

"Okay." John grinned.

"Let's go find some seats." Casey stepped forward and looped her arm through Kate's left arm.

Jen repositioned herself at Kate's right and slipped her arm through Kate's again. The guys followed behind as they made their way into the sanctuary. Kate stared at the ground. She ignored the stares and instead focused on the nearness of her friends and their support. *Friends? Since when…?* As they took their seats, John and Jen on one side of her and Casey and Jason on the other, she looked back and forth between them. Somehow along the way, her heart had lost its walls. These people sitting next to her, she cared about them.

Kate blinked and shook her head. *What am I supposed to do with this?* Her stomach knotted. She folded a piece of her dress and rubbed the fabric back and forth between her fingers. *I have friends…?*

"Good morning. I'm going to pray to get us started, then we'll worship."

Kate looked around and mimicked the postures of those around her. She leaned forward, rested her elbows on her knees, and lowered her head.

"Lord, we thank you for this morning. We are so

grateful that we can gather together in your presence today. I thank you for every person in this room. There are many other things they could be doing, but they chose to come here. As we draw near to you, draw near to us. We want to spend time with you, Lord. We want to meet with you. We humble ourselves before you now and bring you an offering of praise. May it be acceptable to you."

Someone strummed a guitar, and other instruments joined in. There was a rustle around her and Kate glanced up. People all over the sanctuary stood up.

Jen's eyes shone in anticipation as she leaned over. "You can stand up or stay seated if you want to. It's totally up to you."

Kate stood with Jen as the congregation began to sing. She scanned the words on the screens at the front of the church, but they made no sense to her. It was a jumble of letters. Some she recognized, others she didn't. She bit her lip and rubbed the scars behind her ear as the voices around her became one. It should be no problem to follow along, but it was. She turned her eyes from the screens.

Her friends' eyes were closed, their hands raised. Passion, unlike any she had ever seen or heard, filled their faces and voices.

Jason sank to his knees and slowly rocked back and forth to the music. Casey moved past him and lay face down in the aisle. Jen and John swayed back and forth. Jen covered her heart with her hands as tears slid down her face.

Kate frowned. Every song seemed to be about love, sacrifice, and hope. *Why are they acting like this? Is it the words? The tune? Something else I'm missing? Do I even want to know?* She knew God had turned his back on her long ago. That she was an imposter here. But... Jen, John, Jason, and Casey didn't seem to think so. They were glad she had come. They had told her that God cared about her. There was a part of her that hoped against all hope that they were right. That, maybe, she could find a place here. That she would truly be accepted. That God hadn't actually discarded her. She focused on the music and closed her eyes. *God, I... I know I've got no right to talk to you... but... a... are you there?*

The voices around her seemed to fade to the background, but the words of the song, How Deep the Father's Love for Us, became clearer.

A peaceful warmth flooded her whole being and sent tingles through her body. An arm rested across her shoulders and gently pulled her close. Kate gasped and popped her eyes open. She twisted this way and that to see who had touched her. No one was close enough. Everyone was still deeply involved in their own worship. *Who...? What just happened?* Kate shook her head, but she couldn't shake away the warmth across her shoulders or within her heart.

When the worship ended, the pastor stood up with a huge grin. "I'll have to cut this morning's sermon a bit short because worship went long, but man, that was a great time, wasn't it?"

The congregation clapped. A few people shouted, "Amen!"

"Before we get started, I just want to remind you all that you can give your tithes through our app whenever you are ready. There are also some boxes in the back by the double doors. Other announcements are in the bulletin. Please be sure to read them. We have some fun things coming up that you want to be aware of.

Okay, let's get to it. We are starting a new series today. The name of this series is True love: What it is… and isn't."

Kate shifted her weight from one foot to the other and clenched her hands into fists. *True love? Ha.*

"We will focus on one passage this morning. You can follow along on the screen or open your Bible to First Corinthians thirteen. We will read through verse seven, then skip to thirteen. This chapter is titled The Way of Love. This is often used at weddings, but it's addressed to believers, not just married couples. Let's read the word of God together."

The Pastor set the speed as the congregation joined in. His voice was loud enough over the speakers, but when the congregation joined, it was a deep rumbling sound that reached to the very core of Kate's being.

"If I speak in the tongues of men and of angels, but have not love, I am a noisy gong or a clanging cymbal. And if I have prophetic powers, and understand all mysteries and all knowledge, and if I have all faith, so as to remove mountains, but have not love, I am nothing. If I give away all I have, and if I deliver up my body to be burned, but have not love, I gain nothing. Love is patient and kind; love does not envy or boast; it is not arrogant or rude. It does not insist on its own way; it is not irritable or resentful; it does not rejoice at wrongdoing, but rejoices with the truth. Love bears all things, believes all things, hopes all things, endures all things. Love never ends. So now faith, hope, and love abide, these three; but the greatest of these is love."

The congregation quieted, and the pastor continued alone. "Lord, thank you for your word. Holy Spirit, I ask that you would make your word alive and active in our hearts this morning. I pray that we would not sit in these pews, hear your words, and then go on with our lives, but that your words change how we view our lives and how we interact with the world around us. Use me this morning. In Jesus' name."

"Amen," the congregation murmured and sat down.

Kate sank into her seat, slouched down, and made herself as small as possible. Men had told her more times than she could count that they loved her. She knew she wanted nothing to do with love. *What is this love they are talking about? Is this just some gag to draw people in?*

The pastor looked over the congregation. "As we go over these verses, I want you to assess your love life."

There were scattered chuckles through the congregation.

The pastor held up a hand. "Now you know what I mean. Does the way you love people in your daily life line up with scripture? Does it fall short? How can you love better? Love your spouse. Your parents. Your siblings. Your neighbors. The strangers you pass on the street. The people who live their lives in ways you disagree with. In all these things, do you love well?"

The pastor paused and looked around the room. "Self-introspection is rarely fun, but it is an important part of our lives, especially as believers. We need to assess our lives and see if we line up with the way God calls us to live and not with the way culture tells us we *can* live. So, let's first look at what love is NOT. Love does not envy or boast."

The pastor looked up and shook his head. "How easy is it to become envious, especially of people we claim to love? Family members who get to do more than us, travel more, buy more. Friends who get married and leave us singles behind. People who are unmarried and can make their own decisions. People who have kids when you want kids. People who wish at times that they didn't have kids.

This envy leads us to boast about the things that we do get to do. It leads to us one-upping the people we care about, hard feelings, and bitterness. When these situations come up, we should be able to rejoice with those who rejoice. We should share their excitement for the things they get to do and experience instead of whining and complaining that we don't get to. We should pray that God blesses them and their experiences.

Love is not arrogant or rude. It does not insist on its own way. Just think that one through a moment. How many of us act just this way when dealing with people we love?" The pastor raised his hand.

Kate glanced around as people throughout the congregation raised their hands, including her friends on either side of her. *Why are they admitting this? Isn't it a bad thing?*

The pastor smiled. "Yeah, how many arguments happen daily because we just want things our way, especially among family? What would happen if we started asking people what *they* wanted and did that with joy, whether *we* wanted to or not? Do you think people around us would feel loved? Would feel cared for? We need to be aware of our attitudes, not just with the people we love, but with everyone we come in contact with. It's so easy to fall into thinking our way is the right way. Ours are the best ideas. Everyone else should agree with us. But is that really what matters? So what if you are right or your idea is better? Does it not matter more that the person you are with feels loved? I am not saying that we should ignore or agree with sin, that's a different story. We will get into loving people through sin next Sunday, but are you with me, folks?"

There were a few "amens" and "yes, sirs" and an "I'm with you!".

The pastor nodded. "Thank you. Okay, Love is not irritable or resentful; it does not rejoice at wrongdoing. Who here knows how easy it is to get irritable or to feel resentful toward people?"

Kate looked around at the nodding heads. It felt like the pastor was talking directly to her. Like he knew what she had done and her feelings towards others. *Is everyone feeling this way or is it just me?*

"If we are not careful, we can easily find ourselves feeling happy about the misfortunes of our enemies or people we are irritated with. We can even find ourselves doing things to annoy or irritate those people. All these things fall into rejoicing in wrongdoing. But what does God tell us in Matthew five, forty-three through forty-eight? You have heard that it was said, 'You shall love your neighbor and hate your enemy.' But I say to you, Love your enemies and pray for those who persecute you, so that you may be sons of your Father who is in heaven. For he makes his sun rise on the evil and on the good and sends rain on the just and on the unjust."

Memories danced across Kate's mind. JP, Tony, Fran, Juan, all the other men and women who had been involved in making her life hellish. All the men she had served. All the beatings she had suffered. All the pain she had endured. She rubbed the scars behind her ear again. *Love them? Pray for them?* "Ha!" Kate clamped a hand over her mouth. She stared straight ahead, but could see a few people turn her way. She sank down farther in the pew. Jen reached over and patted her shoulder. Kate bit her lip and glanced over. Jen gave her a quick smile before she faced forward again.

"Yeah, it's not easy." The pastor chuckled. "I'm just as guilty as anyone of falling into these aspects of hate. Yes, I said hate. If you don't love someone, you are either indifferent or you hate them. I would claim indifference as a form of hate because it lacks any form of love. Let me just say, if you claim to love someone but constantly fall into these sinful behaviors, I'd ask you to question yourself. Do you really love? If not, ask God to change your heart. If someone claims they love you, but continuously shows these behaviours, that is not love, my friend. Please don't confuse the wrong use of this word with its actual meaning. If you find yourself in ANY type of relationship or experience where this is the case and you need help or advice, please come see me after the service."

Why does it seem like he's talking to me?

"Now, here it gets a little tricky, but I think you all can follow. If I speak in the tongues of men and of angels, but have not love, I am a noisy gong or a clanging cymbal. And if I have prophetic powers, and understand all mysteries and all knowledge, and if I have all faith, so as to remove mountains, but have not love, I am nothing. If I give away all I have, and if I deliver up my body to be burned, but have not love, I gain NOTHING. It doesn't matter how much wisdom, knowledge, faith, power, or understanding we have. It doesn't matter what we do or sacrifice. If we don't have or do those things in love, it's meaningless." The pastor paused for a moment. The church was still as his words hung over the congregation.

The pastor cleared his throat and continued, "Now, for what love IS. Love is patient and kind. Love rejoices with the truth. Love bears all things, believes all things, hopes all things, endures all things. Love never ends." The pastor sighed and smiled. "Sounds too good to be true, doesn't it?"

There were low murmurings through the congregation.

"This is how you check if you are loving well. Do these things represent how you love people? If you can honestly say yes, then God bless you! May He strengthen you and encourage you and fill you with even more love to pour out on people. If these things do not describe how you love, it's okay. You aren't a lost cause. We have access to the One who *is* love, and who teaches us to love others. Let us come humbly to Him and ask Him to teach us. Let us remember the greatest act of love this world will ever know, when Jesus took the punishment for *our* sin on the cross and even while he suffered, He loved us."

A picture of a man on a cross came up on the screen. The man was so badly beaten that Kate would not have recognized him if she had known him. Her heart twisted at the pained expression on his face. Blood covered him as he hung by the nails in his wrists. Kate stared at the picture. *There. There's a man who can understand my pain. I've never been beaten that badly, but if anyone could see my heart or emotions emotions, they would look like that man.*

"We must understand *that* love if we are ever going to come anywhere close to being able to love others in this way. We are not able to love in the way we are called to with our own emotions. This love is only able to be given once we realize and accept the love that *God* has for *us*. Love isn't just a list of dos and don'ts. It's what flows out of us as we learn to understand and accept the grace that God has given through Jesus taking the punishment that we deserved. And let us not forget, faith, hope, and love abide, these three; but the greatest of these is love. I'm going to invite the worship team back up..."

The pastor's voice faded. *Jesus... my parents and Miranda... This is what they believed. Is it possible...?* An emotion she couldn't identify filled her and left her feeling full, but weak.

The rest of the service was a blur. The walls seemed to close in on her again. It got harder and harder to breathe. As soon as Kate realized people were leaving, she bolted to her feet. "Can we go home?"

"Of course."

Kate could hear the concern in Jen's voice, and guilt pricked at her. *I should go home alone and let these guys stay and talk to their friends... but I'm too afraid to go alone. I guess I'm one of those people who don't know how to love. But the pastor said we are not lost causes...*

Jen must have said something to the others because they all stood. Jen gently pushed Kate in front of her. People tried to talk to them, but Jason and Casey politely made excuses and pressed forward, making a way for Kate, Jen, and John to come behind.

Kate let her friend's quiet conversation pass over

her as they walked home. She searched up and down the street as they walked. *What does all this mean?* The feeling that someone watched her tingled at the back of her neck. She glanced back. People stood on the church steps looking their way. *It's just them. Tony isn't here. He used to say he loved me, but what he did doesn't sound anything like what the pastor said. It seems more like...* Kate glanced at each of the people who walked with her. *But how is it possible? They can't really love me, can they?*

As soon as they reached the house and unlocked the door, Kate turned to them. She briefly met each of their eyes. "Thank you," she whispered before she turned and fled up to her room.

JEN

Jen watched as Dawn fled up the stairs, then she turned to her friends. She could read the concern in their eyes. She gestured to the house. "I hope we didn't push her too much. Make yourselves at home. I'll go talk to her."

Her friends nodded and filed into the house. Jen pushed the door shut behind her and headed up the steps. "Dawn?" She pushed Dawn's door open a crack. Dawn sat on her bed, hugging her knees to her chest, and stared into space. "Can I come in?"

After what seemed an eternity with no response, Dawn gave a small nod, then her soft voice reached Jen's ears. "It's Kate."

Jen caught her breath. Dawn looked over at her.

"My name. It's Kate... Katherine." She turned her face forward again and rested her chin on her knees.

Jen entered the room and sat on the edge of the bed. *That was one of the names God gave me for her to choose.* "Kate?" she asked. When Dawn nodded, she asked, "Why did you choose Dawn?"

Dawn, no, Kate, studied her for a minute, then shrugged. "I wasn't sure about you... if I could trust you or not. I wasn't sure if I wanted to... if I... No one has known my real name since I was a kid... Since Miranda died and Juan sold me. To think of trusting someone with that... I couldn't do it."

Jen nodded. *I can't imagine.* "So, why tell me now? And... who was Miranda?"

"I... I trust you." Kate squeezed her eyes shut for a minute, then opened them again with a sigh. "Remember when you asked me if there had been anything that was good in my life?"

Jen nodded.

"Well, Miranda was. She believed like you. If not for her, I..." Kate swallowed. "I would not have survived those first few years."

Jen reached out and laid a hand on Kate's arm. She wanted to comfort her, but what words could you say to someone who had experienced such pain? *God, heal her.* "What happened to her?" she asked quietly.

Kate's eyes met hers. "They killed her." Kate paused, then continued to share the story.

KATE

Twelve Years Ago

Juan entered the room. It was a rare day when he showed up to retrieve one of them.

"What's going on?" Hung asked.

Another shrugged.

"You, let's go." He pointed at Miranda.

Miranda waited a moment before she took a deep breath and stood. Kate knew she had said a prayer. She always did when any of the girls were taken. She prayed a lot.

Juan's phone rang. He seemed distracted and impatient as he answered it. Kate glanced at Miranda and stepped toward her. She looked… different. Determined and peaceful and… like she knew something.

"What is it?" she asked her in a whisper.

Miranda looked at her. Tears shone in her eyes. She smoothed Kate's hair back from her face. "Kate, everyone, if… if I don't come back for any reason… remember what I have told you, all right? Please promise me? Remember what I told you about how much God loves you."

Kate glanced at the other girls. They watched Miranda as if she had sprouted another head.

"Why wouldn't you come back?"

Juan shouted at whoever was on the other end of the call. It gave them just seconds longer to talk.

Miranda shrugged. "I'm not sure, but I think… I have a feeling that today is the day," she answered. She pulled Kate into a hug. "I love you," she said into her hair. "I love you all."

Kate glanced up as Miranda made eye contact with each of the confused women around her.

"Let's go." Juan growled as he disconnected the call.

"Please, don't ever forget the things I've told you," Miranda repeated as Juan grabbed her arm.

Fear gripped Kate so strongly it almost paralyzed her. She reached for Miranda's hand as Juan pulled her from the room. "Miranda?" She wanted to hold on to her. *What does she mean we might not see her again?* She couldn't imagine never seeing her again.

She tried to follow them from the room, but one of Juan's men at the door shoved her back in. "Miranda!" she shouted as he pulled the door closed. Miranda looked back and Kate made eye contact with her one last time as the door shut. Miranda had tears in her eyes, but she smiled. The door shut and Miranda was gone. Kate turned to the others in the room, who looked at each other curiously.

"What was she talking about? 'Today is the day'?" Lyubov asked herself more than anyone else.

"She always was a strange one." Angel shook her head.

Hung and a few other girls giggled. "You can say that again."

They all headed to their own blankets. All except Kate, who paced and tried to pray.

MIRANDA

Since last night, Miranda had had the feeling that her days on Earth were coming to an end. She didn't quite understand it, but it didn't concern her much. Death didn't worry her. It meant she'd be going Home. *How I long to go Home!*

A deep regret gripped her. *I so hoped to see my family and friends again, but that won't happen. Not here on Earth anyway. It kills me that I'll never know what happens to the dear girls in that room... But I'm so excited to leave this terrible place. To not have to suffer this torture anymore. To finally meet Jesus face to face.* She rubbed her arms. *I would gladly trade places with any of them if it could be one of the others getting out of here and going to see Jesus. What difference am I supposed to make before I die, though? I guess the time to act will be soon.*

Miranda stumbled up the steps after Juan. He was furious and pulled her quickly along with him. When they got to the top of the steps, he shoved her ahead of him and released her arm. He gestured toward the hotel across the courtyard, where the men usually waited.

God, please. Whatever is about to happen. Use it for your glory. Use me for your glory. Get these girls out of here, Father. Please. In Jesus' name.

As she finished her prayer, Juan called for her to stop. She looked back as one of the other men approached him. They spoke quietly for a moment. Juan's voice slowly rose to a shout. She ignored them and looked around. It was the same view she had seen so many times. The wall in front of the staircase that led to their room. The small courtyard with a hotel on one side where the men waited. To the right, a wall with a doorway that was always guarded. She wasn't sure what lay beyond there. A few plants with benches decorated the courtyard. To the left, an alleyway led out to the street, and from there, to freedom. There were guarded booths on either side of the alley.

Miranda studied the alley. It looked like the alley in her dream last night. She hugged herself as she let the dream play through her mind again. She'd been running as fast as she could. Men with guns pursued her. To her right and behind her, a group of girls called out to her to help them. To her left, demons ran toward her. In front of her loomed a U.S. embassy. She was so close. She had run harder in an attempt to get past the demons before they cut her off. "God help me!" she had cried. Angels, more than she could count, flew over her head and made a defensive line to protect her from the demons. Just then, one of the men behind her had fired and hit her. She stumbled and fell. Defeated, she lay there. She would fail. "You've got this, my daughter," a kind, gentle voice encouraged from all around her. At the sound of the voice, a new strength filled her, and she rose. As she did, the men fell back screaming, and the battle between the angels and demons intensified. "You can do this. I am with you," the voice said again. With the new energy, she ignored her wound and ran hard. It almost seemed as if she were flying this time. She made it to the embassy gate as a guard opened it and held out his hand. As she took his hand, everything behind her vanished and she felt the pain of her wound. It hurt like nothing she had ever felt before. "The girls." She pointed to where they still stood, calling for help. "Please, you must help them!" She sank to the floor, and he knelt down. "Don't worry, Ma'am. We will get them." She had passed out and awakened.

Miranda wasn't sure how exactly it would happen, but she knew today was the day she had waited for. The day she would make a difference and die. Fear wriggled its way into her heart, but before it took hold, she shook her head. "No," she whispered. "Father, I am yours. Use me. Help me to do what I am here to do. Guide me and give me strength."

The fear dissipated, and she took a deep breath. Juan and that other guy still argued. She wondered what could be so important that they would make a customer wait this long. One of the guards at the door meandered over and soon joined the argument. The other went through the door and pushed it shut. She glanced at the hotel. No one appeared to be watching. She took a few steps towards the alley. The guards were both in one booth playing cards and watching a t.v. show, oblivious to the argument.

"God?" The thought of what she was about to do sent adrenaline coursing through her body. Her heart pounded so hard she could hear the blood whoosh in her ears. She sidled toward the alley a few steps at a time. She turned to watch the men argue as she backed the rest of the way to the edge of the alley. Once there, she took a deep breath.

After one last glance back at the stairway to the room of girls and at the men, she took off as fast as she could run. It wasn't long before she heard shouts behind her. She made it to the street and threw a wild glance both ways before she turned left and took off again. Within moments, she realized she couldn't run for long. Her body was out of shape and sore from the abuses she'd endured. She prayed as she ran. She prayed for help and guidance, for the girls, for energy, that she would be able to complete this mission.

She could hear the men. They were gaining on her. She came to an intersection and paused. Her lungs burned after that short sprint. She gulped air into her lungs. *God, help me.* Something bright caught her eye on the road. *Is it? Yes. Headlights. A car is coming. If they stop, I can make it!* Joy filled her. *I can make-* a bullet tore through her and exited her stomach. She gasped and fell to the ground, a hand on her wound. Pain engulfed her. *So this is how it'll happen. But no… I haven't done anything yet. All I did was run.*

She looked back and could faintly see the men. They had slowed to a walk now that she couldn't escape. The car slowed to a stop next to her. The men froze. Miranda turned toward the car. A woman opened her door and said something in Spanish, then in broken English. "You okay? Need help?"

Miranda nodded. "Yes. Si. Help. Please." She tried to stand, but crumpled back to the ground with a groan. She looked down. Her blood spread across her shirt.

The woman's husband got out of the driver's side and hurried to her. He gently lifted her and laid her in the backseat of his car. As he shut the door, she saw the men running toward them. The man ran to the driver's side, jumped in, and sped away before he even shut the door.

Through hand gestures and single words, Miranda asked to use a cell phone. The woman handed her one. "We go hospital," she spoke to her husband, who sped up even more.

Miranda drew in ragged breaths. She pressed her hand against her wound in an attempt to stop the bleeding, but it was hopeless. She used one hand to scroll through the phone. Finally, she found what she wanted. A notes app. It took longer than she wanted to type out the message with one trembling hand, but she managed. *Ask couple where they found me. Girls trapped in cellar room behind hotel. Save them! Please!*

Miranda let out a shaky breath as she finished. She lifted her hand from the wound in her stomach and looked down at it. *So much blood.* She grimaced and pressed her hand into it again with a groan. She held the phone back out to the woman.

"Here."

The woman looked back at her.

"There's a message." Miranda felt her body growing weaker as her blood continued to drain from her body. She felt a sudden twinge of guilt at bleeding out all over this couple's car and her heart swelled with gratitude that they had stopped to help her.

The woman frowned.

Miranda turned the phone so the woman could see that she had written something. "Please, take it... to... the embassy."

The woman glanced at it, then looked back at her.

"The... United... St... ates... emba... ssy."

The woman's eyes widened, and she nodded. "Si. Si." She took the phone.

Miranda let her arm drop and shut her eyes.

Thank you, God. She opened her eyes again and looked out the window up into the night sky. It was a beautiful, clear night, and she was free.

"Gracias," Miranda whispered.

The woman's face filled with concern. She reached back, took Miranda's hand in hers, and squeezed gently. She spoke quickly to her husband. He glanced back with a worried frown and responded to his wife in a quiet voice.

Miranda smiled and attempted to squeeze the woman's hand back. *It's nice to have someone's hand to hold right now.* She saw the woman's lips move and she let her eyes shut. She was in pain, yes, but she felt peace. Such peace. *I'm coming home, Lord.* She smiled as her hand slipped from the woman's and she gave in to the darkness.

Miranda opened her eyes a moment later. She immediately noticed that she was not in pain. She looked down to where her wound should have been. Nothing. She could not even remember what it had felt like.

Huge double doors that seemed to be bronze but glowed with a bright light loomed in front of her. The light did not come from the doors; they reflected it. An even brighter light shone through all around the doors. Pure light covered everything around her.

Miranda stared at the doors as an indescribable joy filled her. It bubbled out of her in a laugh of pure, childlike excitement. *I'm here. I'm finally here!* With a bounce in her steps, she walked forward and placed a hand on either door. She hesitated a moment.

A voice, unlike any she had ever heard, boomed from behind the door, yet gently surrounded her. It was gentle and kind, filled with love and compassion.

"Welcome, my good and faithful servant. Come, my daughter, and take your place with me."

The joy she had felt moments ago was nothing compared to what that voice did to her heart. She did not know how she could live and contain this all consuming-joy. It filled her to the point where she thought she would burst. *This is it. This is what I've waited for!* She smiled, pushed the doors open, and confidently walked into eternity.

KATE

Kate froze mid-step and spun toward the door. The others whipped their heads in the same direction. Shouts drifted down from outside. It continued on. An uneasy silence filled the room as they strained to hear what was going on.

The shouts intensified. They heard someone run down the steps. Loud, muffled voices came from right outside the door. They could only catch a few words until they clearly heard, "She's running! Stop her!" Gunshots rang out and echoed in the otherwise silent doorway outside of the room.

Everything was eerily silent until they heard footsteps on the stairs again. Juan entered the room with the two guards behind him.

"Who knew what she planned?!" he shouted. His voice warned that whoever answered would pay. Kate pressed her lips together and backed away. She glanced at the others. No one had known what Miranda had intended.

"Well?!" he thundered. "Who knew?!" He stormed over to one of the newer girls and grabbed her by the hair. "Did you know?"

She shook her head with a whimper. He growled and tossed her back on her blanket in frustration. He scanned the room.

All the girls backed away from him. Kate bumped into the wall as she took another step back.

"What about you?" Juan strode over to Angel and grabbed the front of her shirt.

"No!" She shook her head. "No one knew. She told none of us!"

"She told none of you, eh?"

Kate's fear for Miranda overrode her self preservation. "Where is she?" she asked from the corner.

Juan turned to her. "You. She was fond of you. I find it hard to believe that she told none of you what she planned." He swung his arm out in a sweeping gesture as he made his way to stand in front of Kate. "You all expect me to believe that?"

"What did she do?" Kate pressed back against the wall with nowhere else to retreat to.

"What did she do? What did she do? I'll tell you what she did." He leaned in until his face was against Kate's. "She ran. She ran and now she's dead." He straightened. "She's dead," he said louder. "And if any of you try to run like she did, I will kill all of you!" He turned and marched out the door, followed by the guards. They pulled the door shut and slammed the lock.

Dead? After a moment of shocked silence, Kate ran to the door and pulled at it. "No! She isn't dead! Miranda! Miranda! Come back! She isn't dead!" When pulling on the door did nothing, she slammed her fists on it. "Let me out! Where is she?"

Kate turned her back to the door and sank down. "She can't be dead," she whispered. She wanted to keep screaming. To shout and beat the door down. To know exactly what had happened. But as her shock wore off, she had to face the truth. Miranda was gone. She wasn't coming back. She pulled her knees up to her chest and sobbed. Angel sat next to her and laid a hand on her shoulder, but said nothing.

JEN

Five Months Ago

Kate finished her story with tears in her eyes and a small one-shouldered shrug.

"I'm so sorry, Daw-" Jen paused and corrected herself. "Kate."

"It was a long time ago." Kate gave a full shrug and blinked her tears away. "It's weird to hear that name."

"Do you want me to keep calling you Dawn?"

Kate frowned. "No. It... will just take some time to get used to hearing my real name again."

There was silence for a few minutes, then Kate spoke again. "How do you do it?"

Jen tilted her head. "Do what?"

"Live... like the pastor talked about? Until I met you, Miranda and I think my parents were the only people I ever met who came close to living like what the pastor said we should live like."

"Oh, well." Jen pursed her lips and glanced out the window. *God, how do I explain this?* She looked back at Kate. "It takes self-control. It's more of a learned thing than just something you start doing. I could not even attempt to live this way if I didn't have God's help. If I did not understand His love for me and for others, there would be no way I could even begin to love people in the right way. But, when you start to understand how great God's love is, first for you, then for those around you, you see things and people in a different way."

Kate frowned. "Okay. But... what about when he said to love your enemies? Does that mean I am supposed to... love Tony and Juan and all those other men who..." Kate's voice was laced with bitterness and pain. She squeezed her legs tighter to her chest. Her knuckles turned white as she gripped her arms. She shook her head. "I can't do that."

Jen didn't respond right away. She looked down at her hands as she rubbed them along her thighs. *God, I don't want to say the wrong thing here. I don't want to say something that will harden Kate's heart to you. I can't imagine what she has gone through. Please speak to her heart, Father. Soften her heart to you.*

"Jen?"

Jen raised her head again and met Kate's gaze. "Yes?"

"I really do want to know what he meant." The bitterness and hurt had left Kate's voice. In its place was desperation.

Jen nodded and sighed. "It's a weird thing, Kate. We are to hate the sin but love the sinner. If someone hurts you, you can love them, but that doesn't mean you need to trust them. I think, my understanding is that we treat all people with love and kindness even if they do not treat us that way. That we do not attempt to get revenge, but leave that to God. That we pray for those that hurt us. That we realize that they have hurt in their own lives and often they hurt others due to unresolved hurts. So, our job is not to add to that hurt but to try to give them a new experience. One of love, of kindness, of forgiveness." Jen watched Kate closely as she worked through her answer. Kate seemed to accept what she said. A hardness had started to enter her eyes, but she closed them, shook her head and, when she opened them again, the hardness was gone. Jen shrugged. "That's how I understand it."

Kate drew in a deep breath and nodded. "I... I suppose that makes sense. It sounds like something Miranda might have said. It seems impossible. Even to think about."

"True," Jen agreed with a dry laugh. "It is not easy."

"But you and the others... you live like it's no problem at all."

Jen raised an eyebrow, then smiled. "We have been living this way for most of our lives. It's still something we need to practice and remind ourselves of, though. When our own human nature decides to try and take over, man. It can get ugly. Kind of like that time Jemma came home drunk."

Kate tilted her head. "What do you mean?"

"I was furious with her," Jen could hear the anger in her tone and feel it rising up in her even now. "Everything in me wanted to slap the drunkenness right out of her."

Kate smirked and coughed to cover her laugh.

"I'm serious!" Jen smiled before she continued. "I was so angry. I'm still so angry. And what she said... I know she was drunk, but if God didn't give me patience right then, I would have said a lot of things I would regret right now. I would have added to the pain in Jemma's life and likely given her even more reasons to drink." Jen drew in a breath. "A story that really encourages me is one I heard about Corrie Ten Boom." At Kate's blank expression, Jen briefly explained the Holocaust. "Corrie was in one of those camps. Years after the war, she was at an event when a man who had been a Nazi approached her. He asked her to forgive him for what he had done. I don't know how, but she did. She had allowed God to work in her heart to the point she could forgive that man for the horrendous crimes he committed." Jen shook her head. "I don't think I could have done that."

"I... think I understand." They were silent for a few moments before Kate spoke again. "I want to try and live like the Pastor talked about. I don't want to be selfish and always thinking of myself."

Jen tilted her head. "Okay."

"Where... how do I start? I don't want to just live that way. I... I want it to be real. Like you and the others. Like Miranda."

Jen's heart leaped within her. She drew her brows together. "Are you saying you want to follow Jesus?"

KATE

Is that what I want? I want the assurance that they have. I want their confidence. Their love, contentment, and peace. They only have that because they follow God. They've claimed it more times than I can count. Can he give me the peace I'm looking for? Can he really heal me like they say he can? She bit her lip and rubbed her scars. *I don't know… but if that's what it takes to get what they have, I'll do it. I don't mind following someone who understands my pain. If what the pastor said is true, Jesus can understand it better than anyone.* "I… I think so. Yes."

Kate jumped when Jen let out an exuberant squeal. She clapped a hand over her mouth and met her eyes with a wide, joy-filled gaze. "Really, Dawn? I mean, Kate?"

Kate had never seen Jen look this way. She seemed so energized that Kate thought she might bounce out of her own skin. Her heart expanded. Never had she thought a decision she made could bring such joy. She nodded again. "Yes."

"Okay." Jen nodded back. She seemed to have gained control, but her eyes shone. "Well, the Bible says if we confess with our mouths and believe in our hearts that Jesus is Lord, we will be saved. God knows what is in our hearts."

Kate cringed. *That's not good.* "How can he accept

me after all I've done?"

Compassion entered Jen's gaze, though the joy did not dim. "That is the amazing thing about it, Kate. He can accept us when we ask for forgiveness because of what Jesus did on the cross. It has nothing to do with how good or bad we are and everything to do with God's love and mercy. We ask for forgiveness. We claim him. We believe he is who he says he is. That's where it all starts."

"Just like that? It's that easy?"

"Just like that. Don't get me wrong, life still sucks sometimes, but when we follow Jesus, we never face anything alone. "

We never face anything alone? Kate never wanted to be alone again. "So, I just tell him? Here? Now?"

"Yes. In your own words. Do you want me to leave?"

Jen moved to stand, but Kate reached out and grabbed her arm. "No, please stay."

Jen sank back onto the bed and wrapped her hand around Kate's. "Okay, I'll stay."

Kate sighed in relief. Her tongue suddenly felt like sandpaper. *Am I really about to do this? Yes. If only Miranda could be here now. Her eyes would probably look just like Jen's. So full of joy. Of hope. Of... love?* Kate swallowed.

She did not know what would happen after this. Did not know if God would really accept her, but she trusted her friends as odd and terrifying as it was to admit it. *Okay, here goes nothing.* "Uh, God?" She licked her lips. Jen's fingers tightened around hers and she drew strength and comfort from them. "Miranda wanted me to know about you. I know she followed you like Jen and the others. I... I believe what I've heard about Jesus... about who he is. I want what Miranda had. I want what Jen, Casey, John, and Jason have. If... if you truly can accept me, then..." A lump formed in her throat and she tried to swallow it. "Then I want it. I want to be... like these guys. To... to follow you. To know you. Please. If... if it's possible. F... forgive me."

Hope blossomed in Kate's chest. Joy swelled in her heart along with something else. Assurance. She wasn't sure how, but she knew God had heard her. Had listened. Had answered her awkward prayer. Tears sprang to her eyes. Good tears. Happy tears. She opened her eyes to see Jen wiping her face. She grinned. Jen laughed and threw her arms out. Kate did not need more than that. She threw herself at Jen, who wrapped her in a hug.

"Should we go tell the others?"

Kate sat back. *Tell the others?* She pictured John's face. Then Casey's and Jason's. *They need to know. My real name, too.* She hopped off the bed. "Yes." For the first time she could remember, she felt free.

JASON

The stairs creaked. Jason turned to watch Jen come down the steps, followed closely by Dawn. He frowned. *Something's different.* He studied their faces and his heart lifted. There was no sign of the fear and hurt that always lurked on Dawn's face.

She looked up. When her eyes met his, one side of her mouth lifted in a shy smile before she turned her eyes away again. It felt like his heart skipped a beat. Jason rubbed his chest over his heart. *God, she's so beautiful and sweet and she doesn't even seem to know it.*

"Guys," Jen's voice held her barely contained excitement. "We have some news for you!"

Jason couldn't take his eyes off of Dawn. *This is awful! God, I want to get to know her. I want to spend time with her. I... I like her. But she doesn't fol-*

"Well?" Casey's impatient voice interrupted his silent prayer. "What is it?"

Jen let out a peal of laughter. "I'll let her tell you."

"I didn't think it was possible, but..." Dawn paused.

Her quiet, joy-filled voice filled Jason with longing. *If only she could always sound this carefree!*

"But?" John prompted.

Dawn looked each of them in the eyes. "I just prayed. I... I asked Jesus to forgive me. I don't know why... or how... but... somehow, I know that he did."

Casey let out a whoop, grabbed Dawn's hands, and spun her around. "That's amazing!"

Dawn smiled. Truly smiled, for the first time he had seen. Her eyes lit up and her face radiated her joy as she stumbled in a circle as Casey pulled her around. Jason grinned. His heart swelled to bursting with joy and thanksgiving. *Oh, God. Thank you!* He reached out his hand. Dawn hesitated only a moment before she put her hand in his and looked up at him. He wrapped both hands around hers. "I am so happy to hear that," he said. "That's the best news I've heard in a long time."

She flushed and looked away, and pulled her hand from his. Though he wanted to hold on to her and never let go, he forced himself to release her.

John stepped forward and wrapped her in a hug. "Welcome to the family, Dawn."

Dawn's smile faltered. Jason opened his mouth to ask, but John beat him to it.

"What's wrong?"

"My name." Dawn fidgeted. "It's..." She glanced at Jen, who nodded. "My name is Katherine." She tilted her head. "Kate."

Casey grinned. "It fits you."

John smiled. "That's a very nice name. Did you know it means pure?"

Kate shook her head and frowned.

"I know that because it's my mother's name."

"Oh. Maybe... I should pick a new name. I'm not..."

"You know," Jason gently interrupted. *I do not want her to finish this thought if she's going where I think she's going.* "I'm so thankful for the new life God gives us when he forgives us. He makes us a new creation. The old is gone, and the new has come."

Kate turned to him, a frown still on her face. "I don't understand."

Jason smiled. "You will. Kate is a perfect name. Especially now."

"He's got a point," Casey chimed in.

"Oh." The frown disappeared from Kate's face, but confusion remained in her eyes.

Jemma's door opened and a moment later the bathroom door slammed shut. Kate stared up the steps. "Um..." She turned to them.

"I think it might be best if we just use your name in our group. At least for now." Jen smiled at Kate.

Kate sighed in relief.

"Agreed." Casey nodded.

John nodded.

"Around anyone outside this group, you will remain Dawn. But are you okay with us using your name when it's only us?" Jason studied Kate.

"That would be nice."

"I'm glad to hear it." Jason smiled.

"I don't know about you guys, but I think this calls for a celebration! We should order out and eat on the porch." Casey clapped her hands. "A little bit of everything sounds good. Chinese, pizza, fries, soda, chicken wings. Maybe something from that new Thai place that just opened. What do you think?"

Kate stared at Casey. "You want *all* of that?"

Jason tilted his head back and laughed. "This girl can eat. It sounds like a good plan to me."

KATE

Three Months Ago

Kate paced the kitchen as she waited for the tea water to boil. She wasn't sure what she would do with her evening. Casey was visiting friends in another state. Jen had gone on a date with John right after work. *I could see if Jason would come over...* She shook her head. *No. I trust him, but...* She sighed. The teapot whistled, and she turned the burner off.

She grabbed a mug and made her tea. As she left the kitchen, the stairs creaked. Kate winced. *Jemma. I took too long. Now I'll have to talk to her.* Guilt pricked at her. *Will I ever get past my dislike of her?* She knew she didn't feel the love and forgiveness toward her that she should. She sighed and entered the kitchen again. Jemma walked past without acknowledging her.

"Hi." Kate paused. She'd managed to not have to talk much with Jemma, so she wasn't quite sure what to say. "Um, the tea water just boiled."

Jemma opened the fridge and glanced back at her. "Thanks." She turned back to the fridge and ignored her again.

Kate nodded and stood silently for a minute. Jemma didn't say anything. *Maybe she doesn't want to talk? I'm fine with that.* She shrugged and started to leave the kitchen. Jemma's voice stopped her.

"So... you seem to finally be doing better."

Kate gripped her mug in both hands. "Uh, yeah, I guess so."

"That's good." Jemma set the milk and cereal on the counter, then turned and leaned against it.

Kate shifted as Jemma eyed her. *I can just walk away... but I don't want to be rude to Jen's sister.*

"Have any of your memories come back?"

Kate forgot to breathe for a few seconds as she stared blankly at Jemma. She didn't want to lie, but she did not want Jemma to know anything about her life. She might be Jen's sister, but she was nothing like her. Kate gritted her teeth and looked down. *Saying nothing is safe, isn't it?*

"Hm." Jemma turned and poured her cereal. "I can't believe you've spent all this time here and still you can't remember anything." She almost sounded sympathetic, but there was an underlying accusation in her tone. "I don't know if I could handle it. Living every day not knowing how I got shot or who shot me. Not knowing who I was. It sounds awful."

"Mm," Kate made a non-committal noise deep in her throat. Jemma was prodding. Looking for information. She knew Jemma wouldn't remain silent forever. Not with the way she'd been looking at her.

"I don't know what your game is, Dawn, but I just want you to know that I'm watching you. They might seem friendly, but I've talked to Jason. Him and John are watching you, too."

It felt like a knife pierced her chest. She forgot how to breathe for a moment. *Is it true? Were John and Jason pretending to be my friends this whole time? Was*

I wrong to trust them? Do they really agree with Jemma? Kate bit her lip as she pictured their open and honest faces as opposed to Jemma's suspicious one. *Was I that wrong about them?* Peace filled her and settled her anxiety. *No. I'm not wrong about them. I can't be. They love God too much. They're too honest to lie like that.*

She glanced up and met Jemma's stare. "Okay."

Jemma frowned. "Okay? Just okay?"

Kate nodded. "What do you want me to say?"

Jemma folded her arms, and her frown deepened. Kate braced herself for whatever she might say. Jemma opened her mouth but clicked it shut again when they heard the front door.

"Hello?"

Jason's voice sent a shiver down Kate's spine. She could not understand her reactions to him.

"Jason! We're in the kitchen!" Any signs of suspicion or dislike were gone from Jemma's voice.

Kate retreated from the kitchen doorway to the corner by the basement door to make room for Jason. Not that he needed all that room, but she didn't exactly want to stand right next to him. At least, that's what she told herself.

Jason entered the kitchen. "Hey, guys." He smiled, and Kate's stomach did a somersault.

She gave him a small smile and glanced at Jemma, who glowered at her before she turned to Jason.

"What are you doing here, Jay? Come to hang out with me before I head to work?" Jemma's voice dripped with venomous honey.

Kate shuddered to think of Jason wanting to spend time with Jemma. She frowned. *What he does is his business...* She moved to edge past him. Now was as good a time as any to make an escape from Jemma. "Excuse me."

"Actually, I'm here for Dawn. Sorry, Jemma."

Kate froze. She doubted Jemma caught the slight hesitation before he'd called her Dawn, but she'd noticed it. That wasn't what stopped her, though. *Did he just say…?*

"You… Dawn… what?"

Kate glanced up at Jason. He glanced back at Jemma for a second before he turned back to Kate.

"Would you want to take a walk or something?"

Kate's gaze flickered over to Jemma. She quickly averted her gaze. Jemma looked furious. *Does he know what he just did?* She looked up and searched Jason's face. His eyes flicked toward Jemma and he gave a slight shrug. As if asking a question.

"Um." Kate eyed Jemma again. "I don't…" *I can stay here with Jemma and her questions or I can take a walk with Jason. If I go with him, she'll be furious with me…* Neither option seemed completely comfortable, but the walk seemed less stressful.

"Please?" Jason raised his eyebrows.

Heat rushed up Kate's neck. *I can't say no to him…* "Okay."

Jason's grin lit his whole face. "Great. It's a little chilly out there. Why don't you go grab a jacket, then we can head out?"

Kate nodded, set her tea on the counter, and ducked her head as she passed him to run upstairs. As they left the house a few minutes later, Kate could feel Jemma's stare boring into her back. She ignored it until the door shut, then glanced back. *This is a bad plan. I shouldn't have agreed.*

"Don't worry about Jemma. She'll get over it."

Kate looked up at Jason. He gave her a sheepish smile. "Jen told me you'd be alone with Jemma for a bit tonight. I know how awkward that can be. I didn't want you to have to be alone with her."

"Oh." Kate rubbed her scars. *He just saved me... again.*

Jason nodded. "Anyway. How does hot chocolate sound? The coffee shop has some really good hot chocolate."

"That sounds good." Kate smiled. *He is only acting like a brother. He's treating me like he treats Jen. That's all.*

"Great. Hot chocolate it is."

It gave her the strangest sensation to know that he had purposely come to check on her. *He's just being kind.* She told herself over and over. She tried, but she could not keep the grin off of her face as she walked down the street with Jason at her side.

JEN

Jen cupped her tea in her hands. It was way past her bedtime, but she felt off. Unsettled. *God, whatever is going on, please have your way. Who do I need to pray for right now? What are you trying to tell me?* She sighed.

The door opened. Jen glanced up as Jemma walked in.

"Hey, Jem. How was work?"

"Hey, you're up late."

"Yeah." Jen studied her sister. Something didn't seem right. "What's up?"

Jemma tossed her bag on the floor and plopped onto the couch. "Who says something is up?"

Jen tilted her head.

Jemma scowled. "Don't look at me like that. You know I hate it when you do that."

"Look at you like what?"

"Like that." Jemma waved her hand at Jen. "Like you know what I'm thinking. It's creepy."

Jen chuckled. "I don't know what you're thinking, Jemma."

"Right. I wonder sometimes. You always seem to know when something is up."

"So, something is up?"

Jemma rolled her eyes. "I suppose I should just tell you. I met someone."

"Oh." Jen blinked. *I want to be happy for her... but all I want is for her to know you, Jesus.*

"Oh? That's it?"

"Um, where did you meet him? Who is he?"

"I met him online. His name is Alex. He's a construction worker in Philadelphia." Jemma was quiet for a moment. "I'm moving to Philly."

"What?!" Jen's heart sank. "What do you mean, you're moving to Philly? When? Why?"

"Alex and I want to get to know each other better. Besides, there's nothing here for me. I'm tired of this small town. I need a change of scenery."

Jen opened and closed her mouth. "B... Jem, you..." She shook her head. "How long have you known him? How can you just up and move to a new city for a guy you met online? It's not safe!"

Jemma scowled at her. "Look, Jen. I appreciate that you've taken care of me, okay? But you aren't my mother. I'm an adult, just like you. I can make my own decisions." She stood up, paused, and glared at the stairs. "Besides." She faced Jen again. "It's a bit crowded here now."

Jen looked up to see Kate on the stairs. She could read Kate's internal struggle on her face. She gripped the railing so hard her knuckles looked white, even from across the room. Jen's heart felt torn. *How can Jemma act like that? Why is she doing this?* "Jem..."

"Good night." Jemma picked up her bag and ran up the stairs. She bumped Kate with her shoulder as she passed her.

"Jemma!" Jemma ignored Jen's call. Jen leaned back, shut her eyes, and let out a heavy sigh. *God, help me. I don't know what to do. What to say...*

"Jen?"

Jen opened her eyes. Kate had come the rest of the way down the steps. She rubbed at the spot behind her ear. The place she rubbed whenever she seemed anxious.

"I… I can move out. I don't want to come between you and your sister."

Jen bolted up. "Don't be silly. You aren't going anywhere. This is your home." She patted the couch beside her. "She didn't hurt you, did she?"

Kate shook her head as she sank down. "Are you sure? She doesn't like me very much. She might stay if I leave."

"I'm so sorry for how she treats you, Kate." Jen met Kate's gaze. "I don't know why she acts that way… but I don't think it would make a difference either way." Jen sighed again. "Once she gets something in her head, it's almost impossible to change her mind."

Kate looked down and bit her lip. "I might know why…"

Jen tilted her head and raised an eyebrow. "Oh?"

Kate's cheeks flushed, and she looked down. "The other day, when you went out with John?"

Jen nodded. "Yeah?"

"Jemma came downstairs and was…" Kate trailed off. She glanced toward the steps before she continued. "Talking with me."

Jen understood what Kate didn't want to say. *Jemma was bothering her. Prying into her life.*

"Anyway." Kate shook her head. "Jason came by to check on me. Jemma thought he came for her, but he told her he came for me… Then he… he asked me to go for a walk. I did. I should have said no. I knew it would make her angry. I-"

"Kate." Jen patted Kate's knee and smiled. "You did the right thing. You don't need to live your life here making decisions based on what will or will not make Jemma angry. The smallest thing can set that girl off. You'd never be able to do anything if you lived that way."

"But she seems interested in him."

"He's not interested in her. At all." Jen grinned. "Believe me. We've talked about it a few times."

Kate looked at her. "Are you sure?"

Jen nodded. "I am."

"Okay."

"Hey, don't worry about it. I'll talk to her again tomorrow." Jen paused. "You could pray for her... and for me. I need wisdom with how to talk to her."

Kate nodded. "I can do that."

Jen smiled and hugged Kate. "Thank you. We should get to bed. We have a long day tomorrow."

"Okay." Kate hugged her back. "Good night, Jen. And thank you. For everything."

KATE

Two Months Ago

Kate grabbed her blanket and pillow from her bed and jogged down the steps. Jen was already sprawled across the chair. "Taking a fast shower before the movie, huh?"

Kate shrugged sheepishly. "Sorry. The water felt so good."

Jen laughed. "Understandable. Tea water is ready."

"Thanks." Kate tossed her blanket and pillow on the couch and ran to the kitchen. The guys had come over earlier to help get Jemma packed up. No matter how many times Jen had tried to talk her out of it, she refused to reconsider her decision to move. From what she said, things were going well with the man she'd met online. *I can't imagine...* Kate shook her head. *It's not my place... God, protect Jemma. I may not get along with her, but I don't want anything bad to happen to her. Especially for Jen's sake. She would be heartbroken...* She grabbed a mug from the cabinet and set it on the counter with a sigh.

After they saw Jemma off, the guys had left so they could have a girls' night. *I wish Casey could be here, but she's off on another mission trip.* She grinned and shook her head as she poured the hot water into her mug. She stirred some honey into her lemon tea. Jason had been right when he said Casey was always off to some new place for missionary work. Kate was happy for her, but she was more than content to stay home. She'd be happy if she never had to travel again.

She hurried into the living room, set her mug on the table, and plopped onto the couch. "Okay, I'm ready."

"Finally." Jen laughed.

Kate threw a couch pillow at her.

"Hey. I didn't think you'd ever get comfortable enough to throw something at me."

Kate grinned. "Play the movie."

"Okay." Jen grinned back and pressed play. She put the remote down and threw the pillow back.

"Oof!" Kate hugged the pillow to her chest and tried to scowl at Jen. She failed and shook her head instead. *I can't even pretend to be mad at Jen. She's done so much for me. I wish I could even begin to show her how grateful I am... I'd do anything for her.* She pulled the blanket over her and settled in to watch the movie, but her mind wandered.

In a few months, it will be a year since Jason found me. She could not believe how her life had changed in so short a time. *I'm so lucky. No, not lucky. Blessed.* Why God had listened to people's prayers on her behalf and then her own desperate cries, she would never know. But she was beyond grateful.

Some days, it still shocked her that this was actually her life now. That she had close friends. That she was free. That she was a part of a community now. It felt like she had been with these people for years.

Her friends had been right when they said God

would heal her if she let Him. Her heart had begun to mend in ways she'd never imagined would be possible. She bit her lip. Her old habits truly were hard to break, though. She still looked over her shoulder often. She still got nervous around men. She still had trouble trusting people, but she was learning.

Her friends' reactions when she had admitted she could not read, write, or do anything really, had not been what she'd expected. They had immediately agreed that they would teach her. She still struggled with some things, but she wanted to learn. Jen and the others had been very patient as they helped her through.

Jen insisted on giving her a job in the mechanic shop, even though she knew nothing about cars or office work. "I'll just train you as we go." Jen had declared. And she had. She had learned the basics of office work, computers, phone calls, scheduling, filing, and more.

Kate sighed. *I doubt my nightmares will ever go away, though.* She often still woke in a cold sweat. She sometimes felt as if she were being watched. *That's to be expected after the life I had, though, isn't it? That's what the others think... They're probably right. I haven't seen anyone that looks suspicious. I'm probably just overreacting.* Kate shook her head and focused on the movie once more.

Halfway through the movie, she reached for a handful of popcorn from the bowl on the end table between them. She was so focused on the movie that Jen's panicked whisper startled her.

"Kate?!"

Kate glanced over. Her blood ran cold before her

gaze even landed on Jen. Her eyes widened and her breath caught in her throat. *No! No, no, no, no, no.*

Tony stood in the doorway. Two men she didn't know flanked him. The dining room floor creaked. Kate jerked her head around to see another man. This one she had seen before. He had been with Tony since he purchased her.

She forced herself to look back at Tony. His lips curled in an ugly sneer. *We're trapped. This has to be another nightmare. It has to be!* That old, familiar twist of terror knotted her stomach and throat. She opened her mouth, but nothing came out.

"So you haven't forgotten me," Tony's voice held that terrifying calm before he snapped tone.

It's not a nightmare... A chill snaked up her spine.

"I was worried you had forgotten me... and what you did to me."

Kate tried to swallow, but all moisture had left her mouth. She said nothing.

"Who's your friend here?" Tony turned a critical eye on Jen.

She knew that look all too well. *No!* "T... Tony..." Kate stuttered, then tried to moisten her dry throat. *I can't let anything happen to her! After all she's done for me... If I had just left when I had planned to... If I had died before Jason found me... She wouldn't be in danger now... God, help us!*

Boldness filled her, and she was able to breathe normally again. Spit filled her mouth and loosened her tongue. "I'm what you came for, Tony. You don't need her." Despite the boldness that filled her, her voice still trembled. She forced herself to stand and move between Tony and Jen.

"Tony, we don't have long," the guy who had come in the back warned.

"Yeah, yeah. I know." Tony waved a hand dismissively. "Sit back down, Baby," his voice was calm and cool.

Just like I remember it. Like it always is when he's angry. Just before he loses control. She swallowed. Her boldness wavered. She knew that look in his eyes. He had seen Jen and now he wanted her. *I can't let that happen. God, help me!* "We... we can leave now, Tony." Kate wanted to look back at Jen but was too afraid to take her eyes off of Tony. "She won't call the police. Just leave her. We can go." She shoved down the fear and revulsion that swirled in her gut as she stepped forward. Her hand trembled as she reached out and laid it on Tony's chest. She drew up all of the soothing, sultry tones she could. "C'mon Handsome." She forced her lips into a small smile. She was sure it was more of a grimace, but it was the best she could manage. "Let's just go. You, me, and the guys. Like it used to be."

Tony placed a hand over hers, and his eyes met hers. Hot desire flamed in his gaze. For a moment, she thought he would listen to her, but then he shook his head. He tightened his grip on her hand, pulled it from his chest, and yanked her closer.

She gasped as she stumbled into him.

His fingers dug into the tender skin of her face as he gripped her chin. "You're coming with me no matter what." His tone hadn't changed, but the glint in his eyes became deadlier. "Now, I said sit down." He shoved her backwards.

Kate flailed her arms and stepped back to try to regain her balance, but the back of her leg hit the coffee table. She twisted to avoid landing on it and toppled onto Jen.

"Kate!" Jen's arms wrapped protectively around her as she tried to find her footing again. She resisted the urge to rub her burning cheeks as tears pricked her eyes. There was no doubt her cheeks would bruise. *How could I forget the pain? How could I have let my guard down? How could I be so stupid?* Guilt and despair clawed at her chest and made it hard to breathe. Kate blinked up at Jen's terrified face as she eyed Tony.

"Stand up."

Kate's eyes darted back to him. "Tony," she pleaded.

"Shut up!" He grabbed Jen's arm and pulled her up. Kate tumbled off of her onto the floor.

Jen's pained yelp tore at Kate's heart. While she had a lifetime of experience with this pain, she doubted Jen had ever experienced anything close to it.

Kate watched as Jen stood frozen in place while Tony took his time looking her up and down.

"You will do very nicely." He nodded. The color drained from Jen's face and she wobbled.

Panic flooded Kate's senses. She lost all thought of self preservation. She shoved herself up off the floor. "No! Tony, ple-" Kate snapped her mouth shut as Tony shoved his gun into Jen's neck. Jen squeezed her eyes shut and her lips moved silently.

"I couldn't care if she lives or dies, Baby. That's up to you. Though I would prefer if she lived. I'm sure you don't want to kill someone who took you in." He studied them for a moment. When he spoke next, Tony's normal, harsh tone was back. "Does she even know what you are, you useless whore?"

"She is no-" Jen's voice cut off when the gun pressed harder into her throat.

Kate took a half step forward and raised her hand. She wasn't sure why. *What do I do? Appeal to his human side? I have to try something. God, what do I do?!*

Tony cocked an eyebrow. "So you have told her. Shocking." Tony ran his hand back through Jen's hair and she cringed.

"I'm so sorry, Jen," Kate whispered. She wanted to tear that ugly grin off of Tony's face. She wanted to disappear into the ground. *I should have died back then! If Jason had never found me, this wouldn't be happening right now.*

Tony scowled as his men shifted impatiently. When his eyes came to rest on her again, Kate resisted the urge to cower.

"It's time to leave," he growled. "You try anything and I'll shoot her, got it?"

Kate closed her eyes, nodded, then hung her head. If he kept hold of Jen like that, there was no hope. *God, I just need a small opportunity. Just some way to get Jen out.*

"Good. Now let's go." Tony held Jen's arm and kept the gun on her until the guy from the dining room opened the door. Tony shoved Jen forward and motioned for Kate to follow.

Kate's heart leapt. *He let her go! Maybe I can… Thank you, God. Help me.* The other guys filed into line behind them. Tony and the guy who held the door open brought up the rear.

Kate's mind whirled. She came up with and discarded idea after idea as she slowly followed Jen to the door. Nothing seemed like a good plan. As she approached the door, she glanced at the men and swallowed. *Good plan or not... This is it. It's my only chance to get Jen out of here.*

She leaned forward. "Run!" She reached out and shoved Jen across the porch. She waited only long enough to watch Jen jump down the stairs and take off before she partially turned and jumped at the men.

There was a surprised shout before she collided with the first man. He stumbled back into the others, just like she hoped he would. Kate attempted to stand but stumbled on the man. She jumped forward as she fell and reached for Tony. She missed his shoulders, but wrapped her arms around his waist and dragged him to the ground with her. She caught a glimpse of his face as they fell. Complete and utter shock. Disbelief. Anger. She felt a brief moment of elation before they hit the ground.

Tony shouted at her. He cursed her with as much foul language as he could manage, but she'd heard it all before. She kept her arms wrapped as tightly around his waist as she could while he twisted and turned in an attempt to get out from under her.

Finally, Tony turned his curses on his men, who were still trying to get untwisted from her legs and each other. "Get her off me!" he grunted.

The man holding the door finally recovered from his surprise. He grabbed her legs and tossed them aside. The other men scrambled to their feet. The doorman reached down and hoisted Tony to his feet.

Kate's grip slipped, and she dropped back to the ground. She scrambled up and tossed a glance over her shoulder to see Jen round the corner. Relief flooded her. *I did it. Jen's safe. Thank you, God!* As she turned back, she caught a glimpse of the doorman's face. His eyes were filled with amusement and something else. *Respect?*

Before she could analyze the look further, pain exploded in her jaw. Her head whipped back and slammed into the doorframe. Everything went black, and she crumpled to the ground.

Kate blinked her eyes open and found herself staring up at Tony. Her head pounded and her jaw throbbed, but the sight of him seething at her brought some joy. The muscles along Tony's jaw ticked as he clenched and unclenched his fist.

"You're gonna regret that," he growled through his teeth.

Kate smiled. "Never." She shook her head and instantly regretted it as everything spun. She tried to ignore it and get to her feet, but Tony's boot caught her in the side. Her breath left her in a raspy gasp. Pain enveloped her. She collapsed back down, curled in a ball, and tried to blink away the white haze.

The last time she'd felt pain like this, her ribs had been cracked. She was sure that was the case now. Her lungs refused to draw in enough air as she gasped in each breath.

Tony's boot connected with her side again. The next one landed on her back and an involuntary cry escaped her throat. She arched her back in an attempt to escape the pain as his boot connected with her back again.

Tony's fist curled in her hair, and he pulled her head up. The pain on her scalp seemed minor compared to the rest of her body. He pressed his handgun into her bruised cheek. Kate winced but didn't attempt to pull away. It was too late for her now, but at least Jen was safe. *Jen's safe. Thank you, God. He'll just kill me and leave.*

"I should've killed you the first time you talked back to me," Tony growled.

A dry chuckle escaped before Kate clenched her teeth together. "Yeah, you've said that before."

Tony twisted his hand farther into her hair.

"Ah!" Kate reached up to grab his wrist in an attempt to alleviate some of the pressure.

"Tony, we need to go. NOW."

Tony looked at the man, then took a deep breath. "You're right. Bring... this." He released Kate's hair and her head thumped on the ground as he turned from her.

Wait... he isn't going to kill me?! "No," Kate tried to rise. Fire engulfed her. Her body refused to do what she wanted it to. Too much pain. She bit back a whimper. *No. Don't take me back. Kill me!*

She gasped as two of the men lifted her off the ground and tied her hands behind her back. She tried to struggle, but every movement brought searing pain and darkened her vision. Kate let her body go limp as despair enveloped her. They dragged her to the car and the open trunk.

No, not the trunk. She tried to pray, but the pain obscured all thought. The men lifted her and dropped her in the trunk. She felt like she was a child again, being taken for the first time. No one had rescued her that time, and no one would this time either. She looked up into the eyes of the guy she recognized as he lifted a hand to shut the trunk. He had always treated her better than anyone else. She grasped at her last chance. "Please," she whispered.

He hesitated as he made eye contact. His eyes softened and shook his head. "I never did like this kind of thing. Someone wants to sell themselves, that's their deal, but this?" He muttered something under his breath. "I'll see what I can do." He slammed the trunk and left her in darkness.

Fear gripped her. Her breath came in short, quick gasps. Every breath wrapped her in a haze of pain. *So much pain.* She tried to steel herself against the nausea that threatened to overwhelm her. *That man. He was my guard. He always said I was too young and tried to limit the times Tony and his men came in to me. He was kind and took care of me when Tony or his men hurt me. It was his phone I stole to call the police. Does he still care? I'm not a kid anymore. Will he still help me?*

The car rumbled to life and the hope Kate had just felt dissipated. She bit her lip to keep it from trembling. Her head bounced and her body weight pressed onto her bound arms as they went over a bump. Stars danced across her vision and bile raced up her throat. She swallowed and squeezed her eyes shut in an attempt to ward off the pain.

A cool gust of air hit her face. *What?* She opened her eyes to see light filtering in around the trunk lid. Her heart leapt into her throat. *Can I get out?* She gritted her teeth against the pain and twisted around. She blinked, trying to push away the darkness at the edge of her vision. *I can do this. God, help me do this. Don't let me pass out now!* She forced herself up and pushed the trunk lid up with her shoulders. Kate didn't let herself pause to consider what she was about to do. She leaned over the side of the trunk as the car picked up speed and let her body fall. She hit the ground in an explosion of pain before everything went dark.

JASON

Jason rolled over in bed. He could not fall asleep. *The last time I had this much trouble sleeping was the time I found Kate.* The thought made him even more restless. "God, what's going on?" He jerked to a sitting position as someone pounded on the door. He glanced at the clock. 11:30. *Who in the world?* The pounding stopped only for the doorbell to buzz.

Jason threw the covers off and grabbed his pajama pants. He stumbled as he tried to pull them on and walk. He opened his door to see John rush past. Jason ran down behind John as the buzzing stopped and the pounding started again.

"John! Jason! Wake up!"

Jen's voice. And she sounds frantic.

"John! Jay! Come on! Wake up! Hurry! John! Jason!"

Fear curled in Jason's gut. *What happened to make Jen so upset?*

John unlocked the door and yanked it open just as Jen started to yell again.

"Joh- Oh, thank God!" Jen grabbed John's arm.

Jason took in her appearance before she turned and started to pull John towards the steps. Her hair was disheveled, her eyes wide and panicked, and tears streaked her cheeks.

"Hurry! They have her! We have to go back!"

Everything seemed to slow as Jason processed what Jen said. *It can't be. God, not that. Please. Not that!*

"Is everything okay?"

The question startled Jason into action. He glanced at his neighbor's house. Mrs. Wong leaned out the window.

"Call the police! Jen's house!"

Mrs. Wong's eyes widened before she nodded and disappeared back inside.

He hurried to catch up to John and Jen. John's voice calmly pierced Jason's thoughts as they quickened their pace. "Jen, what happened? Who has Kate?"

"Tony and his men," Jen panted as she ran. "No, time. Hurry!" She released John's hand as he pulled ahead of her. John glanced back and Jason waved him on. He quickly left them behind.

Jason ran next to Jen and looked over at her. He wanted nothing more than to pass by her and get to Kate as quickly as possible, but he would not leave Jen behind. Not without knowing she'd be okay.

"Jen?"

She looked over at him. "Go. Help John. Get Kate," she gasped.

"You'll be okay?"

She nodded and waved him ahead. "Hurry!"

Jason squeezed her shoulder before he stretched his legs into an all-out run. *God, please let her be okay!* He prayed as he ran. Fear leant speed to his stride, and he rounded the corner.

It took a moment for him to take in the scene. The brake lights of a car shone in the dark. A man silhouetted by the lights strode toward a dark bump on the ground.

"Hey!" John shouted as he ran even faster toward the man.

Jason followed only a few steps behind. Sweat beaded on his forehead and it was not because he was hot. The man glanced up. Jason could not make out his expression. The man started to raise his hand. *Gun. He has a gun.* "John, gun!" John veered left but kept running toward the man. Jason veered right to come at the man from the other side.

The man cursed and looked toward the form on the ground.

"Don't!" Jason called as he gained ground. His heart sank as he glanced down. *Kate.*

Police sirens pierced the night.

"Tony!" a man shouted from the car.

The man cursed again, spun around, and darted for the car.

A police cruiser turned the corner as the car screeched away before the man was fully in it. The police sped by after the car. Another police car slowed to a stop.

Jason ignored everything and dropped to his knees next to Kate. It was dark, but the streetlights, combined with the police lights, cast enough light to see by. She lay half on her side, her arms tied behind her and one leg bent at an odd angle. His pounding heart seemed to block out all other sounds. "Kate?" He brushed the hair from her face and froze. Her face was red and swollen, bruises already formed along her jaw. "Kate?" He gently pressed his fingers against her throat and sighed in relief at the feel of her strong pulse.

Kate moaned and moved her head. Her eyes

flickered but didn't open. Jason pushed back her hair again and rested his hand lightly against the side of her face. *God, touch her. Please ease her pain. She told us about her life, but I still never imagined...*

"Jay, we need to move. The medics need to get to her."

"What?" Jason shook his head and looked up. *When did the ambulance arrive?* The medics already had a stretcher out and surrounded him. "Oh." Jason ran a hand through his hair. The last thing he wanted to do was leave Kate's side.

"We need to let them do their job. They'll help her."

Jason looked down at Kate once more. He knew John was right. He nodded and reached for John's hand. His friend pulled him up and he backed away with him as the medics took over.

KATE

Pain radiated through her body. Kate groaned and mentally assessed her body. *Cracked ribs? Most likely. Leg? Broken?* She tried to move her leg, but something hard encased it and the pain dissuaded her from another attempt. *Dislocated shoulder. Head hurts so bad! Bruises. Lots of bruises. Nothing new.* Something warm and firm lightly squeezed her hand. She automatically grasped it.

"Kate?"

Jason? Kate blinked her eyes open. White tile ceiling. She dropped her gaze to see Jen. Her head rested on John's shoulder. She looked to be sound asleep. John's head rested on Jen's. He, too, was asleep.

Kate's eyes wandered the rest of the room. The hospital room. *What happened?* Her eyes landed on Jason, who sat next to her. He smiled. Relief shone in his eyes. A small smile formed on her lips in response to his. She still gripped something. She dropped her eyes to her hand. Jason's hand enveloped hers. Her stomach flipped and heat rushed up her neck. She bit her lip and started to pull her hand back.

Jason's grip loosened and Kate paused, her hand still in his. She didn't want to move her hand. She felt safe with her hand in his. She liked the feel of his strong hand as it surrounded hers. *Does he mind? He loosened his hand so fast. Does he want to let go? Why did he hold my hand in the first place?* She drew her eyebrows together and lifted her eyes to his in question.

Jason's grip on her hand tightened again, and he brought his other hand up to cover her's completely. His brows drew together. "How are you feeling?"

The depth of concern in his eyes felt like a punch to the gut. Kate tightened her own grip on Jason's hand in response to his firm but gentle hold. The heat crept from her neck to her cheeks. She hoped he would not be able to see in the dim light. She opened her mouth to say something, but nothing came out. She cleared her throat. "I… I feel… like I was hit by a bus. What happened?"

"What do you remember?"

Kate frowned. "We were watching a movie…"

Jason nodded.

"And…" Her eyes widened and fear gripped her heart in an icy hold. "Tony!" She bolted up and let out a pained cry as her injuries protested the movement.

"Woah! It's okay." Jason jumped up and supported her back with one hand as he maintained his hold on her hand with the other. "I've got you. Lay back down."

Kate sank back without argument and let Jason support her weight until she lay against the pillows again. "Aaaaahhhhhh…." She squeezed her eyes shut and scrunched her face as if that would help the pain.

"Kate?" Jen's voice sounded right next to her.

"Can I get you anything?" John asked.

"I'll call the doctor."

Kate forced her eyes open to see Jason reach for the call button. She forced a breath out as she focused. "No." She lightly shook her head. "I'll be fine."

Jason paused, and his eyes met hers. "Are you sure?"

"Yeah." She realized she was squeezing his hand and quickly forced herself to release him. "Sorry," she muttered as she twisted her hand into the sheet.

"It's fine." He smiled.

The corner of Kate's mouth quirked up in a half smile before she frowned. Tony had broken into Jen's house and almost taken her. Her eyes filled with tears. She looked up at Jen. "I'm so sorry. It's all my fault. I should have left like I planned to. I-"

"Don't you dare," Jen interrupted softly. "It is NOT your fault."

"But-"

Jen shook her head. "No buts. I'm the one who needs to apologize. I thought you were behind me," Jen's voice caught. She covered her face with her hands. "I never would have run if I knew you were not with me. I thought... I thought we lost you. I'm so sorry I just left you there!"

Kate's heart overflowed with love for her friend. She reached out and touched Jen's arm as Jen sank onto the bed next to her. "I couldn't... they would've... I couldn't let them take you."

Jen dropped her hands and glared at Kate with distraught, tear-filled eyes. "But you'd let them take you again? Kate, I don't know what I would have done... What could we have..." She grabbed Kate's free hand. "What if they had gotten away with you?"

John rested a hand on Jen's shoulder. "They didn't get away with her, Jen. Let's not think of the what ifs. Let's just be thankful we are all here together."

Jen glanced up at him and sighed. "You're right."

She reached up and put her hand over John's and kept it there.

Kate glanced at Jason. What would it be like to know he cared for her the way John cared for Jen? To be able to show affection like they did? Jason looked up at that moment and made eye contact. His brown eyes were warm and kind and shone with… *what is that look? If I didn't know any better, I might think it… but no.* Kate shook the thoughts away. *It can't be. He's just a friend. He only cares for me as a sister, like John said. He deserves so much more than I can give him, anyway. It wouldn't be right or fair. I have nothing left to give him, even if what I think might have been there had been. But it wasn't.*

Kate forced her thoughts back to the situation. "I didn't mean to worry you," she said softly. "I just… I know how to survive that life. I couldn't bear the thought of you having to. I… I thought he would just kill me."

Jen's shoulders drooped as she let out a breath. "Oh, Kate."

Jen leaned down and gently placed an arm over her in a hug. Kate returned the hug but winced at the pain even that small movement caused. She looked up at Jason and John again as Jen sat up. She was almost afraid to hear, but she needed to know. "What happened to Tony?"

"He was arrested, Kate," Jason answered.

"He was…" Kate blinked, afraid she had heard wrong. "He was arrested?"

Jason smiled. "Yes. The driver didn't wait for him to fully get into the car before he sped away. He fell out of the car as they turned a corner. The driver and the others got away, but they caught Tony."

"Hah!" The astonished laugh burst from her before she could stop it and fire engulfed her ribs. "Owwww." Kate moaned and wrapped her arms around her middle as her astonishment and pain subsided. "He was arrested?" she asked again. It wasn't that she didn't believe Jason. She just couldn't believe it.

John and Jen nodded.

"He was." John grinned.

Kate closed her eyes. *Thank you, God!* She relaxed completely and sank back into the pillows. She never thought this day would come. She didn't know what to do. How she should feel. She wanted to laugh. To cry. To shout. To dance. To curl up somewhere and be alone to process.

"Are you okay?" Jen asked.

Kate drew in a deep breath. "Yeah. I just... I don't know... all those years... and... now he's in jail?"

"I just wish they caught those other guys."

Kate shook her head, but stopped instantly. Pain lanced through her head and she put a hand to her forehead with a wince. "Don't worry about them. They're long gone."

"How can you be so sure?" Jason frowned.

"The driver," Kate answered. "He helped me. He never did like what Tony did with me. Said it wasn't right to sell someone. I think he opened the trunk for me."

She studied the cynical expressions of her friends. "Really. Besides, they'll go underground after a close call like that. And with Tony gone, they'll have more than enough to take care of."

"Are you sure?" John asked. "I wouldn't want another... surprise."

"I'm sure. Not everyone liked the way Tony did things. They might actually have a fight for leadership." She thought through those who would likely enter the power struggle. "Yeah. With Tony out of the picture, we will be fine."

Kate sighed and tried to sit up. The room spun, and she sucked in a sharp breath. Strong hands carefully and easily lifted her. Kate opened her eyes. John held her up while Jen fixed her pillows behind her back. When Jen moved, he laid her back down.

"Better?"

She nodded. "Thanks."

"Would you like some water?" Jason held a cup out to her.

"Thank you." Kate took the cup. After a few small sips, she handed the cup back and sank into the pillows with a grimace.

"You should try to get some sleep," Jen suggested. She turned to walk away.

Panic enveloped Kate. "Don't leave." It didn't matter that Tony had been arrested. She didn't want to be alone. She didn't care that she sounded frantic.

"We aren't going anywhere," John assured her with a smile. "Just to the chairs."

"Okay."

Jason's hand covered hers again, and a shiver ran up her arm. "Get some rest. We'll be right here."

Kate looked up at Jason. That look was in his eyes again. *What does it mean?* She wondered as she let her eyes drift closed.

KATE

Present Day

Kate bit her lip and rubbed at her scars as she waited for someone to answer the door. She glanced back at Jen and Jason again. They waited a short distance away. She drew in a deep breath and focused on the door again. *Why did I let them talk me into this? This is such a bad idea... I shouldn't disrupt their lives like this... They might be my parents, but we're total strangers. The only reason I agreed was because they said my parents couldn't have forgotten... but it's been so long... They probably forgot about me. Well, that and God. But maybe I just heard him wrong. They have a life here. How can I just come back from the dead like this? How can this be the right thing to do?* Kate backed away from the door. *I can't do this!* She spun away and took a step, but froze when the door opened.

"Can I help you?" A young woman's voice asked.

Turn around. She told herself, but her body would not respond. She opened her mouth, but nothing came out. *I can do this. In Jesus' name. God, help me. What do I even say? What do I do?* She looked over her shoulder. The air left her lungs in a whoosh. A woman a few years younger than herself watched her with a raised eyebrow. "I... uh..." Kate started, but she couldn't breathe.

It's so hot. Why is it so hot? She felt trapped in the woman's gaze and couldn't make herself move.

The woman frowned and tilted her head. "Do I know you?"

It can't be, can it? Kate felt like she was looking at herself a few years ago, except there was no hardness or fear in this woman's gaze as there had been in hers. Everything seemed to loosen. She shook her head and turned to fully face the woman. "No." *It's too late now, isn't it? No, I can still back out…*

"Who is it?" A man asked.

The woman glanced behind the door. "I'm not sure."

The man poked his head around the corner. He seemed close to the woman's age. His features were so similar to the woman's. So similar to her own. A flash of memory startled her. Her, standing next to a play pen staring at her baby brother inside. Her sister beside her.

Her stomach roiled. She pressed a hand to her middle and gulped. *I have siblings. How could I forget that?* She blinked, and her siblings came into focus. They watched her with concern in their eyes. Kate knew she would never have this opportunity again. She knew if she left now, she would never come back. Though everything in her wanted to run, she cleared her throat. "A… Are your parents home?"

They looked her over, and the man frowned. He glanced at the girl, then at Kate again, a question in his eyes. "They're around back." He tilted his head to the side of the house.

Kate stared at the corner of the house. "Thank you." She took a step and paused as fear wriggled its way into her heart and anger filled her. Out there. That's where her whole life had changed. It's where she'd been taken. She hadn't considered that or the fear and anger that would grip her at the memory.

"Is something wrong?" The woman's question drew Kate back to the present.

"No, uh, just... just remembered something." She cast a quick glance at the woman and managed what she hoped was a semi-convincing smile before she forced herself to continue around back.

What she was about to do, it was too much to handle. She couldn't take a full breath. Her hands trembled. She reverted to survival mode and shoved everything to the far corners of her mind. She ignored her surroundings and focused only on taking one step after another.

"Dad, Mom, someone is here to see you."

Kate's head snapped up. She hadn't even realized the man and woman had walked with her or that they had arrived. Her heart contracted. Kate's gaze darted around, taking in the land that she had loved so much as a child. Her eyes welled with tears, but she blinked them away. Her gaze landed on the bushes to the left where she could still remember hiding as a child that day so long ago. She suppressed a shiver and tore her gaze from the bushes. They landed on a small wooden gazebo. *That wasn't there before.* Everything seemed to slow down. There, in the gazebo, sat her parents. She knew it was them without a doubt, even though they were older and she had long since forgotten what they looked like. *Will they know me? If they don't, I'll just... I'll leave. I can't... I just can't...*

Her parents looked up. Kate's gaze darted back and forth between them. *What do I do? What do I say?*

Everything she had gone over and over again in her mind left her. She opened her mouth and shut it again without a word. She had been angry with them at one time. Angry that they had failed to protect her. That she had had to protect them against Juan's threats of sending people after them. But now?

Now, all she wanted to do was throw her arms around them and let them hold her. She remained frozen in place. *What if they don't even want me back?* She stared at her parents and shifted her feet. Her parents stared back at her, confusion clear on their faces. Her dad glanced at her mom, her, the woman next to her, her mom, and back again.

"What's going on?"

The new voice felt like a slap. It knocked Kate out of her stupor. She turned to see another young woman had joined them. She looked like a younger version of her father. Kate clenched her hands and bit her lip. *Another sister?*

"This lady came to see Dad and Mom," the man whispered. "But they are just staring at each other."

"Weird."

The man and the other woman nodded agreement.

"Is it just me, or does she look a lot like us?" One of them asked.

Kate couldn't hear the response through the roaring in her ears. *I have to get out of here! This is too much.* Intent on leaving, she took a step back. Then another.

"Kit Kat?" Her dad's voice was so quiet, so hesitant she almost didn't hear it.

The sound of the nickname from her childhood sent tingles coursing through her body. "I'm sorry."

Kate shook her head and took another step back. "I... I thought..." Her voice caught. Her emotions built up in her chest like water behind a dam. *No. This is wrong. I shouldn't have come.* She shook her head again and whirled to run.

"Wait!" Desperation filled her mother's shout.

Kate faltered to a stop and slapped a hand over her mouth to muffle the sob that wracked her body. A hand lightly, hesitantly, touched her arm. She squeezed her eyes shut, but could feel the tears as they streamed down her face.

"Kate?" Her mother's voice trembled. "Is... is it really you?"

"I..." Her throat closed around the attempted words as more sobs shook her frame. Kate bit the inside of her lip until she tasted blood. *What's wrong with me? Why can't I speak?* She tried to stop her tears, but it was hopeless. The dam had burst. She opened her eyes to see her mother searching her face. Hope and concern shone in her eyes.

Kate wrapped her free arm around her middle. *I'm going to be sick.*

"Kate," her mother said again. This time, it was a statement.

Kate managed to swallow and gave her mother a small nod.

"Oh!" Her mother reached out hands that trembled and cupped Kate's face.

The joy, hope, and disbelief in her mother's eyes sent more sobs tearing from Kate's throat. Her mother threw her arms around her. Kate's legs gave out, and they sank to the ground together. Kate wrapped her arms around her mother and gripped the back of her shirt. She pressed her face into her mother's shoulder and sobbed freely.

"I... I th... ought y... you'd for... g... get... me."

Her mom's shoulder shook. "Never," she mumbled into Kate's hair as she stroked her back. "Never."

Someone embraced her and her mother from the side. Kate lifted her face only far enough to see her father's tear-filled eyes as he pulled her and her mother close.

JASON

One Year Later

Jason laughed and leaned back on his elbows. There was only one thing that would make this day better. He glanced over at Kate. She sat between her mother and Jen. Her siblings sprawled on their own blankets. Her father sat on his wife's other side. John sat with his arm around Jen's shoulders. They had just returned from their honeymoon. *They are a match made in Heaven.* Jason grinned.

Kate's face filled with joy as she grinned at Casey, who currently regaled them all with stories from her latest trip. Plates with leftover food lay abandoned in favor of the stories Casey shared.

Jason made eye contact with Jen. She grinned at him, tilted her head toward Kate, and nodded. Jason blew out a breath. *Okay, then.* He pushed himself up and approached Kate. She looked up at him, her eyes shining with laughter.

"Will you walk with me?" he asked. His eyes darted to her father. He nodded, and Jason focused on Kate again. It felt like a swarm of butterflies had taken flight in his stomach.

Kate tilted her head, concern showing in her eyes, before she nodded. "Sure."

Relief filled him. That could have made things a little more awkward if she'd said no. He reached down and helped her to her feet. They strolled side by side as Jason directed them toward the stream. The place Kate had said she loved as a kid.

"Is everything okay?"

Jason looked over at her and smiled. "Yes." He gazed into her eyes. They were knowing eyes. Eyes that had seen too much. Eyes that showed a world of hurt and pain, of insecurity and confusion, of loss and loneliness. But they were also eyes that showed the hope that still burned in her heart. Eyes that showed that even after all she had been through, Kate was still capable of love, of joy, and of tenderness. That these things burned deep within her heart even stronger than the fears and hurts.

"Kate," he hesitated. *God, please let her say yes!* "My whole world changed when you entered it. The night I found you. It was the start of a new life for me. I didn't know it right away, but it didn't take me long to realize. I… I have loved watching how you have grown in your relationship with the Lord. Seeing your strength and bravery in your friendships with John, Jen, Casey, and myself. In finding your parents and building relationships with your family again. You are so brave, loyal, compassionate, and kind."

"Jay…" Her voice was laden with caution.

He held a hand up to stop her. "No, let me finish." Her cheeks flushed, and she looked down. "Kate, I have grown to care for you so much it hurts. I… I want to be more than friends with you. I talked with your parents and they approve. Is… is that something you would be willing to consider? Would you want to go out with me as more than just friends?"

Kate opened and closed her mouth a few times. She frowned and reached up to rub the spot behind her ear. The spot she always rubbed when she was thinking or uncomfortable. "Jay," she finally got out in a small voice. "You deserve so much better than me." She said it so matter-of-factly that his heart twisted in pain. "I'm not... I can't..." She trailed off and looked up at him, regret filled her eyes. "You know what happened to me. What I've been through. I can never..." She trailed off again and looked at the ground. "I can't give you a family."

Kids. She's worried that she can't have kids. That hurt, to be sure, but they would move past it. Jason took Kate's hands in one of his and gently lifted her face with his other hand. "Kate, I'm not worried about that. When we get married... if we get married... we can adopt if you want to. But, Kate, I love you. I want to spend time with you with the intention that we move towards marriage."

"But... you can do so much better than me..."

"Shhh," Jason pressed a finger to his lips, cutting off the rest of what she was going to say. She closed her eyes and took a deep breath. "Kate, I do not want anyone else. I love you. I want you. That other stuff... We'll work through it. I want to spend the rest of my life with you. Who you are as a person. Who God has made you to be. That is what I love. I think we make a great team."

Kate opened her eyes again and looked up at him. Tears filled her eyes. Her beautiful blue eyes. Eyes that seemed to beg him to be speaking truth but warning him to run. "Are you sure?" she whispered.

"I've never been more sure of anything in my life."

He smiled down at her.

She flushed and smiled back as tears trailed down her cheeks. "Okay." She nodded.

"Okay?" His heart leapt.

"Yeah. Okay." Her smile grew.

"Okay!" He took her hands and pressed her knuckles to his lips. She leaned forward, and he wrapped her in a hug. Delight filled him as she hesitantly wound her arms around him and rested her head on his chest. *We have a long road ahead, but we'll face whatever comes. Together. With God. We will face it.*

* Lyrics from God Will Take Care of You by Fanny Crosby

ACKNOWLEDGEMENTS

First off I want to thank God, the Master Storyteller, for His great goodness and for giving me this story.

I also want to thank my mom, Lisa Baumann, who has always encouraged me and been supportive of my writing. This story started when I was fourteen as a homeschool writing assignment for her. It has come such a far way since then, but I doubt it would have happened without her.

A HUGE thank you to my friends and critique partners who read this story, or parts of it, and helped me make it what it is. That means you Liz Finegan, Sue August, Priscilla Strapp (and our writing group), and all of the makers of the realm in Realm Makers. You may be a Fantasy writing group, but I have learned so much from you all and you have helped shape this story. Thanks also to Lindsey Hough who read this in a very early, unedited version and gave some suggestions that made this book better.

Shout out to Bobbi Prator who did a FANTASTIC job editing my proposal before I decided to self publish. I so appreciate your help with that! (Let me know if you're looking for an editor and I'll try and get you in touch.)

Thank you. Thank you. THANK YOU! to all working to abolish trafficking in all it's forms. Keep up the good work and may God protect you and help you succeed in your work!

BOOKS BY THIS AUTHOR

The Christian

When the government passed the anti-Christian laws, Alex's relationship with the Lord became her arrest warrant. Despite the risk, Alex shares the Gospel with a woman who has lost all hope. To her surprise, the woman doesn't report her-- but someone else does. Alex is soon in handcuffs and on her way to The Island, the most notorious work camp for the worst offenders.

James wasn't a fan of his father's methods for handling the Christians, but it wasn't his problem. Not until his sister, depressed and suicidal, ran out of the house only to return a different person. Kind. Hopeful. Content.

When James and his sister make their dreaded, routine trip to see their father on The Island, a female prisoner tries to duck out of sight. Curious, James decides to find out why. What he discovers may destroy his life-- or free it.

Faith In Fiction: Divergetns, Tributes, Games, & Sandworms

What could the Hunger Games teach us about God? How about the Gospel according to cyberpunk stories or the messianic themes evident in Dune?

This book takes the star-flung, technological, and bestselling works of famous speculative fiction series and teaches biblical lessons alongside the text of beloved stories. Drawing on many different series, six different authors share their faith and insight using both Scripture and classic tales from science fiction and fantasy.

Christians love fantasy and sci-fi. It's okay to geek out with us. Here, we imagine that John's glasses had tape on the middle, Peter's pocket protector got wet after walking on the Galilee, and Jesus saves and rolls for half damage.

Journey through the Old Testament with divergents and visit the New Testament through the Enderverse. Whether you're looking for the perfect nerdvotional or trying to impart biblical wisdom to friends who lean away from Scripture but towards popular speculative fiction, this book is right for you!

Made in the USA
Middletown, DE
20 October 2021